THE INFINITE
MINUTE

EDWARD NEWTON

This is a work of fiction. Names, characters, places, and incidents are products of the author's imagination or are used fictitiously and are not to be construed as real. Any resemblance to actual events, locations, organizations, or persons, living or dead, is entirely coincidental.

World Castle Publishing, LLC
Pensacola, Florida
Copyright © Edward Newton 2022
Paperback ISBN: 9781956788938
eBook ISBN: 9781956788945
First Edition World Castle Publishing, LLC, May 09, 2022
http://www.worldcastlepublishing.com

Licensing Notes

Cover: Karen Fuller
Editor: Maxine Bringenberg

Face froze.
Hands still.
Forever til...
The wind holds its breath.
The sun shuts its eye.
The oceans cease and the moments die.
One, six, nine, eleven
And then…
Midnight never.
Yesterday and tomorrow severed.
Today, today, today, every second.
The end of days but the day without end.
No escape once in it,
The infinite minute.

Table of Contents

Chapter One
19:30
7.16.2023 AD
Hollywood, California

"My mother was just a baby when she died."

Thyme sits at the border, cross-legged and contemplating. She is small with short hair, looking like a pixie at the edge of a petal. After the stylist chopped it short, Mom said Thyme reminded her of an anime version of Tinkerbell. Mom said she liked it. Then the accident happened the very next day. That was a long time ago now. Thyme's hair is still the same length. Nothing ever changes.

Thyme looks like a puzzle that genetics was trying to sort out. She has her mother's midnight hair and almond shape of eyes, but her complexion is softer, and she possesses green irises. Thyme has never met her father, but she knows he must not be Asian like her mother. So she's always blamed Mom entirely for being five foot and never taller. Now Thyme feels bad about blaming Mom for anything. Mom is dead.

She's supposed to get past that. Jiji, her obaasan, urges her all the time to move forward. Her friends have started looking to the future instead of staying stuck in the present. They left her behind, focusing ahead, whereas Thyme just focuses on the dead. Repeat. Repeat. Repeat. It never turns tomorrow. Nothing changes. Nothing ever changes.

Thyme has come out here often since the accident. She finds a place right here on the lush lawn on the gravelly knoll overlooking Santa Monica Boulevard. She can see the tree where Mom wrapped the Escalade around the trunk of a mesa oak. It always rains on the tree, ever since the accident, as if the sky can weep for her mother even though Thyme cannot. It rains and rains and rains, but the tree never grows.

Sometimes Thyme cries, alone and unmoored, drifting without a mother or father, sitting solo in a world without moments, yet things never change. Endless tears, and yet grief never goes. She feels so empty but also still so full—absolutely overflowing with sadness.

"A baby crashed an Escalade into a tree," says the woman standing behind Thyme. "This is a strange time indeed."

Strange time. Thyme checks her watch. Seven-thirty. It's just habit because the minute hand never changes, and the hour is always the same. Thyme is trapped in the moment. Mom has been dead for nearly a year, but really no time has passed at all. She wonders if it ever will.

The woman standing behind her is Mallory Norman. Ms. Norman has come to Hollywood to take Thyme away to school. A new school, far away across the other side of the United States. This will be Thyme's last visit to the knoll where she comes to memorialize her mother. An aircraft waits for them, ready to take them somewhere else—to New York City in 1980. A place that seems to Thyme as big and mysterious as another planet.

She doesn't want to leave, but she knows she can't stay.

Because there's nothing left for her here.

Thyme recalls a poem she read a long time ago by someone whose name she can't remember with a title that slipped her mind. The poet talked about the infinite minute, the point of death when time stops and everything suspends. Thyme thought it was about the poet's own end, life flashing before her eyes, an entire lifetime replayed over the course of minute moments. But now she knows it's about the interminable hours of mourning after a loved one has passed. The infinite minute is experienced by the ones left behind.

It's evening, and the sun is out. It seems like this day has gone on forever. There's no breeze to stir the world, to move it on, to indicate that things are going from here to there. The whole scene seems stuck, like someone made a photograph of life and then tore up the real thing. The world of mornings and tomorrows and mothers who lived to be grandmothers became just a fairy tale.

There's been a fundamental change in the way things work. Mom is gone. She's no longer a part of Thyme's life. It makes a hole that threatens to suck up everything else—a heartache with its own gravity. Thyme has to leave California, or she will fall into the abyss and never find her way out. She's been walking around the edge of it ever since the accident, tottering on the rim, always one weak moment from teetering into a torrent of tears.

The trees all around Thyme are full and green, teeming with life in a mockery of the memorial on this borderland of untimely death. There are clouds across the blue that never cross the sun, never cast a shadow on the gloom of a teenage girl's grief. It's ever bright and blazing in Hollywood on July the Sixteenth,

2023, as if the day is trying to snuff her sorrow. It will take more than this day. This day has tried hard enough for long enough. It's time for somewhere else. Thyme is ready for tomorrow.

"I suppose we should go?" she asks.

"Take as much time as you need," Ms. Norman says, placing a withered old hand on Thyme's shoulder. "There's no hurry. We'll still get there when we get there."

As much time as she needs? She needs all the time in the world, but isn't the world fresh out of time?

Thyme remembers when she was a toddler and still exploring the world, sometimes reaching for something sharp or something hot. Mom would put her in time out. To protect her. To give her a moment to breathe and collect herself. She feels like she's been in timeout for the last year since the accident.

"I'm ready," Thyme tells. It's a lie. It's a lie Thyme will always tell.

"All right," Ms. Norman says. "The others are looking forward to meeting you."

This is a brand-new school, and Thyme Mugen is part of the inaugural class of the Mallory Norman Institute of Time. Ms. Norman founded the school and runs it as headmistress. She chose Thyme specifically from thousands of applicants from every state across the nation. The class represents the diverse population of the new United States. It's meant to squelch the talk of some states seceding and quell the murmurs of insurrection. The institute will have students representing nearly every one of the fifty states.

Thyme hasn't been to a single class since the accident. Days are all the same, one after another, sunny and temperate outside but cold and dark on the inside. Mom is gone, and Thyme was left alone with Jiji, who isn't known for being warm and fuzzy. Thyme could've used a shoulder to cry on.

"Can we stop by Jiji's?" Thyme asks, getting to her feet and brushing grass off her jeans. "I still have to pick up my things."

"Of course. I assumed you wanted to say goodbye."

"She's on the other side of LA," Thyme says. "Jiji spends most of her time at a youth spa up north."

Ms. Norman looks like she's considering the facts, contemplating if she ought to report Thyme's obaasan for something illegal. It doesn't matter to Thyme when she's gone. Jiji deals with the loss of her daughter in a different way than Thyme handles losing her mother. Jiji told Thyme that what happened out there on Santa Monica Boulevard was nonsense and that Rikona Mugen will come back once things get situated. Once the clocks are fixed. As if what's wrong with the world will ever be repaired. It's been a year now since time broke, and things aren't any different today than when Thyme's mother turned into an infant and crashed her car into a tree.

Time stopped the day she lost her mom. And it may never start again.

**

Thyme's obaasan started remodeling the house shortly after her daughter died. "It looks like an old woman lives here," she complained after tomorrow never came. Thyme hadn't even been able to finish her mother's obituary before Jiji started planning ways to seem younger. To turn back time. It began with new paint on the exterior of her house. Pink. Bright. Youthful. Then the white picket fence was replaced with a border made of tempered glass tinted scarlet, like flat polished flames. Lawn gnomes and garden stones became modern sculptures and new-age windchimes.

Now Jiji is off in Brentwood at the youth spa again, gone longer and longer every time she leaves, enjoying somewhen that makes her feel young enough to match their hipster house. So Thyme walks up the stamped concrete walkway, featuring peace symbols and smiley faces, without worrying that she'll get accosted by her obaasan and a million questions. Thyme didn't tell Jiji that she had been accepted to the Mallory Norman Institute of Time. She plans on slipping away while Jiji is gone.

Ms. Norman accompanies Thyme. Looking older than even Jiji when she finally shuffles back home to 2023, Ms. Norman is a curious mix of indistinct ethnicity. Thyme has many mixed-race friends — Britney has an Asian mom and an Indian father, Karsen's mom is African-American, and her dad is Latino, Chantel has a white mom and an anonymous father of obviously non-white origin. Thyme herself is the offspring of her Asian mother and someone certainly of European descent. She never met her father, or ever saw his picture, or even knew his name, but he has to be Caucasian. Ms. Norman's complexion from the future represents a someday that 2023 has only begun to breach. The headmistress looks exotic, beautiful regardless of age.

An old woman meets them at the door of Thyme's obaasan's home. She appears nearer Ms. Norman's age but wears clothes that would look more appropriate on someone of Thyme's generation. Jiji is tiny, as short as Thyme, with hair almost white and wrinkles rippling her sour expression.

"You're back already?" Thyme asks.

"I met someone. He's taking me to Paris. We'll be gone for an e-week or two," Jiji says. "He's only twenty-two when he's from."

Maybe Jiji meant to impress Thyme, but it only makes her

granddaughter scrunch up her nose.

"You can't keep running away, Jiji," Thyme says.

"Well, I can't stay stuck here either, Thyme," Jiji snaps. Then she suddenly takes note of the other old woman, as if Jiji trained her eyes to overlook other elderly. "And who is this?"

Thyme's obaasan wears a top so tight it leaves little to the imagination and bottoms so short they could have been considered underwear. What might've been entirely appropriate someday up in Brentwood is certainly not a good look for a grandmother here and now. Jiji's T-shirt reads "Young at heart."

The headmistress offers a withered hand to the old woman standing before her. "My name is Mallory Norman." Ms. Norman is taller than Jiji by a head, has wrinkled more elegantly than Thyme's grandmother, and sports hair just as white as Jiji's.

"Ms. Norman, this is my grandma," Thyme introduces.

"Just call me Renaissance. Or Ren for short," Thyme's obaasan says with a frown directed at Thyme. "Like I told you."

"Pleased to meet you, Ren," Ms. Norman says politely.

"Can I ask what you're doing with my — with Thyme?" Ren asks arms crossed under her chest, propping her sagging bosom up in a shirt designed for someone a quarter of her age.

"I'm here to escort her to school," Ms. Norman says. "The first semester at the Minute starts very soon."

"The Minute?" Ren asks, obviously uninformed.

Ms. Norman looks sideways at Thyme with an expression of accusation. Hadn't Thyme already informed Ren and gotten proper approval? The teenager had planned on being long gone before Renaissance Mugen returned from Brentwood. Thyme would've rather avoided this scene, and not just because of Jiji's current unfortunate wardrobe.

"She founded a school called the Mallory Norman Institute

of Time. It's in New York," Thyme says. "M.N.I.T. Everyone calls it the Minute."

"How clever," Ren sniffs. "And you think you're running off across the country to some new school? Your family is here. I'm here. And I am in charge of taking care of you, Thyme. I still need to sign off before you can leave."

"At the rate you run off to chase the past, you'll be stuck soon enough on some holiday somewhere, regressed to infancy and wearing diapers," Thyme snaps, temper lost.

"Don't be ridiculous. You're always so dramatic!"

"It comes from being a teenager, obaasan," Thyme says with a loud voice. "I'm sure you're my age often enough that you know what I mean."

Ren huffs and fumes. Ms. Norman looks back and forth between Thyme and her grandmother as if reconciling two different generations of Mugens that look like they share the same wardrobe and the same temperament. Thyme regrets pushing Jiji's buttons because Ren's signature that Thyme forged on her M.N.I.T. application is now invalidated.

"You can't leave me, Thyme."

"I have to go," Thyme tells, looking over her shoulder in the general direction of Santa Monica Boulevard and the tree where her mother died when she was a baby. "I can't stay here."

"You should be here when Rikona comes home," Ren says.

Ms. Norman looks away. She doesn't say it, but Thyme knows. Ms. Norman built a new school and recruited a full complement of students from time zones across the United States. The headmistress doesn't think the clocks will restart anytime soon. Thyme's mother is never coming back.

"I'm going," Thyme says. "I can't stay in one place for the

rest of my life."

"Only if I say so," Ren argues. "Isn't that right, Ms. Norman?"

"Thyme is still a minor even by her equivalent age," Ms. Norman concedes. "But a case may be made in the courts for your capacity as legal guardian, madam." Ren scowls as if "madam" is even worse than "Grandma." "Using passports for extended travel between zones to relive your youth may be deemed as negligent care. Such flagrant narcissism may exempt you as an adequate guardian of Thyme's best interests. I can certainly take it up with some friends of mine in the judiciary."

Ren's countenance appears more like ruin on her aged face than any sort of threatening expression. The old woman looks ridiculous in her teenage attire. Ms. Norman is the headmistress of a federal institute of learning sanctioned by the president himself and has connections that should perhaps cause concern for Renaissance Mugen. Jiji looks like she has come to the same conclusion.

"You'll write?" Jiji asks.

"Every day," Thyme answers drily.

Although that doesn't mean the same thing now as it once did.

***

The physics of the world changed when time stopped. All the clocks quit turning. The sun stilled. One day became all eternity. Calendars were rendered obsolete. The world cracked into thousands of time zones, each a different era set side by side. Across America, fifty distinct epochs are cataloged, all adjacent to one another. Los Angeles is split right down the middle, July the sixteenth, 2023, where Thyme lives, right next to April the first, 1948, when Thyme's mother died.

The borders of each zone act as temporal gateways. Passing through these ephemeral curtains between time zones shifts the age of the person crossing the threshold, making them older or younger, instantaneous changes anywhere along the span of a normal lifetime. One may start in 2023 as a sixty-year-old woman with an obstinate granddaughter and walk into 1948 as a nubile young lady in her twenties. A mother could drive across the border from 2023 to seventy-five years in the past at the very moment time freezes, turning into a baby and crashing into an oak tree. Dead before she even realized what happened.

The equivalent of one year after the Freeze, no one still really knows what happened.

One e-year after the clocks stopped, it's time to make the best of the situation.

Ms. Norman founded the Minute to bring the time zones together. States anywhen from 215,138 BC (in a place that will someday be called Delaware) to 4807 AD (which was once known as Oregon) have to coexist. Some zones still had legalized slavery mashed next to an epoch with advanced bio-silica entities well beyond considerations of skin color. Cro-Magnon cavemen now neighbor Wild West cowboy towns on one side and futuristic federations full of unfathomable advancements on the other. They have all been trying to form the United States of Time. Predictably, there have been problems. Divisions. The states tentatively agreed to recognize Washington, DC, as the federal focus during this trying time, but the discretion of the capitol's control is tenuous. The Institute is supposed to symbolize togetherness, a centerpiece of this melting pot of eras.

Thyme is honored to be a part of the inaugural class.

"President Harrison has a lot riding on the success of

the school," Ms. Norman explains as they sit in a brand new Mercedes retrofitted with AI independent navigation imported from a future, the car moving them from Jiji's house to the airport without either person in the vehicle paying any attention to the route. "There are factions that are resistant to solidarity. Jefferson Davis in 1869 is calling for some zones to secede from the union."

"That guy wants to start another Civil War?" Thyme asks, astonished that history could repeat itself even when you already know the ending.

"There are many opinions as to the impending direction of the United States, Thyme. As many opinions as there are time zones. Those differing ideals bring some of the disparate eras into conflict," Ms. Norman says. "My goal in creating the school is to show everyone that people from every time period can come together peacefully and get along. The future doesn't have to be directed by divergent pasts."

"Lofty goals," Thyme says.

"I want to make a better tomorrow."

"Too bad it's always today."

"It won't always be today."

"It might never turn tomorrow," Thyme argues.

"We all need to think differently than we did before the Freeze. Cause and effect. Destiny and predetermination. Yesterday to today to tomorrow. All those old rules are gone," Ms. Norman says. This feels like Thyme's first lesson as a student of the Mallory Norman Institute of Time. "We can take a different path. We can make a better present. When we eventually turn the page of the calendar, tomorrow will look a lot brighter than it seems right now."

"The California sunshine really suits your disposition," Thyme says.

"When I come from, it's always night. I've spent the last year in the darkness, Thyme. I'm ready for the light."

Bob Hope Airport is in Burbank, at the edge of the border to 2803. A bustling hub before the Freeze, it shut down most services right after time stopped. Crossing time zones can be dangerous and even fatal—if turning into a baby could end tragically in 1948, imagine a planeload of people suddenly piloted by a toddler as a jet passes over a border. Now, the airport serves only an occasional airplane, futuristic flying contraptions piloted by robots or controlled remotely like massive drones.

Such a machine sits out on the tarmac, the only transportation that isn't stashed indefinitely along the empty terminals or shuttered permanently in the massive hangers. The contraption that allows the Mercedes to retrofit to AI autopilot is simple and small—it's much harder to modify a 747. So instead of overhauling existing aircraft, the only vehicles currently in rotation are transports from future time zones capable of nonhuman navigation. Silver and shiny as a sheet of tinfoil, the craft on the tarmac is flatter than traditional jets and as round as a UFO shown in grainy conspiracy theory photographs. The transport on the airport runway seems like a prop from an old science fiction movie like They Came from Mars. Thyme's life seems like it's set in a sci-fi story called The Day the Clocks Stood Still.

Standing outside on the tarmac as Thyme and Ms. Norman pull up is a teenager Thyme's age. He's tall enough to play professional basketball. His arms are crossed in front of him like they're too long for him to properly know what to do with them next, and he stands with his legs apart as if they might tangle if they get too close together. Next to him, a woman poses like she's ready for someone to take a picture. She looks like a blonde movie star from the old films Thyme's mom used to watch on rainy spring days. Clearly, she's proud of her buxom curves, a short dress stretched over her womanly figure. Although the woman displays perpetual postures, there's no one around with a camera.

The car pulls right up to the flying saucer. Concepts like ticket lines and going through security are things of the past. The airport itself is more a ghost town than a transportation center. There's no other aircraft on any runway. Since travel between zones is now strictly regulated by visas issued by the federal government, Ms. Norman has already secured proper credentials for all approved students to travel from California to New York. She passes Thyme her passport as they approach the aircraft.

"Thyme Mugen, I'd like to introduce you to two other new students. This is Efren Cortez, also from 2023. I picked him up earlier. He lives right here in Burbank."

Efren extends a hand that's as wide as Thyme's whole face. His head dangles on a stem of a neck like the wilted head of a flower with heavy petals. His feet are huge and fascinating, and Efren seems as interested in them as Thyme is, although surely he has stared at them his whole life. Everything about him is awkward as if he's made of mismatched parts.

"Nice to meetcha," he mumbles, a faint Latin accent matching his subtle Hispanic features.

"You're tall," Thyme says.

Efren looks Thyme over as if searching for an equal observation to pay her in return. She is shorter than average, not too wide and not too thin, of Asian descent and therefore of unremarkable complexion, black hair styled more boyish than girly, and she wears clothes as generic as anyone else in 2023

SoCal.

"You're pretty," he says.

Thyme blushes.

The blonde butts in, hand out, grabbing Thyme and shaking her hand. "My name is Candy Kane. I'm from across the border in 1948, but I was only fifteen over there," she says with a megawatt smile and enough sparking self-confidence to jumpstart a car. "When I came across the border to 2023, I got these!" She actually grabs her own bosom and gives them a shake. "Ha! Now I look like Veronica Lake. Gotta get my hair styled like a peek-a-boo girl."

"I don't know who Veronica Lake is," Thyme tells. "I'm not sure what a lot of those words even mean."

"Doesn't matter," Candy says. She almost looks shy about it, like a girl from 2023 realizing she's wearing a One Direction tee instead of fawning over solo Harry Styles. Candy stares at Thyme like she has something on her face. Thyme brushes the back of her hand across her nose just in case. "I've never met a girl my age that's from the future. Maybe we can be friends!"

It didn't sound like Thyme would have any say in the matter.

"Your name is really Candy?" Thyme asks. "Candy Kane?"

"It's actually Candace, but everyone calls me Candy."

"Of course they do."

"They say it's because I'm so sweet."

"Of course you are."

"Now that we're all acquainted, we have one more student to retrieve before we fly out of LA," Ms. Norman says. "She's just across the runway. She's from tomorrow. The future cuts across a part of the 2023 airport. She'll meet us at the border, so we don't have to cross temporal zones."

"Another girl from the future?" Candy asks gleefully.

"I know you'll like her," Ms. Norman says with a nod. "Her name is Honor Fitzgerald."

***

The borders that separate the zones—the actual lines where the world has cracked apart and reassembled into a quilt of disparate eras—have a unique look. The boundary between different times glows with a distinctive red light. Like a warning, Jiji would say, on the rare occasion she joined Thyme at the edge of 1948 where Mom died.

Thyme has spent the equivalent of an entire year thinking about the past, but now here she is looking into the future. An actual tomorrow. The year on the other side of the line is 2803. Thyme hasn't considered tomorrow in such a long time that she becomes absolutely enchanted by the sight. A few feet in front of her, it's sometime other than time's eternal today or Thyme's interminable yesterday.

Thyme and her new companions remain a safe distance away from the shimmering curtain of scarlet light as Ms. Norman steps up to the border. On the other side, Honor Fitzgerald stands in the rain, looking back.

Border stations along the demarcations between time zones are controlled by federal workers who attempt to prevent unauthorized migration between eras. Thyme wonders if they had simply repurposed airline employees as border agents. Certainly, the woman behind the booth at the station along the line between 2023 and 2803 could have once sat behind a ticket counter dealing boarding passes.

Now, the ticket-taker looks bored. Where once airline attendants worked in an industry of inertia and energy, things after the Freeze move slowly. The ticket-taker watches television, a replay of a CNN interview of President William Henry Harrison on-location at the White House in 1841. The news scrolling headlines across the bottom of the screen describe tensions between different time zones, instigated especially by the citizens of 1869. Jefferson Davis, former president of the Confederacy during the War Between the States, is banging the separatist drums once again. History repeats itself even when time is on pause. President Harrison is pushing for national unity between the disparate epochs, but Davis leads a growing chorus of dissent that supports all fifty different time zones within the continental united temporal states exercising individual autonomy. Fifty individual nations instead of fifty United States of Time.

While Thyme was distracted with grief, history had marched on, despite the undisturbed calendar. Her world may have come to a crashing halt, but the rest of America hadn't observed her interminable moment of mourning. Time may not march on, but the citizens of America had.

Ms. Norman plans to found the Institute to show people that citizens from all these different millennia can work together. Separated by decades and centuries and millennia, nevertheless, Americans have something in common no matter when they come from. No different from the earliest people to come to this land millennia before the Europeans to the last vestiges of indigenous patriots still living in the far future, the population of this part of the world all come from somewhere else. Now it is just somewhere and somewhen. The differences now are less geography or genealogy and more chronology. But the differences have always been what everyone has in common. The melting pot, ad infinitum.

Yet Thyme doesn't want to leave. And she knows she can't stay.

The border station acting as access back and forth between the 21st and 29th centuries is currently under construction along the tarmac. A plywood shell delineates the building's shape, separate stations for bureaucrats and security and travelers, and a waiting area for loved ones. Security along the border is reminiscent of airport screeners, down to the metal detector archways relocated from inside the Bob Hope Airport terminal to outdoor under the eaves of the new border station. The ticket booth with the bored border agent is entirely empty. Visas regulating immigration from across state lines are rarely granted. Extending left and right out from the station, following the curve of the scarlet screen of incandescent light, is a concrete wall cordoning off random migration, with a wide opening where Honor Fitzgerald currently stands waiting for approval to step into 2023. The tarmac on either side of the centuries is covered in soft mats because occasionally, the transition results in someone on the floor, sometimes a squealing baby or a stumbling senior. Chairs and sofas are arranged behind a glass partition that acts as the receiving room, where Thyme and the other students wait and watch the latest arrival. Ms. Norman obtained special permission to stand right at the portal between timelines to receive her newest pupil.

Thyme has never seen anyone cross zones. She knows the story of her mother, driving along Santa Monica Boulevard in 2023 when the Freeze occurred, crossing over the shimmering, scarlet border into the past without realizing anything had happened. She regressed to infancy and lost control of the Escalade. Many people across the country died at the same instant when time stopped. After the Freeze, crossing between time zones has been strictly regulated across all states and managed through passports granted by the federal authorities.

After the Freeze. Too late to matter. Time never passes, but it's still possible to be too late. Too late to save Thyme's mom.

"Are you okay?" Efren asks, noticing a tear.

Thyme frowns and wipes the terrible teardrop away. She doesn't need to talk to a stranger about her dead mother. She isn't ready to swap sob stories with some string bean teenager. Her tears are none of his business. She suddenly wants to punch him right in the face, but she would need a stool or a boost up for her small fist to reach his stupid nose.

"I'm fine," Thyme snaps.

Now on CNN, Jefferson Davis explains to Anderson Cooper that he supports open borders and fluid migration.

In Honor's era, the 'morrow looks about sixteen and is thin as a rail. Her complexion is an exotic mix of races, hints of the whole world in her features and color. Darker than Thyme, lighter than Khalid, she looks like the child of all six populated continents, a mix of many ethnicities. The girl is entirely bald as if genetically modified to be smooth and styleless.

Thyme watches intently as Honor Fitzgerald steps across from the year 2803 into Thyme's present. As soon as Honor touches the glowing red veil between zones, she flickers forward as if moved in both space and time. She instantly transforms from a teenager into an old woman, wrinkles appearing across her interesting face, stature bending to the ramifications of decades. Her chest drops precipitously, the effects of age and unkind gravity occurring instantaneously. Ms. Norman has a papoose in one hand and a cane in the other. She passes Honor the cane.

Honor is from almost eight hundred years in the future,

so what she wears ought to be strange and otherworldly. When Thyme considers what they wore eight hundred years prior to 2023, she supposes her blue jeans with custom rips and T-shirt sporting a superhero symbol, and hair as short as any boy's would seem alien to someone in a plain brown woolen tunic belted around the middle, paired with a simple headdress and leather shoes. But Honor's attire is simple and practical, a material that seems able to expand with a shift in size, an indiscriminate khaki color that can shrink to accommodate a toddler or stretch to fit a full-fledged adult. Her exposed skin features subdermal tattoos seemingly made from LED lights running in lines like luminous rivers, color shifting up and down Honor's arms and over her face and across her smooth scalp as she moves, shapes and shades changing at whim.

The look would have been new and exciting if Honor hadn't aged to such a degree that she appears more like death a'coming.

Still, Candy rushes up to Honor as Ms. Norman leads her into the reception area. "Ohmigoodness, you're from the future!"

Thyme is also from Candy's future, yet had only elicited about half the awe heaped on Honor. The difference between seventy years into tomorrow and eight hundred....

Ms. Norman excuses herself, taking the stack of forms Honor brought across to the ticket-taker in the booth. The news shows a summit between 2772 Paris and English lords from 503 AD. Europe has its own problems, with prehistoric beasts roaming much of Scandinavia and the Baltic states mostly stuck in the Ice Age.

"There was no one to see you off, Honor?" Efren asks, looking at the lonely zone on the other side of the shimmering scarlet curtain.

"My progeny do not agree with my decision to cohabitate with savages," Honor answers.

"Excuse me?" Thyme reacts, glaring at the 'morrow with hands balled into fists.

"Didn't you have to get your parents to sign off on this?" Candy asks Honor.

"Sign off?"

"Get permission?" Candy rephrases.

Honor sniffs. "Offspring are not considered property in 2803. Slavery is an archaic idea."

"I think the idea is that someone sixteen years old probably won't be mature enough to make a decision that will affect their entire future," Thyme suggests drily.

"Think? Idea? Future?" Honor ticks off. "Do you whippersnappers from the past speak so frequently about concepts entirely beyond your grasp?"

"Is having manners beyond your grasp?" Thyme sneers, getting right up in Honor's face. Something glowing like LEDs moves subcutaneously under Honor's wrinkled flesh. "And who are you calling a whippersnapper? I'm the same age as you are!"

"Please. In the future, intellectual advancements are such that a two-year-old from 2803 is already a more advanced thinker than any sixteen-year-old simpleton from 2023. I really hate when Neanderthals assume they can understand the future."

"No one says 'whippersnapper' in 2023," Thyme says tersely. "You sound like my obaasan. And you look as old as her, too."

This finally silences the girl from tomorrow. Ms. Norman returns from giving the ticket-taker Honor's paperwork. The newcomer is now properly processed through the system. Ms.

Norman looks at the four students she has assembled thus far, notes the lingering animosity like a stench hanging in the air, and frowns a little. Thyme has second thoughts about the success of Ms. Norman's social experiment. Nevertheless, the headmistress loses the frown and smiles so big and bright that it rivals the never-setting sun that has hung over Hollywood for the equivalent of an entire year.

"One more stop, and then we'll be heading to the east coast," Ms. Norman says. "So we will have a little more time to get to know each other better."

All the time in the world, Thyme thinks.

***

Efren Cortez had asked Honor Fitzgerald why there was no one to see her off. Apparently, in the future, sentimentality will become extinct. Thyme's obaasan had to be threatened with possible criminal prosecution to let Thyme go, but she finally relented. Thyme said her goodbye at home, and that was that. But not everyone manages a low-key exodus. A massive crowd of people gathers around the airship parked on the tarmac, dozens of Latinos carrying homemade signs that read "¡Hasta mañana, Efren!" and "¡Te extrañaremos!" Some wear shirts with Efren's face from when he was younger, smiling big from ear to big ear.

Efren Cortez's family is huge. Both in number—some three-dozen mingling around the runway—and in size, his paternal parentage featuring no one shorter than six feet tall. Even a boy who looks a few years younger than Thyme still exceeds six feet. Efren's father is a handsome man with a gray mustache and a black head of hair who towers over all. Seven feet at least, he seems twice the height of Efren's mother. Small and round, Mrs. Cortez cannot be even five feet, the shortest of her family, shorter than even Thyme.

Out of the corner of her eye, Thyme catches a glance of someone moving on her perimeter. She startles, jumping to an impossible conclusion. Mom? It has happened several times since the accident. Out of the corner of her eye or walking through a crowd of people, she might glimpse black hair styled just so or a shirt in a certain color and taste that would suit her mother. Or Thyme might hear a voice that sounds familiar at a store and smile before that smile crashes. Sometimes a laugh peels across a public place, and it sounds like her. But it's never Mom. Then the feeling of her being gone is worse than ever. This time is like every other time—the person Thyme saw out the corner of her eye was just another of Efren's family moving to join the crowd.

Ms. Norman gently informs the gathered family that it's time for the new recruits to the Institute to go. Efren's mother hugs him for the tenth time. She tugs on Efren's shirt sleeve, and he bends down, his radar-dish ear by her face as she whispers something to him. Efren nods solemnly. Didn't he glance quickly at Thyme before agreeing to his mother's words?

Then his father pulls him into a gangly embrace that seems to have more arms than an octopus. He pats Efren roughly on the back and says, "You represent the Cortez name with honor out there in the world. What it means to be a man is timeless. You remember how you were raised, son."

Efren starts down the line of relatives, big and small, pulling him into a warm embrace. Uncles, aunts, cousins, siblings, two sets of grandparents all wish him well, with tears welling in their eyes. Thyme cannot help but stare. She is an only child who only ever had a mother and one obaasan who she considered family. Efren's family seems to go on and on and on.

A voice comes up from a location just below Thyme's ears.

"You take good care of my boy."

Mrs. Cortez somehow slipped close enough to Thyme that she could've reached around and given the girl a hug of her own. Thyme is not a hugger. But she has been known, when her temper flares and yatsuatari suru, to be a slugger.

"The dude is like a tree. I think he can take care of himself."

"Even a tree sways in fierce winds," Mrs. Cortez says. "You two are tethered by this moment, tied together from common origins. There will be many trials out there in this new, strange world. You will need someone to stand with you, and my Efren will need the same."

They'll be the only two students from 2023 in the inaugural class of the Mallory Norman Institute of Time. Perhaps Mrs. Cortez is right. Maybe Thyme needs someone to have her back among fawning starstruck démodés from the past and condescending 'morrows that think they know everything just because it's written in a history book.

"All right," Thyme promises. "I'll keep him out of trouble."

"Oh, I don't know about that," Mrs. Cortez says with a sly smile. "I just want a promise that when you do get up to trouble, you have his back."

Thyme looks at the tall, gangly boy hugging down the line of relatives like a groom freshly married and off to his honeymoon. Efren looks apologetically affectionate and yet unabashedly engaged in each and every interaction. The boys Thyme knew before the Freeze would have scurried away from public displays such as this.

"I promise."

Efren finally finishes and walks back to his fellow students.

Honor moves away when he stands too near her. "That was a garish display of how disease was transmitted in the past. It is no wonder the Black Death ran rampant through the population."

"The Black Death was like, seven-hundred-years ago," Thyme says.

"Exactly," Honor agrees.

Thyme fumes. "There are no hugs and kisses in 2803?"

"Zounds, no!" Honor wrinkles her nose. "I hate any displays of affection, but especially public ones."

"That explains a lot," Thyme tells. "And we don't use 'Zounds' as an exclamation anymore. I don't know if anyone really ever did."

"Well, the more common teenage colloquialisms of 2023 are best not utilized in polite company," Honor says like a snooty teacher giving lessons to imbeciles. "Your archaic four-letter expressions are offensive to most zones outside this one."

"Yes, let's stick with exclamations that avoid vulgarity," Ms. Norman agrees. "And let's also refrain from insults between different eras, both veiled and blatant. Everyone needs to try to get along."

"That'll never happen," Thyme grumbles under her breath.

Honor apparently has better hearing than anyone in 2023. "I believe it is your William Shakespeare that said, 'Never say never.'"

"That was Justin Bieber," Thyme says.

Honor scowls. She looks like a bitter old woman who wants everyone off her lawn, but she's, in fact, Thyme's age and another snotty posh that thinks she's better than everyone else. They would have to be enemies. Thyme doesn't like the future. She doesn't like the present. Thyme prefers the past, and Honor abhors it.

Ms. Norman leads the students toward the UFO parked on the runway. Efren takes one last look back at his parents and the rest of his sprawling family, his wide gait slowing a little. He hesitates as if he has second thoughts. Ms. Norman is already onboard. Candy bounds up the stairs and into the large-scale drone. Honor deliberately takes the steps one by one. Efren stops at the bottom, still looking at his family. Thyme sees it in his eyes. He doesn't want to leave them.

"There's no going back, Efren," Thyme tells. "Time is stuck. We can only try to go forward."

Is she trying to convince Efren or herself? Nothing ever changes. Not really.

"A school made up of students from all different eras throughout history," Efren sighs. "That does sound pretty cool, right?"

"That sounds like something that actually deserves a 'zounds!'" Thyme says.

Efren nods. He ascends the stairs without another look back, taking the steps two by two. Thyme climbs up last. Glancing at her watch, it still says seven-thirty, ever and always on pause. She doesn't know if she will ever see 2023 again, but she doesn't look back. She's ready for another day.

***

Inside the drone, the interior is one circular room, approximately the size of Thyme's homeroom back in high school, back when history was still contained in books rather than scattered haphazardly across the continent. Comfortable cushioned couches face each other in the center, with more individual seats situated outside the nucleus. Efren, Candy, and Thyme take spots in the communal center of the transport. Honor sits alone in a seat, looking out a strange portal in the silver wall. The window is seamless on the surface, a transparent, round shape in an otherwise opaque shell. In fact, the whole of the drone appears poured from a single mold, with no joints visible anywhere. This is certainly technology from somewhen futurer than 2023.

Ms. Norman stands in the center of the circularly arranged seating. "One more stop. We have a student to pick up in 1960, and then we'll be off to New York."

"Will the other students already be there?" Candy asks eagerly.

Ms. Norman nods. "The other faculty has been gathering the rest of the student body from zones all across the country. Most of them should be at the Minute by the time we get back."

"How many?" Thyme asks. When she applied to the Institute, it was to get away from 2023. She couldn't be stuck in the day of her mother's death anymore. She hadn't delved into the details. The only thing she really knows about the Minute is that the Institute is in New York, and that's far enough away. Plus, New York is in 1980, and that's long enough ago. Her mom was born in 1982. She can't be really dead if she isn't even born yet.

"We have a freshman class of seventy-three. A few zones have no students to contribute to the school, but several have multiple pupils, like here in 2023. We'll have kids representing the vast majority of timelines there. You'll be the future of the nation. A beacon of hope."

"I can't wait to meet the exchange students," Candy says breathlessly.

"Exchange?" Thyme asked.

"Yes, ten of the seventy-three students are from across the Atlantic. We have foreigners from such diverse places and times as 2772 Paris to 503 England to 2504 BC Egypt."

"Perhaps the Parisian will be less uncivilized than present company," Honor mumbles from outside the circle where everyone else gathered.

"Apparently, being civilized in 2803 does not include any sort of internal filter," Thyme says.

"Now, now," Ms. Norman chides gently. "The purpose of the school is to celebrate and appreciate the differences between all eras. America is founded on a shared history of people from very different backgrounds. The Institute will illustrate that those principles have not changed. The school seeks to show the world that epochal diversity isn't a detriment but rather the framework for a better tomorrow. We are still the melting pot. It's just the ingredients that have changed. The Statue of Liberty still stands tall, and her words have never been truer. 'Send these, the homeless, tempest-tossed to me. I lift my lamp beside the golden door!' We are all tempest-tossed, torn from our timelines and put together for some purpose. Like the wretched refuse that once teemed through Liberty Island, we're stronger together than standing at odds."

Efren and Candy voice agreement. Ms. Norman's words inspire Thyme. Even Honor, ornery, agrees with a quick nod.

"We're ready to get going," Ms. Norman says, taking a seat outside the circle. "Systems are all automatic. The flight is preprogrammed. The interior fills with a sleeping agent during takeoff, so no one is conscious as we pass through the zones. Remember, you'll each wake up a different age. If any of you arrive in Las Vegas in infancy, you will remain on the drone ship until we retrieve the new student. Memory is muddled in an infant state, so you may not remember the stopover. In that case, you may next regain cognitive consciousness when we arrive in New York."

"I hope I'm a baby when we land in 1960," Honor whispers. "The further back in time we go, the worse it smells."

"I hope you're a baby, too," Thyme says. "I'd rather leave you on board."

Then Thyme yawns. Across from her, Efren nods off, and Candy's eyes close. Honor quits her rude comments. Ms. Norman snores softly in her seat. Thyme feels the saucer-shaped ship start to rise, gently moving into the sky. With every blink, her eyelids grow heavier and heavier.

She has spent the last year of her life stuck in the same moment, the time of her mother's death. Thyme sleeps for a few fitful hours every equivalent day, but horrors plague her dreams. Every time she wakes, it is still the same time. Not even a single solitary second passes. Time froze in the instant of her mother dying.

Now it's time to turn the page of the calendar. Seven-thirty p.m. on July the sixteenth, 2023 is over. It's time to leave the present in the past and look toward the future, even if the future is in 1980. Thyme has to move toward tomorrow.

Last blink. Scarlet flash. She sees Efren turn into an older man, middle-aged, white, peppering his black hair. Candy becomes even fuller-figured, advancing another few years and threatening to overspill her tight top and straining at her formfitting seams. Thyme sees a wisp of gray that is Ms. Norman's head. And behind her, Honor whines like a baby. Thyme smiles.

The sleeping gas takes Thyme away, and the automated drone takes Thyme farther on. Only time will tell if she can leave her grief behind. Because sometimes, one can change the view outside their window and change the time on the clock on the wall, but it's harder to change the tempo of one's heart. Some things are carried with no matter the time or place, no matter how far you go or how many moments you put between now and then. Time heals all wounds, but sometimes there's not enough time in a world where seconds are stuck and hours last an eternity.

All Thyme can do is try. Dreams take her away as the drone takes them east. And in her dreams, her mother dies, again and again and again.

CHAPTER TWO

3:13

2.16.1960 AD

Las Vegas, Nevada

Las Vegas is gaudy and glitzy and glamorous. Time froze in the middle of the night in Sin City, but A.M. and P.M. look little different in a town where the bright lights compete with the sun itself in intensity and inflexibility. The setting accosts the senses, signs and advertisements everywhere promoting fun and freedom. The sights and sounds illustrate an entire cityscape set to the soundtrack of a big top circus.

Thyme stands along Las Vegas Boulevard in front of the Sands. The billboard advertises the Rat Pack playing a show in just two equivalent hours. She doesn't know Dean Martin from George R.R. Martin, but she appreciates that Jiji would fawn over these figures as if they are Greek gods stepped out of mythical Olympus.

Patrons from all over town and from several other eras stream toward the casino to get to the show. Locals wear furs that would have gotten them shunned back in 2023, and plaids that make Thyme's eyes hurt. Tourists mix fashion that flashes forward decades and centuries, or throws back to colonial times with bonnets straight out of the prairie Midwest. There are immigrants from every imaginable era coming to attend the performance.

Thyme sees someone through the throngs of tourists, and that old familiar pang plucks at the strings of her heartache. Mom? It happens even elsewhen, even twenty years before her mother is born. The woman comes closer, and of course it's a stranger. Someone from maybe 696 or 3214. Certainly not Rikona Mugen from 2023. And grief comes in like the tide, washing over her heart, leaving her broken all over again.

"Is it not illegal to wander freely between zones?" Honor sniffs, sounding more whiny than prissy. She came across the border of 1960, less than three feet tall, maybe three years old. "Federal travel visas are notoriously difficult to obtain. It is statistically impossible that so many legal immigrants are in 1960 to attend one single show. Most of these tourists must be lawbreakers flagrantly defying federal law."

"1960 has less diligent enforcement of federal edicts than many other zones," Ms. Norman says. "Tourism is their main trade in 1960, and the zone would wither and die without vacationers. They refuse to agree to certain restrictions from Washington if it harms their local economy and restricts their autonomy. They consider themselves a sanctuary state. Washington is reluctant to enforce immigration over concern that the people of Vegas will ally themselves with Jefferson Davis's 1869."

"Well, we ought to blend right in," Candy beams brightly. "We're certainly not the only fobs in this future."

"Fob?" Thyme asks.

"You've never heard of the term 'fob'?" Efren quizzes. "Have you been asleep the last e-year? Like Rip VanWinkle or something?"

"Rip VanWinkle was asleep while time passed," Thyme argues. "No time has passed at all, Efren."

"But you've never heard of a fob?" he asks, his voice old and his body aged. He looks like he's in his sixties. His tall, gangly form bends like an overgrown willow.

"I was busy with more important things than new vocabulary," Thyme snaps.

"It's short for 'fresh off the boat,'" Candy says, changing the subject. Thyme sighs, relieved. She doesn't want to talk with Efren Cortez about mourning her mother for a whole year. "That's what they call us folks who wander outside our native time zones."

Thyme stares at the scene. Cars like out of some old movie cruise the Strip, buildings that memory suggests should be grainy and blurry are sharp and distinct — a past that ought to be unreal is instead as solid and sure as her own fingers and toes. This place is alive — sounds of slot machines chattering and chiming along the street, changing colors in lights all around, people laughing and shouting happily and singing loudly as they make their way from one attraction to the next.

Most striking is the night sky. The street is as bright as the daytime in 2023 Hollywood, but the sky behind the shining city is black and full of stars. Thyme hasn't laid eyes on the night for an entire e-year, the last long twelve equivalent months spent under a garish sun. She looks past the kaleidoscope colors and shining obstructions at the universe beyond the edge of Earth. Space opens endlessly out beyond the present, an emptiness that stretches forever into the sky. Thyme stares into the void. Somewhere out there, maybe, is the Heaven where her mother awaits, looking back.

"C'mon, Thyme," Candy says, taking her by the hand. "Ms. Norman is getting ahead of us. We pick up the new recruit, and then we can get to New York City." She says "New York" like it's the Promised Land.

"Who is this new student?" Thyme asks.

"Ms. Norman said her name is Scarlett Sloane. Her father is very wealthy."

"Another spoiled brat?" Thyme sneers. "We already have one of those in the class."

Honor, a few paces in front of Thyme and Candy, turns back and sticks out her tongue at the girls. Honor is as small as a toddler and waddles like a penguin at SeaWorld. Her attitude is not diminished with her reduced size.

"Scarlett's father owns quite a few casinos up and down the Strip," Candy says. "Old ones, and even some new ones built after the Freeze."

"How do you know so much about this?" Thyme asks. She has barely had time to speak six words to Ms. Norman about anything besides the accident out on Santa Monica Boulevard and her infinite minute ever since.

"Efren took forever to leave his house when we picked him up to take him to the airport," Candy says to Thyme with a bemused eye roll. "He had to take a picture of the last time he saw every little thing around his house with one of those televisions the size of a Cracker Jack box that you all carry in your pockets." She looks ahead at Efren with the same starstruck swoon as she favored Thyme. But not the abject fawning that she reserves for just Honor. "Ms. Norman told me all about Scarlett while we waited. And Efren. And Honor. And you." She pauses, the last words inflicting the first change in tone Thyme has heard from the girl. Always too upbeat, her voice falls flat, like a soda left out too long. "I'm sorry about your mom."

The words still cut. What do you say? Thanks? Not a chance because the comment is never a gift. It's all right? No, it isn't at all right. As long as Candy doesn't say, She's in a better place. That one is the worst. Her mother is supposed to be by Thyme's side. There is no better place.

Thyme can't dam the tears. They come on too quickly, overspilling her eyes. She cannot control that. But she can stop them again before it turns to a flood. Thyme has learned to distract her emotions over the last e-year. She starts thinking about something else. She changes the subject so hard she almost needs a seatbelt to keep from derailing the whole conversation.

"Where are we going?" Thyme asks, shaking her head as if warding off a sneeze. Her teardrops flick away.

"The Stardust," Candy answers, taking the turn with Thyme. Candy had arrived in Vegas in her thirties, and her dress barely contains her buxom figure. She looks like a starlet from the Golden Age of Hollywood, like Marilyn Monroe herself in 1960s Vegas. "It's one of the newest casinos built before the Freeze. Scarlett's dad owns the place. It's the crown jewel of the Strip. It's the hot spot to entertain tourists."

"We're not tourists."

"Well, we sure aren't from 1960, either," Honor says.

The fobs pass casinos called the Silver Slipper and the New Frontier, the crowds clogging the street speaking all sorts of American dialects. Thyme recalls the last time she was at Disneyland and the cacophony of discordant languages overlapping — Spanish and Japanese and Arabic and English all swirling into unintelligible noise. Now the language is all the same, but so many words mean different things to immigrants from different eras — cloud, viral, text, swipe, tweet, timeline.

A large sign for the Stardust occupies the whole marquee, a kitschy style featuring stars and planets. The simplicity makes Thyme smile. Like pictures of her mother when Rikona was young — the façade of a more innocent lifestyle.

As the fobs walk up to the front door of the casino, two men with sunglasses and suits tailored to the time stand on each side of the Stardust's entrance. "Ms. Norman," says the smaller, his mouth barely moving. "Mr. Sloane would like to speak with you. Alone."

The larger man, as big as anyone Thyme has ever seen, grumbles in a voice deeper than she thought the human voice capable of. Her teeth chime from the sound. "The students can go ahead on up. Top floor. Miss Scarlet is waiting for them in the penthouse."

Ms. Norman nods. "Go along," she says to her recruits. "I'll meet you upstairs."

Ms. Norman goes off with the two escorts. Honor shrugs and heads to the elevator, the smallest of the students in the lead. Thyme watches Ms. Norman until she turns a corner and disappears. She said she would meet them in the penthouse, but Thyme has a weird feeling something isn't right. The feeling would turn out to be a premonition. Ms. Norman will never make it upstairs.

***

Inside the opulent elevator, the button to the penthouse suite is highest on the board of choices, all like glowing little clock faces featuring unmoving numbers. Honor marches first into the elevator car and stands staring up at the button, too short to reach it. She stands barely to Thyme's belly button. With a wry grin, Thyme pushes the button for the toddler. The toddler calls her a name unfit for the mouth of someone just out of diapers.

Thyme herself entered 1960 as about thirteen, not so different from what she was in 2023. Her adjustment to this time zone was the most minimal of the Institute recruits. When Thyme woke up in the drone, she stood for a moment in front of the mirror in the lavatory, like looking back three years to a shape a little less tall and quite a bit less shapely. When Ms. Norman arrived at Jiji's home in 2023 while Thyme was still packing for the voyage east, the headmistress suggested Thyme wear a spandex sports bra. Now Thyme understands why. She lost several sizes as she reduced in age. Her form is as boyish as Efren's had been in 2023.

Efren is youthful no longer. He added fifty years from when they left their home zone. As old as his grandfather, closer to sixty-six than sixteen, he remains fit and still somehow even looks boyishly handsome. His hair turned the solid sterling of a respectable retiree, his hairline still full. So tall, the effects of an aged skeleton make him stoop under the strain of his elongated frame.

Candy turned from a ravishing twenty-something to a voluptuous thirty-something, sporting curves that would make her a perfect pin-up girl in the era she's originally from. It's strange, never having seen Candy at her true age, imagining the girl as a teenager. Bubbly and bright and childlike in her wonder, she nevertheless looks like a movie star. To think she's an equivalent seventeen under all that va-va-va-voom is a concept crazy to consider even in a world without whens.

"Penthouse suite," Honor says drily. "Is this Scarlett Sloane trying to impress us or something?"

"Maybe," Thyme says. "You know, some people actually care what other people think of them."

"An archaic idea," Honor dismisses.

"That's how you make friends. Trying to get other people to like you."

"Like and dislike? Caring what people think about you?" Honor sniffs like a debutante talking to the destitute. "You people are pathetically Paleolithic."

"I'm starting to think the future looks pretty bleak," Thyme tells.

The elevator stops at the top floor and opens not into a hotel hallway but on a vestibule that leads into the penthouse beyond. They march forward, and Efren holds the elevator door open for the three ladies, more like a gentleman from Victorian England than a teenager from 2023. Candy favors him with a stunning smile, Thyme mumbles a "thanks," and little Honor scowls like he has somehow offended her as if in the future, polite and rude are mixed around.

Sinatra croons from inside the room on a radio, a remake of a Taylor Swift song from 2020. The four students walk forward to find the fifth new enrollee to the Minute. She wears her copper-colored hair in a high bouffant puffed upward toward a vaulted ceiling, pearls as large as jumbo gumballs around her neck, a dress as yellow as the immutable sun from 2023, and a coat that ends mid-thigh that looks extremely expensive.

"Is that fur?" Honor asks with withering contempt.

"Yes, it's sable. And it's authentic," Scarlett replies without any sign of being unsettled. She looks up to the challenge named Honor Fitzgerald. "Is that plastic?"

"It is a polymer construct beyond even your wildest imaginings," Honor answers.

"I dunno," Scarlett replies with a devious wink. "I have a pretty wild imagination."

"We were sent up here to wait for Ms. Norman while she takes a meeting with your father," Thyme says, interrupting the escalating catfight.

Scarlett ends the back and forth with Honor without a clear winner. She sashays around toward the fobs, Honor flinching from the fur as if the sable could still bite.

"Make yourself at home," Scarlett says. "We might be here a while."

The penthouse suite in the Stardust looks like it was built for a sultan in ancient Arabia. Cream and gold evoke sand and sun, like the desert tones of the Middle East have been replicated perfectly. Sheer curtains stream from the ceiling and pin to the walls, flowing in bright colors over the bed and billowing near the open windows. A small hot tub in the corner of the room is surrounded by sand, like a small beachfront respite right here inside the suite.

There are lamps with exotic oils flickering in the corners of the room, an arched brass mirror frame featuring multicolored gemstones, a handcrafted Mashrabiya wall shelf, a Moroccan pouf in blue leather, and a chest inlaid with mother of pearl tiles.

"Are these all authentic Arabian artifacts?" Honor asks the girl standing at the center of it all.

Scarlett Sloane makes a face more derogatory than anything even Honor Fitzgerald has managed. Thyme grins inwardly as the precious princess prepares a rude rebuke. "It was imported from 1143 BC. The Stardust had it shipped directly from the

Hejaz region of the Arabian Peninsula shortly after the Freeze. Chronological legitimacy is the newest fad, don't you know."

Thyme looks at Honor and sees that there's now someone in the group who irritates her more than Thyme Mugen does.

"I'm from the year 2803," Honor sniffs haughtily. "Everything is an antique to me. Even you."

"The future? You must be so smart, with all those extra years of history under your belt," Scarlett says with sarcasm dripping from her sharp tongue. "Ooo, does that mean you can tell me what's going to happen next?"

Scarlett stares at Honor. Honor glares back.

"This looks like a lair," Thyme says, interrupting the tense teenage stand-off.

"A lair?" Scarlett asks. "Like in a James Bond novel?"

"You mean a James Bond movie?" Efren corrects.

"The movies came after the books, dear Efren," Scarlett says. "That is after my time."

Something isn't quite right. Thyme sees no packed bags. Scarlett certainly doesn't look dressed for traveling between time zones. Thyme thinks about her sports bra and then looks again at Scarlett's attire. She wears high heels that would be impossible if she crosses octogenarian and a short yellow dress that would slip right off if she was small, with all kinds of jewelry certainly serving as choking hazards if Scarlett comes across in infancy. Something suddenly feels very wrong about this.

"You could've met us in the lobby," Thyme says. "Why did we have to come all the way up to your lair?"

"You find the villain in the lair," Scarlett says.

"Yeah, and the villain always has a splashy, sinister name," Efren agrees, then frowns as if he's just figuring something out. Like Scarlet Sloane.

"Do you think I'm going to be the villain, Thyme Mugen?" Scarlett asks. "Is that what happens next? Maybe Honor knows since she's from the future?" Sarcasm must be a superpower in the '60s. "You think you know everything, Honor. You see the past as events that have been recorded and certified. Tombstones written in granite with epitaphs summarizing the facts. But the past is still alive. Changing. It's different than you remember. That's how you can be my hostage eight hundred years before you were even born."

Candy blinks like she just heard a joke and can't figure out the punchline. Honor glowers, unsure of the turn of their trade of insults. Efren looks like he is attempting to translate foreign words from the language of 1960 to a 2023 dialect. The words Scarlett said mean the same thing now as they did then, the same thing they will mean tomorrow. It's the thing that always means the same.

People suck.

"This is a trap," Thyme tells him.

Efren tries the double doors between the penthouse and the elevator. Locked from the outside. There's no other way out of the room, twelve stories up. Thyme looks at Candy, who looks at Efren, who looks scared. Scarlett Sloane is the villain, after all.

***

It's all cliché before cliché was even a thing. Scarlett's wild red hair piled in a beehive shape, wearing a daffodil dress that looks squeezed from lemons, in a room fit for one of Batman's foes. All that's left is a lengthy monologue revealing every detail of her master plan, right before the hero thwarts her.

"Ms. Norman is playing a dangerous game," Scarlett pontificates, pacing back and forth in front of the four fobs. "She wants to incorporate the disparate eras. All the clocks might be stopped, but that doesn't mean we can't still take lessons from history. Integration incites amalgamation. Assimilation will lead to the eventual breakdown of what keeps us individual. It has occurred over and over throughout history. Cultures fade and decay when blended together, becoming some bland concoction that lacks distinction. I mean, consider Honor. Eight centuries in the future, and she looks like she should be called Ambiguity instead of Honor. I'm getting bored just thinking about her."

Honor appears stung. Bald as a newborn with average features, colorless eyes, unexceptional complexion, and a functional, forgettable wardrobe, Thyme imagines having to describe her if she lost Honor in a supermarket in 1980 New York and cannot conjure a proper rendition.

"Your hair reminds me of an overripe radish," Honor retorts.

"A millennia from now, and we still resort to name-calling?" Scarlett says. "Well, you look like a Popeye Pez dispenser."

"Where I come from, you have been dead for a very long time," Honor replies.

The girls stare at each other for a while, the teenage Scarlett glaring down at the three-foot toddler.

"You were going to tell us all about your evil plans," Thyme prompts.

"You think of me as the bad guy here, Thyme?" Scarlett asks. "I suppose that depends on the story, doesn't it? We can each be either the hero or the villain depending on the turn of the tale. History casts its characters in one role or the other, but it all depends on perspective. Whether we are good or evil is all in the eye of the author."

"You're holding us here against our will," Efren says.

"That makes you the villain, Scarlett."

"I'm protecting you," Scarlett says. "I'm keeping you safe. Would Superman let a bunch of kids run into a burning building? Would Flash Gordon let a spaceship land on a doomed planet? You wear seat belts in 2023, don't you? For safety? In case of a crash? Well, think of me as restraining you for your own protection."

"Let us go, Scarlett," Thyme demands. She had been a prisoner of sorts in 2023, and now Thyme is stuck in a hotel room in 1960. She wants to move forward, but the world keeps trying to hold her back.

"It's too dangerous," Scarlett says.

In 2023, it's a hackneyed plot device, subject to ridicule after decades of the antagonist announcing their motivation in a grand, pompous soliloquy in so many movies and books. But a girl from 1960 doesn't know that.

Scarlett continues, "Some factions in America are resistant to Ms. Norman's brave new world. They want to keep the zones separated, preserved in time. When the clocks start ticking again, they want things to be as close as possible to the way they were when the moments stopped moving. No travel between zones. No integration of eras. No central government in Washington telling everyone what to do. We want to be free. So we follow the lead of Jefferson Davis from 1869."

The same Jefferson Davis currently talking to Anderson Cooper on a replay of his CNN interview on an RCA television set on the floor in the corner of the hotel room? The colors on the convex screen bleed and blur like someone had left a finger-painting out in the rain.

"You want another Civil War?" Thyme asks.

"Mr. Davis has started a public resistance to President Harrison's plans," Scarlett says. "Behind the scenes, he has gathered supporters to undermine certain initiatives like the Mallory Norman Institute of Time. Mr. Davis plans to stand firmly against all efforts to weaken the borders between the states. He will take up arms against the homogenizers."

"What happened to Ms. Norman?" Candy asks.

"She's in custody. My father will keep her safe. Like in a seat belt, as I said. My father is Jeremiah Sloane, the grandson of Jefferson Davis. There are other descendants and ancestors of the family in various zones. Even beyond family, there are many sympathizers. Well-known politicians and power players from across the fractured timelines are against Ms. Norman's educational experiment. There's strong American resistance to authority, and you lot are a part of the problem."

"We're like the Empire?" Efren gapes. "And you're the Rebellion?"

"I don't understand your reference," Scarlett sighs. "Nor do I want to. I want things to stay like they are. I want James Bond to be on the page rather than on a silver screen."

"For someone stuck in the Sixties, you sure seem to like your anachronistic artifacts," Thyme interjects.

She joins Honor along the far wall of the lair, examining items along a series of shelves nearer the bed. She recognizes electronics chargers, a digital clock, a coffee maker, an old-fashioned phone with a dial and a cord, and a flat surface television in digital color beside a black-and-white screen on a classic Zenith. There are many more things that Thyme cannot comprehend — a device that appears to be made of small rainbows, wafer-thin translucent surfaces, liquid light in a polycarbonate flask, metal tools that might be a thousand years old and serve some mysterious purpose, things ancient and things from a future beyond even Honor's understanding.

"Amenities for the affluent," Scarlett says. "Some things don't change no matter what era you're from. This hotel caters to high-end clientele. Even leaders of this rebellion you speak of must meet somewhere. The Stardust has five-star amenities, and I'm a five-star daughter. We might not be 'morrows to most of you, but neither are we savages."

"Says the person holding us prisoner," Efren says.

Scarlett shrugs.

"What happens next?" Candy asks.

"My father will negotiate a dissolution of the Institute. Once President Harrison agrees to rescind permission for the Minute, then you go home," Scarlett explains. "You go back to when you came from. Back to when you belong. All of you. Along with all the other recruits and instructors."

"Or what?" Thyme wonders.

"Or Ms. Norman stays in 1960 indefinitely," Scarlett says. "There won't be a Minute without her."

Thyme doesn't want to go back. She has been stuck in 2023 for the last year, every day the same. Every day the day her mother died. She is finally moving on, moving forward. Now Scarlett Sloane wants to send her back. Scarlett wants things to stay the same. She fights change. But Thyme needs tomorrow. She needs to turn the page of the calendar.

Honor looks at Thyme, and Thyme sees a reflection of her own resistance in the 'morrow's eyes. For the first time since they met, the two girls agree on something. Neither one of them wants to go back to when they were.

"You don't know what half of these things are used for, do

you?" Honor asks Scarlett. "These devices are like some sort of science fiction that only exists in these books you speak of."

"I don't need to know," Scarlett says. "None of that will matter when the clocks start again."

Honor shrugs. "That might be true. But what happens in the future is not what is happening now. The only future you are facing at this moment is me. And I know how a lot of these things work. Want to guess?"

Scarlett glares across the room. "I'm perfectly content with 1960 as it is, thank you very much."

"You embrace ignorance? Good. Very good," Honor says. "Because ignorance and intolerance always lead to failure. And you will fail, Scarlett Sloane."

"I really cannot stand you, you know," Scarlett says.

Honor replies, "I believe it was Henry Wadsworth Longfellow who wrote, 'The haters gonna hate, hate, hate, hate, hate. I'm just gonna shake, shake, shake, shake, shake, shake it off.'"

"That was Taylor Swift," Thyme tells.

Honor shrugs. She holds a futuristic device in her hand, something beyond the ken of a simple girl from 1960 or even 2023. The 'morrow presses her thumb into the pliable material, and the scene inside the suite stutters, like the whole thing is a movie being played back on a silver screen from this time zone, and the film reel skipped a frame. Efren and Candy disappear, like magicians teleporting away. Thyme startles, then looks toward Honor, mouth hanging open.

"This is an antique Holographic Overlay Device with omni-sound," Honor says. "Scarlett can't see us or hear us."

"No, no, no, no, no," Scarlett rants, searching all around as if unsure Thyme and Honor have ceased to exist or have teleported away. Her mouth moves like a fish trying to breathe air and failing miserably. Scarlett looks from the door to the elevator, firmly locked, to the windows that open to a thirteen-story drop.

Honor steps closer to the window, and Efren and Candy reappear.

"The H.O.D. bends sound and light to make us undetectable," Honor says, setting the device on a desk near a window overlooking the Strip. "The acoustics are affected by simple sound dampeners. I can adjust the range of the device. We can see and hear each other when we are in proximity, but we are invisible to anyone beyond three meters."

"The cone of silence," Efren sniggers.

No one replies.

"Austin Powers?" he asks.

"I know Tyrone Powers," Candy says. "My dad loved him in The Mark of Zorro."

"What did you do?" Scarlett cries out to an apparently empty room, fists clenched at her sides and her face going red to match her hair.

"We need to go out the window," Honor says.

"We're thirteen stories up," Efren says. "How do we get safely down to the street if we go through the window?"

Honor passes out small disks that look like betting chips from when Jiji used to play poker Saturday nights with the other old gals in the neighborhood. "Bouncy," Honor explains.

"What's Beyoncé got to do with this?" Efren asks.

"It's a bouncy. It took the place of the fire escape and parachutes and flotation devices around the turn of the twenty-second century," Honor elaborates. She puts one on her chest, and it stays, like her heart is iron and the poker chip magnetic. "Watch." Honor smiles at the other three fobs, checks the streets below, and leaps through the open window.

Efren lets out an unintended yelp as Honor jumps, but the cone of silence holds, and Scarlett remains clueless to their means of escape for another moment. The three teenagers not from the far-flung future watch an orb inflate around Honor instantly, like an airbag crossed with a beach ball. Honor is in the center, a harness like thin bands around her torso, suspending her in the middle. She bounces. Safely.

Thyme looks at Candy. Candy looks from Thyme to Efren. Efren watches Honor over the ledge. Smiles. And jumps.

Another ball inflates out of the poker chip on his chest, straps securing him so he will bounce safely against the ground in the beyoncé. "'Now all the single ladies…,'" Thyme sings. Candy stares back, clueless. They leap out of the window together.

Thyme went to Disneyland with her mom a year ago, or a month ago (or sixty years from now), just last June. They rode all the rollercoasters, but none of them held the thrill of free-falling in 1960. Before the safety device activates, Thyme feels freer than she has felt since the clocks stopped. Then an orb inflates around her, and she hits the street, bouncing up and down in an inflatable ball. This must be the future of Space Mountain. Beyoncé as a Magic Kingdom ride.

The bouncy stops after a couple of gentle dribbles, settling near Honor and Efren. Instantly it deflates and dissolves, draining into the street and along the gutters in a thin stream of goo. Outside again, the lights of the Las Vegas Strip illuminate the fobs like they're under a spotlight.

"The H.O.D. will run out of power any moment," Honor says, looking up at the open window of the penthouse suite.

"1960 has not ionized their atmosphere for perpetual recharge."

The three students from the 'morrow's past stare at Honor like she's speaking Asimov.

"It is no wonder you are all extinct where I come from," Honor mumbles.

"What do we do now?" Efren asks, watching as Scarlett appears at the open window and looks down from thirteen stories up.

A Mustang so red it makes Scarlett's crimson tresses look colorless in comparison pulls up to the curb in front of the Stardust. Behind the wheel sits a boy who might have been straight out of a progressive remake of Rebel Without a Cause from 2023 that recast Jim Stark as a teenage boy of color. He's dark and handsome — skin a little browner than his leather jacket, face chiseled from a billboard advertising a weekend in 1960 Sin City, hair black and curly and as shiny as the body of his growling Ford.

"You freams aren't from around here," he says.

Thyme glances up at Scarlett. Several heads appear out the window around her. Security. Thyme turns back to the bad boy with the dangerous looks. Being "bad" in the Sixties is like being an angel in 2023. This guy doesn't know bad. Thyme leans into his driver-side window and flashes him her most dangerous smile.

"You want a ride with the future, hot stuff?"

The driver looks past Thyme at Candy, buxom and blonde. "Is she coming?"

Thyme realizes she's thirteen in 1960 and about as alluring as a firefly flitting among the neon glare of Las Vegas Boulevard. But Candy is a bombshell.

"We're kind of a package deal," Thyme tells.

"Then get in," the kid says.

***

Efren probably should have sat shotgun in the front seat of the Ford Mustang if the decision had been made by determination of size, but Thyme isn't going to let the two boys ride up front while the three girls crowded into the backseat like a trio of helpless damsels. They may be stuck in 1960, but it is so not 1960 anymore. So Efren is folded up like a beach chair behind the passenger seat, Candy directly behind the driver, while Honor, only three and small, sits between them. Thyme rides shotgun. The driver tilts the rearview mirror to point back at Candy, and he glances into it often. Thyme sighs. Boys are the same, from Fred Flintstone to George Jetson.

Thyme also looks back regularly, checking the side-view mirror for a tail. It's only a matter of time before Scarlett's security guards track them down on the streets of Vegas. She didn't come all the way from 2023 trying to put her feelings behind her just to get killed twenty years before her mom is even born.

"What's your name, Mr. Blast-from-the-past?" Thyme asks, studying the African American teen with a greasy pompadour, a leather jacket, and black-and-white wingtips.

"Jay Stone. And I might be blasting, but this is the present, baby," he says. Thyme isn't sure if "baby" means something similar in 1960 as 2023 or if he is addressing her apparent immaturity.

"I'm sixteen, you know. Seventeen in e-years. You can't be much older than that yourself, baby."

"Don't have a cow, dolly," Jay says, driving like he could hardly be bothered to pay attention to the road. "I've never talked to a fob before. I heard crossing zones messes with the biologics, but I've never seen it up close before. Is your voluptuous friend in the backseat sixteen, too?"

Jay Stone's black eyebrows waggle in a way that might have been bad boy back now but is juvenile in 2023.

"Close enough," Thyme says with a roll of her eyes. "You're staring so hard at her, I figured you could see right through her exterior appearance."

"What are you freams doing in 1960?" Jay asks, finally tearing his eyes off Candy.

Thyme glares. If he weren't black, she would wonder if "freams" is a racial slur. Or maybe it is anyway.

"Running," she says, catching a glimpse of a security vehicle coming up the Strip fast on their tail. "So, Jay Stone, you fast?"

Then Jay gives her an authentic, timeless, better-buckle-up bad-boy grin. Fast enough.

Jay accelerates. The wheels squeal, and the inertia presses Thyme back into the seat. For a moment, her head gets woozy, and her heart makes a tympani beat. This is the thrill of being alive. Of moving forward. She spent a year stuck in an infinite minute, and now she feels propelled forward into the future. Finally.

"What do they want from you?" Jay asks, taking a corner on two wheels.

"They don't like the idea of the future colliding with the past."

"I don't like the idea of this death trap colliding with an immovable object," Honor huffs from the backseat.

"Well, you freams sure know how to make a guy's day a lot more interesting," Jay says with a dazzling, dangerous smile.

"Can you outrun them?" Thyme asks, digging into the dashboard with her fingernails.

"Depends on where we're running to." Jay looks down the length of the Strip—plenty of room left to really open the throttle. "I can move fast enough to stay in front of them. But I probably don't have enough gas in the tank to outlast them. They ration fuel for the lowly citizens in this zone, y'know."

"Can you get us back to McCarran Field?"

"The airport?" They're heading in the opposite direction up the Strip. Jay checks his mirrors, this time not even sneaking a peek at Candy. Thyme looks, too. Now there's a squadron of Las Vegas police cars behind them. The cops are surely in Mr. Sloane's deep pocket. "In a roundabout way, maybe. You up for something unreal?"

"The world has been unreal all year," Thyme tells. "Do it."

Jay pulls hard on the wheel and points the Mustang due east. "Hold on to something. I'm gonna goose it."

Thyme has never been in a car without seatbelts in her entire life. Her mother would remind her to buckle every time she got into a vehicle. Now her still-alive daughter is drag-racing through 1960 Las Vegas without a seatbelt anywhere in the near vicinity.

From the backseat, Candy caterwauls a big "Yee-haw" like she's more Maybelle than Monroe.

It's night in 1960, the zone stuck in perpetual darkness. The lights of Las Vegas Boulevard offset the effect of the never-ending night. But on the outskirts of town, where the neon lights fade and darkness looms across the open desert beyond, the scope of always being 3:13 a.m. is more apparent. The night is cloudless, an eternity of sky above them going on and on forever. The stars are a myriad tapestry so bright and clear, unobstructed by smoke or smog. Thyme has never seen anything like it. Like something from a fairy tale.

Enchanting, Thyme thinks.

"Enchanting," Efren says, as if reading her mind.

Eerie.

The universe is on pause, but the light from the stars takes eons to travel across the cosmos. Thyme gazes up at worlds that still turn, where days still pass, and the cycle of life and death still plays out in all the thousands of different galaxies scattered across the sky. She sees a past where time still moves. The day when the clocks stop is still in their future.

Thyme has seen enough of the past. It follows her whenever she goes. History is alive all over the world. She doesn't need to gaze up at the stars. Thyme looks away from the twinkle of the night sky. Outside the windshield, she stares into a void.

She's resisted the abyss for the last e-year. The darkness constantly pulls her closer, the loss of her most loved like an anchor trying to drag her down. Thyme feels it every time she closes her eyes. The gravity of grief. The whisper of ruin. But now the abyss is real. She stares into it with her eyes wide open. The void is close, and Jay is speeding right toward it.

Darkness. Complete. Unending. So deep it feels as if it has substance.

"What is that?" Thyme whispers.

"That's the Dark Zone," Jay says.

"Is it the future or the past?" Thyme asks softly, afraid of an answer.

"No one is sure," Honor contributes from the backseat. "All anyone knows is that it is somewhen else. And when you go in, you do not come back out."

Jay accelerates directly toward the Dark Zone, with six police cars in hot pursuit. The roads all ended, so they are speeding across hardpan desert, dust making a cloud that at least obscures their tail. Jay flips off a switch, extinguishing his taillights and the headlamps to further confound their followers. The shimmering scarlet border that delineates the time zones glows softly before them in the night, like the subtle warning of a red light. Jay speeds closer, like a madman racing toward the edge of a cliff.

Thyme's fingernails scrape trails along the dashboard.

"I don't want to die," she says.

"This isn't what dying looks like, dolly," Jay Stone says, smiling like the devil making a deal. "This is living."

Jay Stone pulls the steering wheel into a hard right at the last possible second, the driver's side so close that if Jay reached out his window, his left arm would be in a different era. Five of the six cars chasing them manage to avoid the border, but one vehicle couldn't turn in time. Thyme watches Scarlett's hired security's car as it enters the Dark Zone, the driver turning older by several decades. At least he didn't turn into a baby.

Then the car is plucked off the ground by something with tentacles made of vine, some amalgamation of plant and predator. The vehicle is lifted up and away, the octogenarian driver leaping out of the car door and falling back through the border on his way to the ground. He crosses back through the scarlet veil, this time without mechanical transport. He bounces across the desert landscape of 1960 as his original age, less prone to broken bones as a man in his twenties than if he was still elderly.

Then the scene disappears in the rearview mirror. Jay tears along the border, but the five police cars still behind him keep pace. "Those cars must be hopped up. Future tech."

"They import hemis from 2023," Efren says behind him. "My dad works in the factory."

"Cheaters," Jay grumbles.

Jay weaves in the sandy surface, wheels drifting on the unstable ground, threatening to make the Mustang slide into a tailspin. It kicks up more sand, obscuring their wake. The border unexpectedly curves, and Jay expertly avoids the Dark Zone. The five patrol cars behind them also manage to avoid the eerie neighbor to the east but less expertly. One vehicle spins out and ends up high-centered on a small dune of sand.

"Nice driving," Candy compliments, her smile dazzling like the full moon from the backseat. Thyme expects Jay to howl like a werewolf.

"Thanks, dolly," Jay says instead, flashing his killer smile toward the backseat. The expression definitely has hints of a dog.

Thyme looks past the drooling predator driving the Mustang and into the Dark Zone again. Things move in the other epoch, strange shapes that don't make any sense. When she was little and had a nightmare, she could go to her mother's room and snuggle next to her in bed. The terrible dream would always fade by morning. Now, the nightmares don't go away even when her eyes are open, and there's no morning coming anytime soon.

Something big and aggressive touches the scarlet border between time zones, the effect pulling the creature from the other period fully into 1960. The transition makes it turn smaller, younger, whatever it is, at least still affected by age. It looks like the trunk of a tree spliced with a hippo/hedgehog, big and barky with fur made of fir. On the other side of the border, it had been as big as a single stall garage. Luckily for the car that crashes into it behind them, it comes over the size of a port-a-potty. The impact launches the thing back into the Dark Zone, enlarged and enraged, and the police vehicle spins out in the opposite direction, smashed and incapacitated.

The last three police cars chase them the final leg back to McCarran Fields. The airport is on the south end of the Strip, and Jay has managed to already circle almost entirely back to the airport. Thyme can see a jet with "Southwest Airlines" written on the side coming in for a landing. At the end of a runway sits the silver drone they'd arrived in with Ms. Norman.

"There," Thyme points.

"You mean that thing that looks like a rocket ship on Teenagers from Outer Space?"

Thyme peers at Jay like he might be pulling her leg. He looks serious. They really made a movie called Teenagers from Outer Space? Simpler times.

Then one of the police cars paces the Mustang, and a cop leans out of the passenger side, shouting, "Pull over, sooty!"

Sooty? Now that's certainly a racial slur. Maybe simpler times, but certainly not better.

Between the silver drone on the landing field and the caravan racing across the desert is a deep ditch that has to be circumnavigated. Or….

"You ever see Happy Days?" Thyme asks the kid who looks like Jaden Smith playing the Fonz. Thyme's obaasan used to watch it all the time before the clocks stopped, and Renaissance Mugen started taking trips to other zones to turn back to her twenties.

"Must be after my time, baby," Jay says.

"Well, it's a television show where a character named Fonzie uses a ramp to jump over a shark on water skis," Thyme explains.

"Why is the shark wearing water skis?" Jay asks.

"Fonzie is wearing the skis, not the shark," Thyme corrects. "Or it would be silly."

Jay looks at her as if he isn't sure if she's pulling his leg.

"Whatever," she dismisses. "Just tell me, can you jump that ditch?"

Jay scans the landscape. There are dunes rising along the desert here and there. He finally nods. "I think so. I'm not sure how my hot rod is gonna look after, though."

"You can't stay here anyway," Thyme tells him. "Those racist pigs will…. I'm not sure what they do in the Sixties. Is there still lynching?"

"What?" Jay yelps. "You're an oddball, fream." Jay concentrates on choosing the right sloped dune for the jump. "Fonzie sounds like the name of a nerd."

"Nerds are kinda hot in 2023."

"That's nowhere, baby," Jay snorts. Then he stomps the gas, aims like an arrow, and meets a dune at full speed.

The rollercoaster ride hits that sweet spot where gravity is erased. But in the Mustang, there's no harness, no safety straps, no air brakes. Aloft, Thyme feels like they're in a flying car out of some time zone from the future. For a moment, the last piece of physics fails, gravity as gone as the next minute. Weightless. No tether to anything anymore. Fully free. Thyme closes her eyes and smiles.

Then they land.

Thyme hits her head against the ceiling hard enough to make new stars to compliment the clear night sky. Cries of pain ring out from the backseat. But no one dies instantly, not even the Mustang. Several parts fall from the chassis as they make the last hundred yards to the airfield, and the Ford only makes it the last leg with a ruckus of squeals and squeaks.

The last three cop cars refuse to make the same attempt that Jay achieved, choosing instead the long way around.

Jay pulls right up to the silver drone. Candy, Efren, and Honor erupt from the back seat and race toward the ship. Thyme stands beside the sputtering Mustang as the cops circle around the dunes. Jay stays behind the wheel of the car.

"You can't stay here, Jay Stone. Come on board. Ms. Norman will sort this out."

"Ms. Norman's a teacher?" he asks.

"Yes," Thyme tells. "She brought us here. She can fix it."

"If she brought you to 1960, then it seems like she's the one who landed you in this hornet's nest in the first place," Jay says. "Besides, I've never been the teacher's pet. They don't ever seem to like me much."

The cops are getting closer. Thyme and Jay only have a few seconds to get aboard the drone. Once locked from the inside, Thyme is sure they will be safe until Ms. Norman can get this mess cleaned up.

"Please, Jay. You saved us. If you hadn't stuck out your neck, we would've been arrested. Locked up. Or worse. Now let us help you."

Jay glances at the cops racing toward them. He turns his gaze toward the drone as Candy disappears into the entrance open on the side. Then he looks at Thyme. Really looks at her this time instead of being distracted by the bombshell Candy Kane.

"Yeah," he says.

He hops out with one last lingering look at his Mustang, and they run toward the drone. Into the open portal. The hatch closes behind them. Immediately after Thyme is aboard, the quiet motor starts to cycle. The drone lifts, carrying them off the runway and away from the last three police cars.

"What's happening?" Thyme demands, like the spaceship works like Siri or something.

Honor is the closest thing onboard to AI. She has the personality of a smartphone. The 'morrow studies the instruments farther future than anything Thyme understands. "It appears Ms. Norman remotely programmed the craft to get us to the Institute without her. She is saving us from 1960."

"Something must have gone really wrong," Thyme says.

"We better get seated and sedated," Honor advises.

"That's the escape plan?" Efren asks. "We run all the way to New York?"

"What about Ms. Norman?" Candy adds.

No one has an answer as to the fate of Mallory Norman.

"New York?" Jay wonders as Thyme leads him to a seat to prepare him for another time zone.

"Well, Mr. Stone," Thyme tells as she sets him up to be sedated, "I guess you're coming to the future."

CHAPTER THREE
17:51
1.14.68,437,912 BC
Mesozoic Sea

The first thing Thyme notices are her fingers. She notices her fingers even before she recognizes the alarms. Feeling like she used to when Mom woke her up for school, groggy and disoriented, she looks around, almost expecting to see her mother standing in the doorway, telling her it's time to get up. Everything before was just a dream. But that had been a different time. Different place. Before her mother died and left her all alone.

Thyme's hands are so tiny. As an Asian, Thyme already featured smallness, but now she's reverted to a size not seen in a dozen years. Thyme is a toddler, maybe four. Her T-shirt has become a dress. Her pants tangle around her legs and slough off her waist. The sports bra, which had seemed prescient in 1960, is now purposeless.

"This isn't New York," Efren says in a slow drawl, shaking off the effects of sedation. He stands in front of a bank of monitors, steadying himself, looking older than even Jiji. If he was a senior in 1960, he's even older now.

"What is this?" Jay croaks from beside Thyme, sitting up and studying his hands, wrinkled and bony. Jay's greased hair has gone stark white, and his smooth black skin has turned gray and mottled. He looks old enough to be even Efren's father. The brown leather jacket looks odd, like an old soldier putting on the uniform he wore in his youth. It's Jay's first time crossing zones.

"Calm down," Thyme squeaks, her voice more baby and less woman. "It'll change again as soon as we get where we're going."

"Why aren't we in New York?" Candy asks, coming across at forty and looking as bombastic as 2023 Gisele Bündchen.

Thyme, Jay, and Candy join Efren around the monitors relaying the external camera feeds that show endless sea stretching out below them and unending cloud cover above them. The water beneath the aircraft is getting closer and closer.

"Are we crashing?" Efren wonders aloud as if he expects the ship to answer.

"Well, this certainly isn't flyin'," old man Jay wheezes.

They all look to Honor. Honor takes one look back and starts bawling. The 'morrow is only a baby, maybe two months in age. She doesn't even have teeth.

"Something attacked us," Efren says, squinting to accommodate failing eyesight. He points to a screen showing the feed from an exterior camera. The fobs stare at a smoking, sparking hole in the silver surface and one whirling propeller missing most of its blades. "It looks like our enemies have a greater reach than 1960."

"Enemies? We're just kids," Candy cries.

"We're targets because we're students at Ms. Norman's

school. The idea behind the educational institute is a timeless concept," Efren says. "It's a symbol of moving on. But there are a lot of people who prefer to stay stuck in the past."

Thyme frowns at Efren. Is he talking about her? Does he think she likes being trapped by her past? She wants to move on. Thyme wants to get to New York. But things keep getting in the way. The past keeps pulling her down.

One monitor shows towering waves rolling across an endless sea, cresting so high they almost scrape the bottom of the craft. "Hold onto something," Thyme warns.

The craft hits the top of a whitecap, the impact throwing the passengers around the inside of the craft's cabin. Candy had scooped up baby Honor and now cushions the infant in her pillowy bosom. Jay bounces around, brittle bones barely avoiding breakage. Efren is tall enough to safely wedge himself between a console and a seat. Thyme's tiny hands barely hold their grip on one of the instrument panels.

The craft skips several times like a stone across a pond and finally comes to rest, floating on the surface of a roiling sea.

"If this isn't New York, then where are we?" asks Jay.

"I think the right question is when are we?" Thyme says. "This certainly isn't 1960 or 2023."

Efren, taking a seat in front of the console where Ms. Norman had sat on the way from 2023 to 1960, finds the answer. "We're in 68,437,912 BC."

Candy gets to her feet and stands like a sailor on the deck of a boat suffering choppy seas. She cradles Honor against her chest, the baby rocked to sleep by the motion of the ocean.

"How seaworthy is this aircraft?" she asks.

The fobs all look at one another, none of them experts on either boats or futuristic flying contraptions. The aircraft answers for them, water slowly bubbling up from behind a backboard of electronics. A circuit board pops and sizzles, and the screens fall dark as the lights all go out inside the craft.

A flame ignites, Jay holding up a lighter. The glow casts the creased countenances sported by the elderly Efren and Jay into wrecks of wrinkles. The looks of worry, from the very old to toddler Thyme, all transcend age. Only Honor is unperturbed, slumbering soundly.

"Let's check topside," Thyme says. "Maybe there's an island or something nearby. Shine that light this way."

She leads Jay over to a door in the ceiling marked as a maintenance hatch. Thyme opens it carefully. A spray of salty water carried on a strong breeze spatters her face and snuffs Jay's flame. The gray light from the overcast sky dimly illuminates the interior of the drone.

Thyme has to climb up several rungs of the ladder to get high enough to see out, popping her small head out of the portal. Jay appears beside her, his old body wobbling up two steps of the ladder so he can look. He smells like leather and old man. Waves roll as far as they can see in any direction. No sign of land. No sign of anything but endless water.

"This isn't how it was supposed to be," Thyme tells, tears mixing with the salty spray every time a massive wave slaps the side of the silver drone. "I was trying to run away."

"Run away from what?" Jay asks. "Is the future really so bad?"

"My mom died at the moment of the Freeze. The clocks stopped and left me stuck at the time of her death forever. I wanted to get away from that day. A day can only be so long before you have to move on."

"I get it," Jay says. "I was getting tired of February back in Vegas. The shortest month ended up being the very longest."

"I just wanted a different day. Tomorrow. Yesterday. Any other day. I couldn't stay stuck in that moment any longer. But I was supposed to be moving to someplace better. Somewhere safe."

"You're telling me," Jay says. "I don't think I'm in 1960 anymore, Toto."

Thyme smiles. "I love The Wizard of Oz."

"They still watch Oz in 2023?" Jay asks, amused. Saltwater spray soaks his white hair, rivers running in streams along his wrinkles, runnels draining off his sagging flesh of cheeks and neck. In the pale light of prehistory, he still possesses a youthful spark in his gaze despite milky cataracts muting his bright chestnut eyes.

"'There's no place like home,'" Thyme quotes.

"There's no place left like home," Jay disagrees. "We're in some uncharted territory, fuzzy duck."

Fuzzy? Duck? Thyme doesn't know if that's a compliment or insult.

"That's definitely uncharted," Thyme tells, pointing at a part of something massive breaking the surface between waves, the tip of a fin hinting at something big enough to swallow even a whale.

"Get in," Jay hollers, his hundred-year-old body moving down the ladder at superhuman slowness. "Close the hatch!"

"What was that thing?" Thyme cries as she moves aside, letting Candy climb up and haul the door shut.

"I have it on the monitor," Efren shouts.

"I thought everything turned off," Jay says, looking around at the muted red emergency lights that leave everyone glowing like umber coals.

"Efren figured it out," Candy swoons, like Efren is Einstein instead of a normal boy from 2023. The kids of Generation Z were all born with an iPhone in our hand, Thyme thinks. This kind of tech is no big deal.

"We're on auxiliary power, which lets me operate one camera at a time," Efren says. "Exterior camera three shows… that."

Exterior three is on the underside of the hull, some ten feet underwater. It shows the creature swim by, fully five times the length of the drone ship. The wafer-shaped craft would fit in its jaws like a folded quesadilla. Teeth like needles glimmer as it skims a few yards under the surface. A fin shaped like a great white's (yet ten times as big) breaks the surface, but the fin is tipped with a razor-sharp appendage. The tail is thin and looks like a whip that ends in yet another sharp point. This thing has endless ways to kill them.

"Prehistoric," Efren marvels.

And then, as if it doesn't like to be told how old and extinct it is, the creature turns as fast as a viper striking prey, mouth open wide, coming right at the camera. One needle-sharp tooth destroys the electronic eye, and several more puncture the hull, sabers stabbing through the surface all around the fobs and leaking water in thin salty rivulets.

Face froze. Hands still. Forever til…. No escape once in it, the infinite minute.

Thyme isn't ready for this. Jay looks a hundred. Efren's maybe eighty. Thyme is only four. But they're all too young to die.

***

"There's never enough time," Mom had said once while they were sitting around the table a couple of weeks before the Freeze. It was June, the last June Thyme has seen in more than a year. They were poring over college options, preparing for scholarships before Thyme started her junior year in high school in the fall. Thyme had thought that graduation seemed a lifetime away. Little did she know....

"We have plenty of time to look at colleges, Mom," Thyme had said.

"There's never enough time," her mother had replied.

Then time stopped a month later, and they could have had an eternity together. But Mom crossed a border, turned into a baby, and wrapped her Escalade around an oak tree. Then Thyme had an eternity without her.

Thyme could have lived forever in 2023. But she had never really lived at all, stuck in that infinite minute, where the day is always the day her mother died.

Now Thyme is four years old all over again, stuck somewhere between Las Vegas and New York City, sixty-eight million years in the past and descending into the dark deep in the mouth of some prehistoric leviathan. The drone leaks severely, water spraying in through multiple breaches where the teeth puncture the hull. Efren looks at Thyme, who looks at Jay, who looks at, always, Candy.

"I can't figure out what the rest of these things do," Efren says, turning helplessly toward the computer controls and the single working monitor.

"Cheese and crackers. If the thing that can save us is right in front of us and we can't figure it out, Honor is going to be soooo mad."

"My God, Candy, do people really say things like 'cheese

and crackers' in 1948?" Thyme says through gritted teeth. Now isn't the moment for baby-babble.

"Well, we sure as shootin' don't drop four-letter words with the frequency of a prepositional phrase like they do in 2023," Candy claps back, as antagonistic as Thyme has seen her since they met. Imminent death has a way of putting just about anyone on edge.

"All right, fighting with each other isn't going to keep us alive," Efren says, "and I would rather die among friends than around enemies."

Thyme nods. Candy says she's sorry. Honor wakes up and wails as if she knows she's the only one who can save them and can't manage to communicate beyond a meaningful rivulet of drool.

Efren switches to exterior camera five. It points upward, showing the length of the beast that has them in its craw. The thing is bigger than anything Thyme has ever even imagined. A whale would be unto a salmon in comparison. It's like some mutant fish from a bad B-movie. Something worse than Teenagers from Outer Space.

"How deep is that thing gonna take us?" Jay wonders, watching the camera as the view gets darker and darker and darker.

"It wasn't supposed to end like this," Thyme sighs, sitting down in a seat, her feet dangling off the floor. "This is supposed to be a brand new today. I wanted to find somewhen without all the death and darkness."

"There will always be some tomorrow with death and darkness," Efren says. "And you can't run from tomorrow."

"That thing is not tomorrow," Jay says.

The gray sky casts a feeble pallor on the underwater realm, and it diminishes fast as they descend to greater depths, like night falling in the mountains when the sun slips behind the peaks and the world plunges quickly into darkness. Like dying slowly, the dolorous fading of the light of life.

Then, something else.

Something impossible.

But impossible is as extinct as seconds.

The submarine appears over the top of the diving fish, a shadow that passes between the descending camera and the brighter surface in the growing distance. Something launches from the sub, growing larger through the water. The submarine launched a torpedo.

"Hold on to something!"

Efren grips the console in front of him with gnarled knuckles. Thyme braces herself for impact by wedging her small hands into the sides of her seat. Jay grabs Candy and wraps his bony arms around her and the baby, the three of them crouched between two chairs. The torpedo hits the creature, and the impact makes the whole ship shudder. The sea monster makes a noise like nothing Thyme has ever heard, a terrible combination of bird shriek and lion roar. The teeth retract from the hull, the gnashed holes making worrisome spouts of seawater.

"It worked!" Efren says. "It let go."

The drone still has enough buoyancy to start rising to the surface. But the leaks will offset that long before they ever make it above sea level. Efren stares at the instruments like Thyme's obaasan would stare at a smartphone. He even looks across at Honor for a hint. The baby gives him a look that smacks of disgust, and the 'morrow in Candy's arms promptly falls back asleep.

The water is knee-deep and getting deeper. Thyme never paid enough attention in physics to even guess what the point is between the air still trapped inside pulling them up and the weight of the craft and its contents dragging them down.

Exterior camera five shows the surface. Getting closer. Slowly. Then more slowly. The torpedo only bought them a few imaginary seconds. The submarine who saved them is gone like a fleeting feeling disappears before it grows permanent. It takes a while for anything to grow and flourish, even feelings, and they are trapped in a world without whiles. The water inside the aircraft rises to their waists. The image on the screen becomes unchanging, as if Efren's fiddling has put the camera on pause. Instead, it means their ascent is arrested. They are caught between the effects of buoyancy and gravity. For one extended moment that seems to last forever. Like being pulled between the past that haunts and the fate of the future.

"We were supposed to be the symbols of someday," Candy cries, her tears only adding to the problem.

"There is no someday, Candy," Thyme says. "I thought you'd have realized that by now."

"But you are my someday, Thyme," Candy sniffs. "Don't you see it? Just like Honor is yours. Each of us is proof that there's something after the zone we were stuck in. The beauty of Ms. Norman's dream is that we can all move on to something else. We can make another someday together."

Thyme had been stuck in 2023 for an e-year. All she wanted for so long was to turn today into yesterday. Now that's finally behind her. She made her own tomorrow by leaving home. Candy is right. This can't be her someday. This is the past, millions of years ago. Like Thyme is stuck on a reality show called

Previously On…. There's no way Thyme Mugen is going to die along with a bunch of dinosaurs.

"Right," Thyme agrees, her eyes scanning the cabin. When she flew to Kansas a couple of years ago to visit her mom's cousin Cole, the stewardess gave specific instructions on what to do in the event of an accident. "Check under the seats for a crash kit."

Jay, Efren, and Thyme collect bright red objects from under every seat, each a little disc the size of a poker chip. They are just like the safety bubbles they'd used to jump out of the thirteenth floor of the Stardust back in Vegas—the future's version of an inflatable life vest. Thyme takes the first beyoncé and shoves it into one of the holes in the hull spraying water, pressing a button on the surface of the chip. It inflates instantly, the large bouncy plugging the gap, looking like a balloon inflated half in and half out of a hollowed-out peephole. Jay and Efren follow her lead, and they have enough beyoncés to stopper ten out of the twelve leaks.

The image on the screen stays static. They avoid sinking, but they have taken in too much water to regain their ascent.

"Well, at least it will take longer to die," Jay croaks sarcastically.

An infinite minute.

Thyme shakes her head. "No. We aren't going to die like this. Candy said it. We are the future."

And then, as if obstinance is antecedent to the impossible, the drone begins to rise. The image on exterior camera five shows the surface getting closer and closer. Within e-minutes, they resurface, the stormy sky showing through the beaded water on the lens. Efren switches to external camera eleven, and the fobs see the catalyst for their salvation. The hull of the submarine beneath them stretches out into the distance. The words USS

Hammerhead are embossed on the steel surface. They are saved once again by the submarine, rescued from a prehistoric fate by something that should not even exist sixty-eight million years ago.

Thyme ought to know by now that she should not believe in should nots.

***

Last year, Thyme was asked out on her first date. Everett Lee wanted to know if Thyme would like to attend the autumn formal. Her mother reluctantly allowed it and enthusiastically took Thyme on a shopping spree. A new hairstyle was required.

"Try something different," her mother pressed.

Thyme looked in the mirror at the salon. She had had short hair, the same style she had worn since she was tiny(er). Her mother urged her to evolve, maybe get it dyed or change to a curly style, but Thyme shook her head, trimmed the ends, and looked the same exiting the salon as she had going in. Nothing really changed, and that was okay with Thyme.

Aboard the USS Hammerhead, Thyme feels even smaller than she did back inside the drone. Candy carries Honor, making Thyme the shortest one among five fobs and six sailors walking down a narrow corridor through the submarine, more a tunnel than a hallway. She has always been short for her age (the Asian disadvantage, Jiji calls it), but this is ridiculous. At the physical age of a four-year-old, she barely comes to the sailors' waists. Thyme takes two steps for their every stride.

They were greeted by this complement of sailors as they'd exited the drone and made their way along the slick deck of the submarine to the exterior hatch that allowed entry into the boat. One of the sailors took Thyme's small hand and helped her down the ladder like a gallant gentleman. Their manners suggested these boys are not from 2023. They're from the past. Just not sixty-eight million years in the past.

The kind young sailor marches right in front of Thyme as they make their way through the passageways, deeper into the submarine. Behind them, another sailor aids the ancient Jay. A third isn't much younger than Efren, but he stays close as the tall octogenarian from 2023 ducks through every doorway along the hall. Candy is flanked by two navy officers, both sharply dressed and apparently youthful. They each look like they haven't seen a woman in forever. Certainly, the last woman they saw likely looked nothing like Candy Kane.

"When are you from?" Thyme asks her escort as they wind their way along the claustrophobic corridor.

"1945, ma'am," the sailor answers. Thyme had never been called "ma'am" before in all her original sixteen years. "We are the crew of the USS Hammerhead. SS-364 was assigned to the Gulf of Siam during the war."

"I'm sorry, was there a very important battle there?" Candy asks, fluttering her eyelashes at the sailor. "I was never very good in school. I was always better at being a little bad."

The sailor appears too young to chase a woman who looks forty, but nevertheless, he blushes bright red. Appearances are misleading.

"Cougar," Thyme coughs.

Jay frowns, looking around. "Cougar? I think we would be wiser to worry about another dino-fish."

"This is so freaking cool," Efren says in an old man rasp. "A World War II submarine in pristine condition."

"This boat is from World War II?" Jay asks, maybe for the first time since 1960, considering something other than Candy

Kane's décolletage. It seems his interest can perk up at something other than only things that are already perky. "How did you get all the way out into the middle of America?"

"After the Freeze, we started back toward Fremantle, but the seas west of Australia predate the oceans itself, a molten mix of lava that Skipper says dates back billions of years. We changed course toward California. On the way, we saw…." The sailor pauses, shudders. Things better left unsaid.

He continues. "We refueled in California and restocked on supplies, but we got new orders before we could even unload the boat. That brings us here. Now. To the middle of America in a prehistoric sea."

"What are your new orders?" Thyme asks. She wonders if it has anything to do with Ms. Norman being kidnapped and her four missing students.

"I'll let Skipper tell you the rest," the sailor says.

A lot of people want to stop the school from opening. It seems numerous forces are working against Ms. Norman's dream of a new tomorrow. So many want things to stay the way they are. There seem to be acolytes like Scarlett Sloane and her father in so many different zones, all following the lead of Jefferson Davis. People that don't want things ever to change.

The sailor leads them through one last doorway into a room smaller than Jiji's kitchen back in 2023. Standing a little taller than Thyme herself at three and a half feet and wearing clothes that look like the kid borrowed them from his dad's closet, the captain of this submarine turns as the fobs enter the control room. He sports a scowl that can be achieved only by years and years of cantankerousness. Thyme imagines he has a mustache in his future, but his future is not now.

"You need to tell me how in the blazes the five of you came to be floating on a sea sixty-eight million years before any of you are ever born," Skipper demands.

"We are students on our way to New York City," Thyme says. "Ms. Mallory Norman is starting a school for kids from across all the zones. But she was abducted in 1960, and we escaped. Until someone tried to stop us."

"Seems they succeeded. You would all be bobbers but for the saving grace of the United States Navy," Skipper says, his little-kid voice squeaking. "I'm fully aware of the Minute. And I know factions are working against the school. They don't want any sort of collusion between the time zones. Some folks prefer things to stay the same. Forever. At any cost."

"They shot us out of the sky," Efren says.

"This is war, kid," the six-year-old informs the elderly man. "That's why we're out here in the Mesozoic Sea. Lucky for you. Radar picked up an unidentified civilian aircraft crashing into the ocean. We were close enough to get here before you ended up as a prehistoric snack."

"You saved our lives," Thyme tells. "Thank you."

"It's what we do," Skipper says, then turns to the sailor escorting Thyme. "Yeoman Cooper, get these riders to the mess hall and let them rest for a bit. I'll be down as soon as we dive to the optimal depth."

Yeoman Cooper takes them through another doorway, down another ladder, then through a portal into a small dining area. Three sailors sit around eating up food that looks more like paste than sustenance. They stare at the five fobs like they're prehistoric fish the size of a doublewide trailer instead of merely 'morrows from their near future. Most of the gazes are directed at Candy. Every time they cross zones and change age, Candy gains ten years, and her dress seems to get shorter and tighter. Thyme swears her bosom goes up a size with every decade she accumulates.

"Coffee?" Yeoman Cooper offers.

The fobs all nod. Cooper gets them each a cup and fills them up. It's strong, cheap, and hot. In clothes still wet from flailing about their sinking drone, the steaming beverage hits the spot. Exhausted, the five fobs gather at a table, all sitting silently for some time. They're safe. For the moment, they're okay. Not so long ago, they were all about to die.

Thyme catches herself wringing her hands. Stops. She left 2023 to escape the grief over her mother's death, not to run headlong into her own demise. For so long, she was reluctant for change. She was stuck for a long while in the infinite minute. Now she's trying to move forward, but here she is sixty-million-years ago. It seems the past isn't quite done with Thyme yet.

"You okay?" Efren asks, his voice full of sand and marbles.

Thyme gazes at the tall boy towering on the bench right next to her. His head droops like a large flower at the end of a long stem. There's something in his eyes when he looks at Thyme. It reminds her of Everett Lee when he picked her up for the autumn formal last year. An expression of enchantment and expectation. Is Efren crushing on her? She doesn't need to deal with that right now.

"I'm fine," Thyme says.

Still, Efren has noticed that she isn't actually fine. He seems to catch a lot about Thyme. What's the story with Efren Cortez?

"You know any guys from the 332nd Fighter Group?" Jay asks Yeoman Cooper.

To make conversation, or something more? Thyme

wonders.

"The Tuskegee Airmen? Who hasn't heard the stories? A whole squadron made up of black pilots. Heroes all, but I never met any personally," Cooper says. "You have a grandson over there, old-timer?"

"I'm only seventeen," Jay says in a raspy reply as if offended. "And I'm from 1960."

"You're all really from the future then?" Cooper asks, looking at each of them in turn.

"I'm only a few years beyond you," Candy says. "But yes, we're all tomorrow people."

"I guess the future isn't so…white."

Thyme notices for the first time that Yeoman Cooper is darker than most of his shipmates. Thyme is Asian. Efren is Latino. Jay is black. Honor is whatever Honor is. Candy is the only white one in their circle. To Thyme, it just seems like a slice of America. But it isn't a slice of Yeoman Cooper's America.

"Yeah, we made some progress, I guess," Thyme tells. Race relations might seem unseemly in 2023, but she suddenly thinks she might not know what unseemly really means.

Skipper enters, standing barely to Yeoman Cooper's midsection yet undeniably in command. He looks over the fobs as if he considers them hazardous cargo and is eager to get them off his boat.

"We will get you to safety," Skipper says in a thin voice filled with authority. "The next zone over is 2118. They're friendly to Washington and will grant you safe passage eastward."

"Did you contact the authorities?" Thyme asks. "Did you tell anyone you found us?"

Skipper remains silent. He looks like a kid who took a cookie and refuses to confess. Thyme glances at Cooper, who looks away.

"Mi familia must think I'm dead," Efren says.

Skipper looks hard as stone, a cold expression on the tender flesh of a child. It chills Thyme to the bone. "This boat was launched in '43. Now, we have communications capability, but whatever we send and get will be heard by everyone with ears across America. They shot your drone out of the sky with a satellite from outer space. What will they do if they know you're now safe and sound aboard the Hammerhead?"

"You plan to dump us in 2118 and take off?" Thyme asks, aghast.

"I saved your lives. That's what we do," Skipper repeats, struggling to keep his bottom lip from pouting. "The rest is up to you. I'm sure the 'morrows in 2118 can help you."

There's nothing more to say. Skipper won't risk his crew's safety by relaying the fobs' rescue. The submarine will merely facilitate transport to the next zone. Then Thyme and the other teens are on their own. They still have more than half a continent to travel, with no airship to fly them the rest of the way and no known allies to give them aid or succor.

"A word of advice," Skipper adds, back to his gruff and unapologetic self. "Stay clear of 1869. It borders 2118, and it's bad news. Jefferson Davis is behind these shenanigans. He probably was the one who authorized the strike that downed your drone. He calls his proposed union of zones the Chronfederacy. There are plenty of people sympathetic to his cause. War is coming, kids, and he is the enemy."

"He has allies across other zones," Efren says. "His grandson is the one who took Ms. Norman captive in 1960."

"He means to stop her Institute from ever opening its

doors. Make sure you see he doesn't succeed." The Skipper pauses, stretches, and yawns, arms reaching up and still not as tall as even Candy. It must be past his nap time. "Get some rest, riders. You have a long way to go to get to the Big Apple. Something tells me you'll need all the energy you can muster."

Thyme nods. The rest of the fobs follow her as Yeoman Cooper leads them to some bunks. If the next stop is 2118, this will be the last chance to sleep for the next sixty-eight million years.

CHAPTER FOUR
18:45
9.28.2118 AD
Ketchum, Idaho

It is eerie. The USS Hammerhead had descended to a depth of several hundred feet. The maneuver had to be perfect. The submarine eased so the front section of the boat is in 2118, only a few feet of the three-hundred-and-twelve-foot length extending into the future. They have to do something with air pressure and science that Thyme doesn't understand. Science has been wonky since the Freeze, but apparently, people a lot smarter than she can figure out these new laws of physics. The five fobs end up climbing out of a torpedo chute and onto a patch of soft green grass in a zone where the sun shines and the birds twitter.

Thyme looks back, the majority of the Hammerhead submerged in an ocean that extends up like the rock-face of a high cliff and down into murky depths. The scarlet sheen of the temporal border makes the water resemble blood, and she hopes it isn't an omen for the sailors aboard Skipper's boat. The visual is disconcerting, gravity suspended between the zones like weather and time and atmosphere, nothing crossing over unless enough inertia takes it across. Like babies driving an Escalade.

The submarine reverses, the nose retreating into the sea. Skipper leaves the fobs all alone on the side of a mountain in a time zone that none of them are familiar with. Honor won't be born for another seven centuries. It's a future in which Thyme and Efren and Candy and Jay would all be dead.

The future. Thyme looks around. It's about a hundred years after she turned into a teenager. Almost a century from the endless present she left behind. This is tomorrow. Somewhere, all the answers are recorded in a newspaper obituary or accessible in online archives. Thyme could read about her entire life—children, jobs, milestones, successes, expiration date. She could know what happened next. But what happens next in 2118 isn't what happens next in the Freeze. This time is no more her someday than Monday in her time zone, where it's actually perpetually Sunday. The public record in 2118 is filled with lies, accounts of a life where Thyme's mother didn't die in a car crash and made memories maybe long beyond July 16th, 2023.

Tears prickle her eyes as she looks up at the ominous wall of water, an impossible ocean reaching up along the horizon. It offends the very nature of science. Mom is dead. Thyme is all alone. That seems impossible, too. But impossible ignores science. This world exists despite shoulds and coulds and supposed to bes.

Thyme checks her watch. It still shows seven-thirty. Always and forever. The minute that lasts unto infinity. No escape once in it. She blinks away the tears and leaves them behind her. It is past. For the moment.

Efren puts a hand on her shoulder. Thyme turns away,

shrugging it off. He notices her every moment of sadness, but she doesn't need him noticing. Thyme saw how Efren had his doting mommy and daddy saying goodbye in 2023. He doesn't know how she feels. And she doesn't want him to pretend like he does.

"This past isn't any better than the last one," Honor says with a scowl, aged to fifty years old when they went across the border from BC.

Thyme came through into the future back to being a teenager again. It feels good to be in her own skin, more or less. She examines the craggy peaks of the autumn mountains, a chill coming down off the slopes that portends of a winter that will never come. The sun is bright, shining against high evergreen mountains as the lower trees along the base turn red and orange and yellow under a sky as blue as La Jolla Cove in San Diego. Or it was in San Diego. Thyme isn't sure if San Diego is in Candy's 1948 or somewhen else when maybe the Pacific isn't even there anymore. Everything in 2118 looks like the world observed through a neon filter, something almost unreal about the amped appearance.

"I think this place looks happy," Candy says with a spectacular grin spread from ear to ear. She seems to be the same age as Thyme this zone around, closer to the beginning of being a teen than the end, and still pretty as a princess. Thyme glares, wondering if there's any age when Candy loses that classic beauty. At least she doesn't have curves from here to Havana in this time zone.

"It's too bright," Honor grumbles. "I hate it."

It didn't take long for Honor to shake off the inefficacy of her infancy and re-embrace her natural cantankerous superiority.

Efren gazes toward the burnt sienna sky, still older but not as old, maybe sixty, with hair as white as the snow-capped peaks of the Rockies. One alabaster eyebrow is higher than the other as he ponders upward. "They shot the drone out of the sky with a satellite."

"That's what Skipper said," Thyme says.

"They had to see us," Efren observes. "To know it was us. To aim."

Thyme peers into the blue and wonders who's looking back. Can they shoot lasers from the sky and put a hole through her right where she stands? Can they drop a bomb and blow the five of them to smithereens? Or is it like finding a needle in a haystack, and they're looking and looking and looking? Easier to track an aircraft flying through the sky than five individual teens on foot somewhere along middle America. Or perhaps the enemy believes they're all dead from the first attack?

"Let's not wait around to see if they can see us back," Thyme says. "We need to find shelter."

They start off along a craggy path down a gentle slope, trees wending their way along the incline, rocks as large as vehicles parked haphazardly here and there. They may be marching through the future, but the landscape seems timeless, eternal, without anchor. Thyme likes the feeling of being unmoored from the precepts of clocks, unhampered by the page of a calendar, existing in a moment that isn't future or past but merely here and now. Neither today nor tomorrow nor yesterday, her mother may be alive and well around any corner instead of dead and gone or not yet born.

But time, like pain, cannot be ignored. It's incessant and insistent. As a toddler cries for attention, time needs to be observed, acknowledged, and obnoxious.

"Maybe we were supposed to crash into BC," Efren

suggests as they follow the looping path down the mountain. "Maybe this is something we're destined to see."

"We almost died," Thyme says. "I don't think that defying death is our destiny."

"But maybe this adventure is our fate, Thyme."

"I don't believe in fate."

"I hate fate," Honor says.

"Now you made me agree with Honor," Thyme groans with a roll of her eyes.

"I didn't say I don't believe in fate," Honor corrects. "I just hate it."

"No one tells me where I'm headed or what I'm going to do," Thyme says, Efren's words getting under her skin.

"How can you ignore the fact that there's such a thing as fate, Thyme?" Efren asks, as if as offended by her as she is by him. "The future is right in front of us. We are walking along a path in 2118. This whole patchwork quilt of time zones that makes up the United States is about connecting the dots from the past to the future."

"There is no past, Efren. No future. Not anymore," Thyme snaps. Her legendary temper is starting to spark. "It's always today, every day. The present is all there is. We can make the next moment whatever we want it to be."

"You can find out your whole future with a simple Google search."

"That isn't my future," Thyme dismisses, pondering the winding path down the mountainside leading to someone else's tomorrow. "My mother wasn't supposed to die."

"None of this was supposed to happen. That doesn't mean we can ignore where we're intended to go."

"We don't have to let it define us either," Thyme says.

"There's a well-worn path that leads down the mountain and will take us where we need to be," Efren says. "Are you saying we should leave the route and blaze our own trail?"

"Sometimes you make your own way," Thyme agrees.

"You're quite a rebel, Thyme Mugen," Jay says. "Cool."

It's the first time Jay has seemed to notice anything besides Candy since this adventure began.

***

The way down the mountain becomes difficult and long. It seems that the five fobs have been walking forever by the time they crest a ridge and see a small town down the slope at the bottom of the hill. The roads in the town are arranged in perfect geometric squares, every street black with bright yellow lines painted perfectly down the center. Each building is a pastel color, square, one story, with a picket fence and cobblestone walkway and rows of rosebushes along the front foundation, all alike, as if this place is the municipal equivalent of the monotonous minutes after the Freeze.

"Well, doesn't this look like the charmingest little town?" Candy says, clapping her hands together.

Thyme and Honor exchange a look. It's worrisome that Candy feels so cozy in a place as fake as her eyelashes. Maybe being a teenage girl in 1948 isn't so different from being a robot.

A sign at the edge of town reads Welcome to Ketchum. People work on their yards, tending flowers that will never bloom and pruning shrubs that look perfect already. A man in a hat (featuring an automated brim that adjusts to the angle of the sun as he moves) stands watering a lawn that will never get more or less green or grow an iota, even if he irrigates for the next hundred e-years. The Nile is a river in Egypt (at least some of the times), but denial runs through the mountains of Idaho.

Or is it something more sinister?

Billboards along the street read Happy is the only way to be! and Smiles are for everyone! and Joy to the world! The citizens toiling in their yards all wear wide smiles, rictus repeated address after address. Thyme wonders if it's a mandate or medication. Everyone can't be ecstatic all the time. Something's wrong with these people. Everyone seems happy, but no one says "Hi."

A van creeps slowly up the street as the five fobs follow the sidewalk. The strangers are garnering stares and generating gossip. There are lights on the roof of the cab that suggest it's a police vehicle, but the side doesn't say Ketchum Police Department. Instead, it reads Nirvana Resort Security.

The van pulls up to the pedestrian fobs. An entirely generic person with little features and scant indications of character blinks like a fool trying to make heads or tails of an unfinished puzzle. A wide, vacuous smile creases an otherwise unanimated face. Fake as a fortnight.

"You folks staying at the resort?"

"We needed some fresh air," Candy says, oozing sweetness.

The driver appears unaffected by Candy's charm. A first. "Tourists are instructed to stay within the confines of the resort."

"We got lost," Efren tries. He looks at Thyme. She shrugs. What is this "resort"?

"I need to take you back to the resort," the security guard declares with a methodical expression of politeness.

Well, they can't trek through the rest of 2118 on foot, anyway. The mountains to the east are steep and ominous, this valley just a brief respite from an impossible route. Thyme would bet a hundred bucks that not one of the five fobs knows the first thing about scaling cliffs. They need to find someone who can do more than grin like a creepy circus clown and converse with the robotic inflection of a smartphone app.

"Take us to your leader," Thyme says, starting to wonder if this future was taken over by brainwashing alien bugs.

The van door automatically opens. The fobs get in—age-old warnings against getting into a stranger's vehicle echo through her thoughts in her mother's voice. Efren looks at Thyme. Thyme glances at Honor. Honor rolls her eyes as Candy slides into the passenger seat and starts a cheerful conversation with the security person. She isn't giving up on winning over the bland van driver.

Candy asks the person sitting in front of Thyme a string of endless questions. Name: Pat. Marital status: single. Age: thirty. Hobbies: shabbing, holovids, romtech. Favorite food: vintage chocolate. Music: electromonica. Most of it makes no sense to Thyme and even less sense to Candy, but Candy bobs her head like a puppet on strings.

"What did you do before the Freeze?" Candy asks.

"Pardon me, miss?" Pat says.

"I suppose it would've been September 27th around here," Candy says. "Before the clocks stopped."

Pat's head just shakes back and forth. "Same as today. Same as tomorrow."

Wash, rinse, repeat.

Wash, rinse, repeat.

"Do you remember yesterday, Pat?" Candy asks.

"Yesterday?" Pat muses, taking his eyes off the road. The vehicle is driving itself anyway. "Why, I guess I don't. This has been a long day, I can tell you. Absolutely endless. Today seems so long I can't rightly recall yesterday."

Doesn't Thyme understand what Pat is experiencing? The infinite minute. Stuck in a stretch of experience that never ends. Mourning made afternoon, evening, all night, next day, next week, all year. Thyme wants to think about something else. Anything else. She wants to feel some other emotion than sadness and anger and fear. She wants a tomorrow brighter than today, but today is so long she can't even remember yesterday. There's no hope it will ever turn tomorrow, no matter what the calendars say.

She blinks and looks around at the faces in the van. Jay and Honor peek outside, but Efren stares right at Thyme like her grief is some sort of magnet for his attention.

The van pulls aside, and Candy still flashes Pat her dazzliest smile. "Thanks for the lift."

"They'll take care of you inside, miss," Pat replies without inflection, then drives off.

"That was weird," Thyme says.

"This is even weirder," Jay says, pointing.

The building in front of them is massive. The entrance feels welcoming and modern, glass with embedded LED lights making the message on the sheer surface change every few e-seconds—Welcome to Nirvana Resort. Leave your problems in the past. Forget your worries at Nirvana Resort. The past is the problem, and Nirvana is the solution. Signs along the path to the front entrance repeat the mantras Thyme saw walking into town—Happy is the only way to be! Smiles are for everyone! Joy to the world!

"I don't like this," Thyme tells.

"I hate this," Honor mumbles.

Candy peers back at the happy citizens working in their

yards along the street, whistling and smiling and dancing a little. "They seem friendly. Let's ask them for help."

"Those ninnyhammers are clueless," Honor says. "We need to find someone who can manage an expression other than a stupid smile."

The grin finally falls off Candy's face.

"Ninnyhammers? Really, Honor?" Thyme snaps. "I think you're starting to make this stuff up as you go along."

"Would you prefer niddy-noddy?" Honor asks with no little snark, the shifting glow of her subcutaneous LED lights seeming to mock Thyme along with the 'morrow's words, shapes and colors that seem offensive forming along Honor's smooth scalp.

"Maybe call them zombies. Or brainless. Or something," Thyme sighs, exasperated.

"You're a zombie," Honor says under her breath.

Yet Honor follows Thyme and the other fobs as they march up to the entrance of the Nirvana Resort. The doors open silently as they approach, the interior lobby like something out of Star Wars. Bright and futuristic, the patina pops like fireworks, colors churning under an amorphous surface turning happy reds to fun blues to exciting oranges. The person behind the front counter has a grin that might make the Joker jealous, but it falters a bit when five unscheduled fobs come marching through the front doors.

"We don't have any guests scheduled to arrive this e-evening," the receptionist says, as if addressing a figment of the imagination instead of five real and weary customers.

The receptionist has hair cut as short as Thyme's, bright lipstick as fresh as Candy's, thick eyebrows like Jay's, and attire reminiscent of Honor's innovative garb.

"We're lost," Efren explains again. "If you could direct us to someone who might be able to help us, we would —"

"Come with me," says a voice from behind them.

Thyme turns and faces the first person since they arrived in Ketchum who doesn't feature a ridiculous rictus. The person wears a doctor's jacket with a Nirvana Resort logo on one side of the chest and a name tag on the other that reads "Dr. Cortez." Thyme looks at Efren. The doctor features a crewcut, eye shadow, and a tattoo on the neck that is a mix of pink and blue. The name may be Hispanic, but the appearance is as amorphous as Honor's as if the future had figured out how to cure prejudice. When the doctor looks at Thyme, does Thyme see something familiar in the eyes? Is this doctor somehow related to Efren?

"This way," Dr. Cortez says and takes off down a corridor, leaving no time to decline.

They pass rooms that are less like hospital rooms and more like hotel rooms. Some doors stand open and showcase people inside smiling like more mindless idiots, while they occasionally meet other people along the hallway who don't look at the five eclectic fobs twice. The people inside the resort are different from the ones outside in Ketchum. The guests inside are all tourists from different zones. Thyme recognizes styles from 2023, 1960, 1948, and the nineteenth century. And others. From everywhen. These are all immigrants. Other fobs.

Dr. Cortez leads them into an empty room. It looks like a suite from a future adaptation of Willy Wonka, more blue and green and violet than anything this side of a rainbow.

"How did you get here?" Dr. Cortez demands after closing the door behind them.

"We crash-landed in the next zone," Efren answers, his

head tilted sideways as he studies the doctor with the same last name as his. Thyme wonders if Efren is also considering if they're related. Cortez is probably a common enough name. "We barely made it to 2118."

"I suppose you're wondering what kind of a place this is," Dr. Cortez says, appearing a little ominous as if the doc is resisting the urge to rub his hands together and laugh maniacally.

Mad scientist, much?

He seems more strange than Efren has ever acted.

"The past is a precursor to pain," Dr. Cortez explains. "I'm a doctor. I evaluate affliction and advise treatment. Our harmful memories of the past are causing the symptoms of the present. Imagine if you could pluck out those terrible thoughts, exorcize them like cancerous tumors. Take away the bad feelings that tumble and jumble every day. What would that make you in the future?"

"Happy," Candy answers immediately.

Thyme thinks about her mother, the crash, the last equivalent year of mourning. What if that memory of the worst thing that ever happened could be wiped away? She thought about those ninnyhammers wandering around Ketchum and shuffling up and down the halls of the resort. They looked like souls absent gravitas.

Honor steps forward and appears as if she wants to speak, but Thyme shoots her a glare to warn the 'morrow that one word will get her an elbow in the ribs. There's something strange here, and Thyme doesn't trust Dr. Cortez enough to ask for help. Not yet.

"We could use some rest," Thyme tells.

Dr. Cortez nods. "Certainly. This room and the adjacent room are available until the next guests arrive. Please peruse the menu of options for our services during your stay. We can scrub those bad thoughts away and turn those downtrodden expressions into bright smiles." Dr. Cortez pauses upon exit beside Candy, examining the ebullient teen. "Except you, my dear, who already looks happy enough for all of you."

Then the doctor is gone, and the fobs are alone. Even Candy's smile falters. There's something off about 2118. They should all be worried. Escape should be imperative. Instead, Thyme can't stop thinking about the allure of just forgetting.

***

Food comes served by smiling androgynous custodians. The five fobs haven't eaten in a long time. Fluid physics made food less necessity and more of a hobby after the Freeze. Death only comes from accident or intent. Disease has been arrested. Aging annihilated. Sickness, like seconds, extinct. Murder and mishap are now the only ways to die. Crashing a car into a tree or being blasted by a laser beam from outer space.

Food is just a luxury. A pastime. And taste is a blessing that has at least survived the fizzle of physics and the cessation of seconds. Hunger is a habit that's hard to let go of, like keeping track of the days when the sun never sets or marking Christmas on a calendar when it's evermore September. Yet flavor is a familiar pleasure in a patchwork world with too much pain. They eat—raspberries, marmalade, chocolate wafers, slices of pecan pie, sweet juice. Thyme doesn't count a calorie. No one gains a pound in a world where consequences can be shunted to a tomorrow that's never going to come.

The five fobs are scattered about a room painted pastel pink, reminding Thyme of cotton candy from the circus where Mom had taken her when she was ten. There was a fortune teller there that had offered to tell Thyme the future for five bucks, and Mom wanted to hear what was in store for her little girl. The soothsayer gazed into her crystal ball and predicted that Thyme was due for a fantastic adventure. Indeed.

Candy stares at a painting of brightly colored balloons hanging on the wall opposite a set of bunk beds. Jay stares at Candy. Efren reads a Ray Bradbury book he brought all the way from 2023. Honor looks like she's meditating.

"I don't like this place," Thyme says, taking a big bite of a chocolate dessert.

"I hate this place," Honor agrees, her eyes remaining closed and her face expressionless. "There is no way everyone can be so annoyingly happy all the time."

Candy smiles brightly. "I'm happy all the time."

Honor frowns. "That is a sign of a mental disorder."

"There's nothing wrong with looking at the bright side of a situation, Honor," Candy says. "It's called optimism, not insanity. You should try it sometime."

"Maybe tomorrow," Honor says dryly.

"There's something off," Thyme tells. "I'm getting a serious American Horror Story vibe."

Efren gazes up from Fahrenheit 451, marking his place with his long wrinkled thumb. "What are you thinking, Thyme?"

"I think it's time to play Sherlock."

"Is that the vampire?" Honor asks.

"Yes, Honor, the plan is to go door to door and suck the blood of every time-tourist we can find," Thyme deadpans.

"I'm not drinking blood," Candy cries.

"Thyme is being sarcastic," Efren assures Candy. Then he says to Honor, "You're thinking of Dracula. Thyme is talking about a famous detective. She wants to go sleuthing."

"Ooh, I like a good mystery." Candy actually does a little dance, her dress sashaying like a pendulum and two boys watching like they are being hypnotized. "What are we trying to solve?"

"There must be something in the Kool-Aid here in 2118."

"Really?" Candy asks, mouth puckered, pushing away a cup filled with a bright red drink. "Like poison?"

Jay sighs, saddles up to Candy, and puts a leather jacket arm around her. "Don't have a cow, dolly. Jay won't let anything happen to you."

"Do you play more than one note, dude?" Thyme finally let irritation turn into invective. "We don't have time for puppy-love. If you can't control yourself around a pretty girl, then I'm going to slug you so hard you'll wake up in a different time zone."

"What's your tale, nightingale?" Jay snaps. "I can't show appreciation for a lady who is stacked?"

Thyme steps forward, eye to eye with Jay. "Does 'stacked' mean what I think it means?" Candy looks down at her impressive chest. Jay shrugs. Thyme punches him in the face so fast he doesn't even have time to flinch.

"Ow!" Jay hollers, holding his nose. "You're crazy!"

"Welcome to the future," Thyme tells. "Where pigs get punched."

"It was a compliment, you crazy bird," Jay says through pinched nostrils.

"Save your 'compliments' for another time," Thyme warns. "Girls don't ride in the backseat anymore, Jay Stone. Women do not stay home and raise the babies while the big, strong men make the money. We don't wait to be asked to the dance. We don't want you to protect us. And we sure don't need your drool.

The past is past. So leave it behind."

Jay looks properly taken down a peg. Honor gives Thyme an appraisal that might have elevated a level.

"If we have a mystery to solve, then we need a lead," Honor says.

Efren glances at the door. "Dr. Cortez."

"Probably not a coincidence that he has the same last name you do," Thyme suggests.

"Probably not," Efren says.

Thyme's obaasan would recognize the look in her eye. She had that gleam when she meant to swipe some cookies from the jar, no matter how high Jiji put the container. Time to get up to trouble.

Thyme opens the door and peeks out. The corridor is empty. In a world without time, schedules form for sleep and eat and play. The sun still hangs in the west, suspended forever at 6:45 p.m., but the residents of the Nirvana Resort are mostly asleep. Thyme steps into the hall and sneaks away from their room. She doesn't look back. When Thyme gets to the first room with an open door, she pauses. Only then does she realize all four of her new acquaintances have followed her. She would have gone with or without them.

"Excuse me?" Thyme says.

A fellow in his thirties looks up as Thyme enters his apartment. He isn't from 2118. Thyme can tell from his 2023 hairstyle and his contemporary outfit and the iPhone that seems glued to his left hand. He sports a big vapid smile indicative of the Nirvana Resort, empty and eternal.

"Are you new tourists? 'Cause you're not from around now," the fellow says, noticing their anachronistic attire and especially Honor's intriguing appearance.

"We just arrived," Thyme tells.

"I'm Henry. I'm from 2023. So, what package did you get?"

"The, uh, basic one," Thyme answers. "And you?"

Somehow his smile gets bigger. His head is fully split in half. "They made me forget all my favorites," he exclaims loudly, as if the fobs were all as old as Efren and maybe hard of hearing.

Thyme checks his room. Henry has books scattered here and there. Actual hardcover books, not electronic readers with glowing screens. Harry Potter. All seven books. Game of Thrones. To Kill a Mockingbird. Romeo and Juliet. Murder on the Orient Express. Then there are movies. Star Wars. All of them. Even the bad ones. The Sixth Sense. Se7en. The Shawshank Redemption. Pulp Fiction.

"So, you had them take out your memories of these movies and books?"

Henry nods eagerly. "Erased them all. Now I can start over. I made a list of all my favorites, and now I can experience them for the first time. All over again!"

"But you didn't have them take out the bad stuff?" Thyme follows up, bewildered.

"The bad stuff is what makes you who you are, kid," Henry replies. "The reason I appreciate the good stuff is because I survived all the bad."

A hand reaches out and takes Thyme's. It is Efren. "C'mon. We better go."

"Yes, Efren. Don't forget, you're here to get some answers," comes a voice from behind them. It's Dr. Cortez, standing in the doorway, a tall figure slouching in a familiar way, as if trying to diminish his height. Just like Efren does. "I will tell you everything, Granddad. Follow me." The doctor points at Thyme.

"And bring her with you. After all, her destiny is all wrapped up with yours."

***

Thyme and Efren sit across from Dr. Cortez. Thyme sees the resemblance — in the eyes, the mouth, the tall and lanky shape of the doctor. It's like finding similarities of the original in the shadow of an object. They traveled a hundred years into the future and find one of Efren's descendants. Efren wears an expression on his face akin to a toddler trying to cipher a calculus equation. And Thyme tries to estimate the odds of coming across another Cortez in all the fractured zones in America. She told Efren she didn't believe in destiny, but this smells like fate.

"So, Dr. Cortez, you're in charge of the resort?" Thyme asks as Efren remains speechless.

"Please, call me Theodore." Efren's grandson sits behind a desk with his hands clasped together in front of him, an expression suggesting he's about to convey a difficult diagnosis to a suffering family. "I'm one of several scientists and physicians who pioneered the procedure of memory extraction."

"That sounds like a fancy way to say you perform voluntary lobotomies," Efren says, rediscovering his voice.

Theodore smiles. Not the eerie rictus that affects the citizens and tourists in Ketchum. He gives a genuine grin, a small expression of appreciation for his grandfather's concern. Even the smile seems familiar, something that Thyme has seen before. What did he mean about Thyme's fate being wrapped up with Efren's?

"We provide a service. The people of 2118 had a hard time accepting the Freeze. In the future, stress is regulated to achieve a minimum, and memories are mediated until manageable. When the clocks stopped, people turned to the Nirvana Resort to alleviate their anxiety. They wanted to forget. They'd rather things be the way they were."

Thyme thinks about life before the Freeze. Her mother had been alive. The world had turned, a bad today turning into yesterday, behind her, moving on. Days had been boxes on a calendar, predictable and easily marked off, slices of time cut into sections like a pie. Now the pile of moments became indistinguishable and amorphous, like a broken hourglass spilling its grains along an endless expanse of beach.

Theodore Cortez can take away the memory of her mother's death. He can make it all better. Thyme could be a smiling citizen of Ketchum instead of the mourning adventurer trying to make it across America without being murdered.

"How did my own grandson become some brainwashing expert?" Efren challenges.

Theodore's smile fades. "It's not brainwashing. Quite the opposite. The research originated in efforts to find a cure for Alzheimer's. My father was a pioneer in the field, working day and night to find a cure for the ailment. He was obsessed with the project."

"The technology you use to remove memories was originally designed to preserve them?" Efren asks. "You perverted the altruistic works of your own father? My son?"

"Sometimes remembering can be as painful as forgetting," Theodore says.

Efren looks away, as if it hurts him to see his hereditary future. The past haunts Thyme, and now Efren will be haunted by this future. In a world where future and past are the same, Thyme and Efren have a connection.

"You know, we never did see eye to eye," Theodore says

to his grandfather. "You and my father were always of a sort. You wanted to remember everything. But I argued that some things aren't worth a memory. Recollection is simply reliving a moment over and over again. Why do we want to remember every heartbreak? Every bad day? Every terrible tragedy? The people of Ketchum voluntarily forget why the sun never sets. At the end of every e-day, they come to me. This is the happiest place on Earth. I mean, look at me."

Theodore's smile is big and bright, not like Efren's at all. When Efren grins, he always looks smug, like he has a juicy secret. His grandson's expression is easygoing and innocent. Yet still familiar....

"You've undergone your own procedure?" Efren asks.

"Oh, yes. So I don't know what happens to you. You might be alive or dead in 2118. I don't remember. I can't be upset by something I cannot recall. I remember the good times, Granddad. I know we had our intellectual debates over the ethics of memory extraction. If it ever escalated into a fight, I don't know. If it eventually caused a falling out, I intentionally forgot."

"I think it's causing a falling out right now," Efren says. "I suppose you'll erase this whole conversation once I'm gone?"

"You might be Efren Cortez, Granddad and patriarch of the Cortez clan," Theodore concedes, "but your past isn't my past. I might not remember everything about you, but I do know that Efren Cortez never came to Ketchum, Idaho in all my history."

"We're strangers," Efren says.

"I'm afraid so," Theodore agrees. "The man you'll become now isn't the same future you would've had otherwise. I don't know if I'm a part of your tomorrow anymore."

"You don't know?" Efren repeats. "But of course you are! You're right here."

They stare at each other across the desk and Theodore finally looks away, down and left, his gaze sweeping away in a familiar way. Thyme's mother would grow uncomfortable with eye contact after a few seconds, always looking away in that manner. The memory hurts to revisit. Theodore could take it all away. Make her forget. Then Thyme thinks about what Henry had said. Maybe the reason I appreciate the good stuff is because I survived the bad.

"Jefferson Davis and his Chronfederacy are searching for us," Thyme says, changing the subject. "We need to get the word out to someone who can help us."

"Do you know who your allies are, and who is your enemy?" Dr. Cortez asks.

Ms. Norman thought that Mr. Sloane was an ally back in 1960, and he betrayed her. The only person Thyme trusts is Mallory Norman. And Ms. Norman is a captive of the Chronfederacy. Thyme shakes her head.

"We need to get to 1980 New York. We're students at the Mallory Norman Institute of Time," Thyme tells. The Institute has to be the safest place in the United States. Theodore might be a mad scientist from a science fiction movie, but he's also Efren's kin. She hopes she can still depend on family in the future. "Can you help us?"

"You're recruits to M.N.I.T.?" Theodore asks, watching Efren avoid his grandson's gaze. Then the doctor nods to himself. "Of course you are."

"You know about the Minute?" Thyme asks.

"Oh yes. One of my colleagues took a position as a teacher at the school. He escorted one of our brightest pupils to 1980 a few e-days ago. The headmistress asked me to join the faculty, but I knew that would be...." Theodore looks from his grandfather to Thyme, then back to Efren again. "...awkward."

"It ended up being awkward anyway," Efren says.

"Yes," Theodore agrees. "It's quite surreal seeing you both so young."

"Both?" Thyme asks. What does Theodore know about Thyme's future? His comment about the intertwined fates of Thyme and Efren resurfaces in her mind. And Theodore's familiar mannerisms, the ones that didn't seem like Efren....

"You don't know, do you? She didn't tell you when she recruited you?"

Thyme's blood turns cold. The one person she has trusted since she agreed to leave 2023 has been Ms. Norman. She fears that Theodore has some terrible secret about the headmistress of the Minute. Thyme shakes her head.

"As I said, my father was obsessed with finding a way to cure Alzheimer's. It was a personal passion. His grandmother had suffered from the disease, slowly sliding into dementia. I remember when I was little, going to visit her in the home, and she would sometimes recognize me, sometimes not. She called me 'Teddybear.' She was nice until she forgot how to be nice. Toward the end, she couldn't remember anything. My father never found the cure in time to save my great-grandmother, but he persisted even after she was gone. The breakthrough came five years after she passed."

"You chose to remember that?" Thyme asks.

Theodore nods. "Some memories make up the reasons we do what we do. It is destiny. I needed to remember that to lead me to this right now. Especially after the clocks stopped. Because this patchwork world has its own rules, its own filigrees of fate. Maybe I never forgot because you need to hear this story."

"What does that mean?" Thyme asks.

"I didn't know for sure until Grandad said your name back in Henry's room," Theodore says. "You are so young. So... different. You see, your mother is the reason for my father's research. Rikona Mugen is the woman who used to call me Teddybear, before she got too sick. Someday, you are my grandmother."

CHAPTER FIVE
07:47
5.09.1869 AD
Promontory Summit, Utah

Thyme crosses into 1869 about ten years younger than she had been in the future. She stands across the shimmering scarlet border and observes the past, on alert. Skipper had warned them against going into 1869, but Theodore promised them he has someone they can trust in Promontory Summit. And he is her grandson, after all. The future descendant that she will have with Efren Cortez. A future that crashed into her present.

Thyme glances at Efren, coming across in his twenties. He looks like he will in 2029 when they get married. But that's what happens back in Los Angeles in a world where time never stopped and mothers didn't turn into babies driving cars. Thyme and Efren will have a son that will try to save Thyme's mother. And fail. Then a grandson, who will take the technology and help people forget. She can't help but stare at Efren, and he cannot bring himself to look at Thyme. The whole idea makes her feel weird. Does fate still work when time is broken? Can destiny arrive when there's never a tomorrow?

It's overcast in 1869, the rainy weather lending a mood in the past tailored perfectly to Thyme's future. In a world where it's always and only present, do somedays even matter anymore? If time starts ticking again right now, will they move on from this moment, stuck in 1869? Will she still fall in love with Efren, and have babies that will grow up in the nineteenth century instead of the twenty-first? Will her mother still be born in 1980 or not? Will Rikona Mugen still suffer dementia, slowly forgetting Thyme and Teddybear and seventy years of her life?

Or does everything reset when time starts again, all of this a dream that never really happens?

No one knows. The only thing Thyme is sure of is that she won't be bound by the future. She's already too affected by the past. She can't survive being torn in both directions. Whatever her future grandson said, it won't influence her decisions. It isn't the map she will follow on her path forward. What happens with Efren will occur because it does, not because it should.

She isn't going to fall in love because the ghost of Christmas future urges her to.

The rest of the fobs come across into 1869. Candy ages a decade older than she has ever been, now sixty and still as sexy. It seems impossible, but then again Thyme is standing at the site where the transcontinental railroad was completed a hundred-and-fifty years before she was born, so what's impossible nowadays? Candy wears every wrinkle like it's jewelry that only enhances her allure. Gray highlights her blonde, somehow making her more striking instead of less. Her curves defy gravity and logic. Thyme's obaasan used to always lament the decline of quality of everything from appliances to socks. Candy was built in 1932—maybe they don't make them like that anymore.

"I made a scale model of this with my Lionel train set for my history project when I was in fourth grade," Jay says, staring at the site of the railroad. He came across looking like he's still in the fourth grade. "This is the most."

Honor stands nearest the border, as if reluctant to get any farther away from the future. She alone has come across elderly in this zone, her aged countenance a match for her sour attitude. Her puckered face is wrecked into a thousand wrinkles. Her implanted LED tattoos seemed muted by a condition like epidermal cataracts. All she's missing is a Rascal and blue hair.

Three androgynous 2118ers come across after the fobs. They appeared similar before they came across, maybe brothers of an age in their original zone. In 1869, they look like three generations from the same family—one a teen, one about forty, the other around seventy. They silently march down the slope and board the last car in the train. The one in the middle carries a case of a shape and size that might contain a laptop.

"An envoy to President Harrison," Honor says. "I overheard them talking on the other side of the border."

"You mean you were spying on them," Thyme says.

"We have enhanced hearing in 2803," Honor reveals. She moves her cold eyes from Thyme to Efren. "We can even hear through walls." A small smirk appears on her face, transformed by endless wrinkles into some kind of nightmare.

Does Honor know about Efren and Thyme's future family? It seems so.

"What are they taking to 1841?" Efren asks Honor while avoiding Thyme's gaze entirely.

"That I don't know," Honor says. "But they are following the rule of three."

"Rule of three?" Candy asks.

"It's a traveler's rule. Unmitigated migration between zones is illegal, but that doesn't stop people from the unauthorized crossing of the borders. Teddybear Cortez doctored us up these visas with fake names to get us across 1869."

She knows, Thyme realizes. She knows I'm supposed to marry Efren and have a family. She knows my future.

But this is the present.

And the future is on the other side of forever.

"Guides called travelers break these rules and move freely through the zones. But there are certain precautions. Crossing a zone with one or two people can result in death. What if you cross over as an infant alone into a waterlogged future and drown? What if two people step across a border as octogenarians and neither can fend off some prehistoric predator? The rule of three supposes a mathematical average based on the random results of age as one moves across zones, versus the instance of dangers posed as one travels. It could still go bad even following the rule of three, but it greatly increases one's chances of success."

"You think you know everything, don't you?" Thyme is angry about Honor eavesdropping on Dr. Cortez and that she now knows the secret of Efren and Thyme.

"I could know everything if I wanted to. I'm from your future," Honor says. "I just do not care enough about most things to bother to find out."

"You had the capacity for limitless knowledge, and you wasted time getting glowy tattoos and a perfect tan," Thyme attacks. "Maybe if you spent less time on your wardrobe and more time figuring out what happened to the clocks, we might see another tomorrow."

"What can I say?" Honor snaps back. "Wasn't it Emily Dickinson that wrote, 'We are living in a material world, and I am a material girl'?"

"That was Madonna," Thyme hollers, hands balling into fists as if she might finally haul off and hit Honor.

"I am a far superior physical specimen to you, Thyme Mugen," Honor says.

"And I fight dirty, Honor," Thyme threatens. "Your own name suggests that you won't do the same. So I'm gonna kick your—"

"All right you two, I think that's enough," Jay interrupts. A kid drowning in a leather jacket five sizes too big, he stares down the mountainside at the train steaming on the track, his brown eyes as big as peanut butter cups. "We have our tickets and our visas. Let's get on board that train!"

***

The 1869 countryside rushes by as the steam engine chugs along the transcontinental railroad. Growing up in SoCal and only rarely leaving the city, Thyme has never seen so much green in all her life. Spring is in full bloom along the route of the railroad. The train passes through lush valleys in what will eventually be the states of Utah and Wyoming. The rising mountains are still capped with snow and will remain so evermore, the feeble light of dawn unable to penetrate the gray cloud cover that's an even sheen across the entire sky.

Thyme took a seat with Candy and Jay. Younger, Jay doesn't seem to have an utter fascination with Candy in 1869. He is all about the train. Finally, something that fascinates him more than the girl from 1948. Thyme believes that the lack of hormones plays a part in his switch in interest. Jay investigates every aspect of the train, acting like he has won a thousand dollars in a 1960

Las Vegas casino. Like one of those brain-blasted zombies from 2118, Jay can't quit smiling.

Efren and Honor sit behind Thyme. Honor appears to be sleeping with her eyes open, meditating about something that is probably beyond the ken of Thyme from the twenty-first century. Efren is reading his book again, Bradbury's Fahrenheit 451 open to somewhere in the middle of the novel.

Thyme can't deal with what she learned in 2118 right now. She wishes she had had time for Dr. Cortez to scrub that from her memory. No good can come of knowing that in every future across America exists a record of Thyme and Efren's relationship. They don't have a relationship!

"My mom told me stories of Dad traveling across Europe in a train," Jay says, as if he has transported himself to another place and time instead of being stuck in this one.

Thyme recalls his questions for Yeoman Cooper aboard the USS Hammerhead. "Your dad served in World War II?"

Jay nods, assuming a gravitas that she frankly didn't think the punk capable of. It seems his face should be too youthful for such a serious expression. His hair, long since it lost all grease to tame the wild black curls, sticks out in corkscrew strands every which way. Just ten, Jay reminds Thyme of a kid in those Our Gang shows that Jiji had on DVD when Thyme was little— someone with a name like Alfalfa or Quinoa or Buckwheat. That show was in black and white, but the past is in color. His jacket drowns him, but Jay doesn't take it off, not even when seated on the train.

"He served in the 332nd Fighter Group," Jay says, and Thyme recognizes the tone in his voice. It sounds like her mother when she told her friends that Thyme won the solo competition for the Los Angeles County high school choir finals. She was supposed to go to state, but instead time stopped. Now it seems like someone else's life. "His plane went down before I was even born."

The jacket. It isn't just any leather jacket, like the one she saw in Grease when Jiji made her sit through it after Thyme said she wanted to sing—she still wonders if her obaasan thought that watching Travolta croon to Olivia Newton-John passed for voice lessons. It's a bomber jacket. An authentic World War II artifact presented to a boy who had lost his father.

Candy is listening to his story and looks like she's about to bawl.

"I'm sorry, Jay," Thyme tells.

Jay blinks, chasing away tears of his own. "Don't be. He died a hero. Most kids I know, their dads eventually disappoint them. It's hard to stay a hero if you live long enough. My dad didn't get a chance to disappoint anyone."

They all stare out the window for a while as the landscape rolls across the horizon, massive mountains tapering to large hills. The green never stops. In fact, as they descend into lower elevations, the snow disappears off the tops of the rises, increasing the already copious complement of green. The gray sky remains unending. All the way, trees line the route, full and bright and countless. Tree after tree after T-rex.

"Is that a…?" Jay pauses, as if he can't quite manage to make the word. "…dinosaur?"

Thyme watched Jurassic World III with Ramon Rios a couple of weeks before the world changed. She remembers over an e-year later thinking dinosaurs in that film looked more realistic than even the real ones probably had. She was wrong.

The Tyrannosaurus rex at the edge of the clearing along

the transcontinental railroad is terrifying, like a great white shark swimming in circles around a small rowboat. Thyme feels defenseless as the massive predator watches them pass. Is a steam engine any match for a killing machine if the T-rex decides to chomp?

Tyrannosauruses.

Two more appear, even larger.

The trio of Tyrannosauruses stare as the train passes, like hungry patrons at an all-you-can-eat buffet trying to choose between endless enticing entrees. They must have come across some border from a time long before chug-chug-chugging prey. Thyme thinks about the rule of three and wonders if the three dinosaurs travel in a pack by chance or by design. The powerful predators stand still among pine and spruce and fir, their hungry eyes tracking the passing train.

The steam locomotive pulls sixteen cars, and Thyme and the other fobs are sitting in the second to the last car. The dinosaurs watch them move, clickety-clack, clickety-clack, clickety-clack. The caboose finally passes the prehistoric predators and Thyme exhales. The dinosaurs probably don't know what to make of the train. Surely there are plenty of easier prey to hunt than a mechanical monstrosity worming its way across the landscape.

"Ain't that a bite?" Jay says with wonder, craning his head to see behind them, wanting one last look at the Cretaceous beasts. Trains and dinosaurs!

"Y'know, I really hate 60s slang, Jay Stone," Thyme tells, exhaling, then looks herself.

Behind them, the three dinosaurs start sprinting along the tracks after the train, gaining on the caboose at an alarming rate. The biggest, larger by far than the entire rear car on the train, opens its mouth as it gets within striking range. The huge head darts forward, turning horizontal, and chomps down on the caboose like the metal teeth of junkyard equipment grabbing garbage. With one violent yank, it rips the caboose away with a jolt to the entire train, and then there's nothing left between the fobs' car and the pack of attacking Tyrannosauruses.

***

The five fobs stare out the back of the speeding train car. The steam engine races forward despite losing the caboose. What other choice does the engineer have? To stop is certain doom. The three dinosaurs would make quick lunch of the passengers on the train.

Luckily, there were no passengers or crew in the caboose when the predators attacked. As the three extinct avatars of death finish poring over the first casualty of their attack, a disappointing victim made of mere wood and iron, they all three simultaneously turn toward the escaping train. As one, they sprint after the row of escaping cars.

"I am not going to be eaten by some prehistoric lizard with a brain the size of a pea," Honor declares, as if her offense to the idea is enough to dissuade the hungry beasts. "I have not come this far to be food for something you primitive démodés use as fossil fuel."

"One taste and they will probably spit you out anyway, Honor," Thyme says. "Not that you'll survive the first bite."

The predators gain on the train. Thyme feels helpless, like all she can do is watch her impending end getting closer and closer and closer. Like speeding toward a tree and being too tiny to turn the steering wheel or reach the brakes. Imminent death. She closes her eyes, but the tears still squeeze through the tight lids. This is how her mother must have felt in her final moment.

The dinosaurs don't make any noise. They advance silently, even the stamp of their feet unheard over the whine of wind and the chug of the engine. Thyme opens her eyes, prepared for the last thing she'll ever see—teeth and tongue and certain horror. Nearly. They are close. Fifty yards away, the dinosaurs' empty eyes lock on Thyme's, and she feels like she's staring into the abyss of her own ending. It looks like she won't be able to figure out what her future self back in 2023 ever saw in Efren Cortez. They only had about thirty e-seconds left to live. Not enough time to fall in love.

But the locomotive has reached a wide arc in the tracks. The bend makes the cars at the front of the line more attainable if the dinosaurs take a shortcut straight across the curve. The cars closer to the front are filled to capacity, dozens of delectable passengers staring out of the windows at the prehistoric spectacle, a more enticing target for three big hungry lizards. Acting on instinct and prudence rather than any advanced logic, they turn and bolt across an open field, running toward the buffet at the front of the train.

"We're safe," Honor exhales. "They are going for the fuller cars."

"Those cars are in front of us, Honor," Thyme tells. "If they derail any of the remaining cars, we're going to crash."

"Better than being eaten," Honor says.

"What do you think will happen after we crash?" Thyme asks, exasperated. "For a 'morrow, you don't ever seem to bother much about what happens next."

Honor, rebuked, goes pale, the LED lights running beneath her skin standing out starkly against the gray of her flesh, like sad neon lights in midnight Vegas advertising nothing but despair.

They watch the Tyrannosauruses intercept the train cars nearer the front. As the dinosaurs attack, mouths wide and teeth bared, a dozen men with guns appear at the open windows and take aim. Locals from 1869 more accustomed to train robbers than two-story dinosaurs defend themselves nonetheless. The fobs can hear the gunshots over the steaming locomotive and the wail of the wind. The predators flinch as every shot hits its target. They falter, but do not retreat. The three Tyrannosauruses shake it off and renew their attack.

"Look." Jay points beyond the bend of the railroad. The curve aligns perpendicular to a valley on the horizon, a bridge connecting the near side with the east side. Just a half-mile ahead. If they can make it across the bridge, the dinosaurs cannot cross the tracks after them. They have to fend off an attack for the next e-minute or two.

The largest T-rex snaps at the third car in the row, teeth glancing off the carriage roof and pulling free a section of the car. The carriage totters back and forth on the tracks, and the five fobs brace, ready for the section to derail and cause a cataclysmic train reaction. But somehow the wheels stay on the track, everything moving forward.

"We're nearly there," Efren hollers over the sounds of new gunshots.

The 1869 passengers in the first-class cars near the front coordinate an attack, all of them aiming at one muscular leg on the biggest T-rex, the one in the front. Multiple injuries are enough to make the big beast stumble, a dozen slugs all hitting one leg at once. The fifteen-ton creature face-plants on the prairie, the two dinosaurs behind it tripping over the tumbling Tyrannosaur and crashing too, an epic fail that would have blown up Youtube. But there's no cell service in 1869, and the pile-up of deadly dinosaurs like a wreck on the I-405 will have to remain a mere memory, a good thought to balance all Thyme's bad ones.

"Noooo," Jay moans.

Thyme sees it. Right before the bridge. A brontosaurus as big as a Winnebago trudges across the tracks like an enfeebled octogenarian crossing the street. The five fobs are thrown forward as the engineer attempts to brake in time, but it's too late. Everyone was so intent on tracking the Tyrannosauruses, no one noticed the big beast on a crash course with a choo-choo.

The T-rex with the wounded leg manages to get upright, and the two healthier predators are already up and chasing the train, like a lover late for the last departing airplane at the end of a romcom. They could never have caught any of the fifteen remaining cars at the speed the locomotive was going unless the train never made it across the bridge.

It never makes it across the bridge.

The steam engine hits the brontosaurus with a wet squelch that turns Thyme's tummy. The fobs are thrown across the passenger car as the front of the train crumples, cars colliding and spilling off the track. Thyme catches the briefest of a glimpse of the Tyrannosauruses descending on the crashing cars near the middle of the line. Then a wall comes rushing at her, and she supposes that if a T-rex could enjoy YouTube, the formerly foolish-looking fossils would have a vengeful chuckle at her expense.

Pain. Then everything is dark.

***

When Thyme was nine, there was a neighborhood dog called Bruiser that had absolutely terrified her. It was a pit bull and she had Googled enough stories about what a pit bull could do to a small girl to feel that her fear was justified. It came to a head six calendar summers ago — or a hundred-and-fifty-years from now, actually — when she was riding bikes with Lizzie Wang. Bruiser was off his leash. The killing machine came cruising around the bend of the block, barking, teeth click-clacking like a racing train. Thyme and Lizzie peddled for dear life. They made it to Thyme's backyard, dived off the bikes, and slammed the wooden gate shut on the backyard fence. Bruiser stood outside the gate, not making a sound. It was as if the pit bull thought by being quiet enough, the girls would come out and let him have his bite.

That's what will happen in another century and a half. Because that's what happened already. Just like she is supposed to marry Efren. Because it has already happened in someone's past. But that's someone else.

Thyme wakes up to a gray world, the train car turned on its side and the contents spilled everywhere. The windows face up like skylights, broken out. Beyond the wooden walls and roof and floor of the car is something that wants to have a bite. The T-rex is out there, Thyme is sure. But it doesn't make a sound.

She looks around. Jay is already on his feet, silent, understanding the situation. Perhaps Thyme underestimated the originally hormonal teen. When he isn't in a post-puberty body, Jay is perfectly acceptable. Candy's eyes flutter open and Thyme puts her finger to her lips. Efren stirs closest to her, and she vaguely recalls him trying to get to her before they crashed. Trying to save her. She frowns at him as he opens his eyes. Thyme doesn't need Efren to save her. She's perfectly capable of saving herself.

Honor remains unconscious beside her. Thyme crawls over her and peers out the window in the door that used to connect two cars. It's now horizontal. She glances out in the direction of the bridge. When the engine derailed, the first cars piled up in a chaotic mess. The last few cars jumped the rail and rolled down the slope from the tracks. From Thyme's vantage point, she can see one of the Tyrannosauruses chomping through the pile of train cars. She can't see the other two man-eaters.

They need to move. Waiting will only reduce their chances of survival. The predators will hunt down every last piece of food. These killers are hardwired for survival.

Thyme slaps Honor. She has wanted to do it since she first met the smug 'morrow. Honor's eyes flutter open, the subdermal tattoos on her wrinkled face sparking a deep, disturbing red. Surprise and defense turn to simmering rage, her gaze narrowing into dangerous slits. Thyme wonders about that enhanced strength and Honor's temper.

Instead of inflicting injury, Honor rolls over and surveys the scene. Biologically older than any of the other fobs, Honor will be the one that slows them down no matter how much futuristic physical speed she possesses. The stakes are as high as they have ever been since the plan changed back in 1960, but when the chance for survival is decreased by being last in the line of a scurrying human buffet, things are most ominous for the slowest member of the group.

"A plan?" Honor mouths.

"We run," Thyme mimes back.

Honor rolls her eyes. "Typical antique thinking," Honor says soundlessly. Or something like that, maybe with a curse word or two from tomorrow.

Thyme looks at Efren, Candy, and Jay. She tilts her head toward the bridge still a hundred yards away. The three fobs all nod. Thyme moves forward, the bumps and bruises from the crash making her feel as old as Honor appears. She eases the door open, horizontal so that she must step over and through, swinging a leg over the jamb like stepping over the tailgate of a pickup truck. Outside, she sees the second T-rex through the gap between the car they were in and the one in front of them. The dining car has been peeled open like a can of tuna fish, and the dinosaur has its snout inside the food stores like a hungry kitten.

The fobs move slowly along the line of crashed passenger cars. Other survivors of the destruction start poking their heads out of the derailed train. The fobs are joined as they move toward the bridge, Thyme trying to keep her eye on the deadly dinos as they get closer and closer and closer.

The roar is like something out of the cinema, Dolby surround sound making Thyme's very bones shake. The biggest T-rex, the one with the injured leg from multiple gunshot wounds, rises on the other side of the car they are currently passing. Thyme doesn't want to think about the feast she interrupted.

"Stay still and the T-rex can't see us," Thyme tells her companions.

"And where did you get that ridiculous notion?" Honor hisses.

"Movie science," Thyme says.

"Cro-Magnon logic," Honor insults.

The T-rex uses its massive head to batter the car between it and a dozen passengers. Candy screams like a horror movie queen. Honor grabs Thyme by the wrist in a viselike grip and starts racing. With a train car between them and an injured T-rex, they have a chance. More passengers escape the cars and start dashing toward the bridge, dozens of people running toward safety. And three deadly predators with scurrying snacks to choose from.

The T-rex feasting on the contents of the dining car looks up and considers the new prey. The other T-rex nearest the bridge is eating the remains of the brontosaurus that the engine made into roadkill. It starts watching the people sprinting in its general direction, pondering a full feast versus fresh morsels. The big T-rex with the lame leg makes its way around the car behind them and gives chase.

Candy is still screaming. Thyme feels her own terror building inside her, ready to burst out of her mouth. The race to the bridge should only take a few e-seconds, but it seems like she is running a marathon. Her life since leaving Los Angeles has become a series of infinite minutes, extended moments that drag on forever.

Honor holds onto Thyme, either in solidarity or to slow Thyme enough to increase Honor's chance for survival if the T-rex catches them. Fifty-fifty odds. Jay runs on the other side of Thyme. He could run off ahead, but he keeps pace. Candy is a mess, smile as gone as the dinosaurs are in 2023, running as if her hair is on fire and outpacing the other four fobs. Efren must have injured his leg in the crash. He has a limp, just like the pursuing predator, keeping pace a few feet behind them. He might be her future husband, but today he is mostly a stranger, and Thyme won't risk her own life to die with Efren if he is the slowest of the lot.

Thyme gets to the edge of the bridge. The tracks extend past a steep drop off and traverse a deep valley. Candy has already moved out onto the bridge. Thyme balances on the ties, stepping gingerly over the edge and out along the span that offers safety. Honor is right behind her. The Tyrannosauruses cannot follow them out onto the bridge. Thyme and the other fobs have all managed to avoid being lunch for a fossil.

There are dozens of other passengers still trying to get to the bridge, too many ever to make it. Thyme turns away before the bloodbath commences. Then she hears it. Sirens. Even the Tyrannosauruses give pause, turning toward the sounds coming from the south. It's a squad of vehicles marked with "Border Patrol." The vehicles are imports to 1869, of course — police SUVs from 2023. There are guns mounted to the roof of three vehicles, automatic weapons spattering the ground near the dinosaurs as a warning. The three Tyrannosauruses retreat. Two of the vehicles are ambulances, medical support ready to treat the passengers injured in the crash.

"The cavalry," Candy cries, her patented smile blooming as bright as a sunrise.

The other passengers that found safety on the bridge start straggling back toward the group of cars, rescued. There were two dozen passengers that had arrived at the safety of the bridge. All but five head back toward the crash. Thyme remembers what Skipper warned them about. "Don't trust anyone from 1869."

"No," Thyme decides for the whole group. "We need to move on. They could be the enemy. We shouldn't trust anyone from this era."

Honor nods, agreed. Efren silently concedes. Jay never considered options — he'll follow the rest of the fobs whenever they go. Only Candy's gaze lingers on the border patrol helping the traumatized passengers and tending the injured victims. Candy watches intently like she is considering going back. She just wants to be happy, and the future on the other side of the bridge probably promises more strife.

Thyme turns away and starts across the bridge. She doesn't look back until she gets to the other side. Honor follows nearest her, then Jay and Efren. Candy is the last one off the bridge, but she has chosen. The five fobs stay together, headed toward the next future.

CHAPTER SIX
15:16
8.18.2033 AD
Denver, Colorado

"The future is better, but things have to get worse first," Honor says.

"Sounds like life," Jay says

Time passes. Time stays stuck. Thyme loses track of the e-minutes as they make their way eastward, avoiding every town along the way until they can figure out whether the new zone sympathizes with Washington, DC, or with the Chronfederacy. Strangers entering any small town along the way would certainly be too suspicious, so they sneak past one population center after another, walking and walking and walking.

Honor was sure she knew the exact date of the new time zone when they crossed the border shortly after traversing the bridge near Green River, Wyoming. They are in 2033, a nearer future to Thyme's present than the last one she'd seen. Somewhere in this year, she would be twenty-six and probably married already. To Efren Cortez. She didn't want to think about that.

It's summertime, midday, and it is a scorcher. The sun beats down on them, and not one of them was wearing the right attire for a heatwave back when they were ambushed in February of 1960. Candy's dress is certainly not conducive to a cross-country trek consisting of hundreds of miles. As they skirt the border of 1869 again around a mining camp near Sweetwater, Jay and Candy scurry across the border and swipe some laundry hanging on a line along the river. Jay transforms from seventeen to seventy to seven in a matter of moments. Candy switches from thirty to twenty to twelve. She changes into bib overalls and a denim shirt. After that, for the first time since Thyme met Candy in 2023, the woman looks more like a boy than a bombshell. Preadolescent in 2033, her blonde is bland, her chest is flat, and her figure is less Barbie and more toy soldier.

They walk three-hundred-and-fifty miles before they come to a metropolitan area big enough they believe they can blend in. They look down the mountain at Denver, keeping off the main interstate going west out of town to prevent being spotted by passersby. From afar, Thyme can see that the passengers in the passing vehicles probably wouldn't notice them anyway, transportation automated at some point in the next ten years. No one watches the road — everyone reclines back and stares off into the distance as if they are daydreaming.

Above the roadway are black gnats in a stream along the same routes as the cars. What first resembles a swarm of flies is upon closer inspection revealed as a great number of automated drones ferrying goods from place to place. Many have an Amazon logo on the side, while others advertise Starbucks, McDonald's, as well as a dozen other brands Thyme has never heard of. There are drones by the hundreds.

"We have to risk talking to someone, Thyme," Honor says, looking away from the assembly-line future. "We need to get new information. Maybe Ms. Norman has broken free of Mr. Sloane. The events in 1960 took place a couple of e-weeks ago now. Perhaps she is looking for us."

Thyme turns to Efren for his opinion, but he's a newborn and merely wobbles his head like a loose nut on a short bolt. Candy will do whatever they tell her to do. Jay….

Jay already strides down the slope, that swagger of a kid born at a time when boys had to be tough or they were taunted and teased. All his life, Jay Stone might not have been able to walk into whatever restaurant he wanted to or take whatever seat on the bus he preferred, or maybe he had to go to a different school than the white Nevadans, but no one will ever make him think he's less than anyone else. He's seven in 2033, a lot younger than when he left 1960, but he walks like a full-grown man.

Thyme is ten and as short as seven-year-old Jay in 2033, although the two of them will never see eye to eye. She sprints after Jay. Honor easily keeps pace, her age presenting at about twenty years old. She has an athlete's stamina despite carrying baby Efren in a makeshift sling made of Candy's discarded dress. Candy is twelve and klutzy, clamoring to keep up.

"We stick together, Jay," Thyme scolds, catching up. "We weren't done making a decision."

"You don't look old enough to be my mother, Thyme, so maybe I'll make my own choices."

"You're making choices for all of us when you run off without permission," Thyme snaps.

"Permission?" Jay grumbles. "This isn't a team, Thyme. I'm here because I saved your bacon back in Vegas. Since then,

I've been shot out of the sky, almost drowned in a prehistoric sea, crashed in a train in 1869, and narrowly avoided becoming a Tyrannosaurus turd. Maybe I don't want to hang around with you anymore."

"The Chronfederacy is looking for us," Thyme says. "They tried to kill us back in BC."

"They tried to kill you," Jay says. "I'm not going to your dumb school. I'm just the guy caught in the crossfire."

Thyme pauses. He's right. She has kind of lumped Jay in with the rest of them since 1960, but he really is only an innocent bystander. Jefferson Davis and his loyal Chronfederates want to stop the symbolic school from opening. They're targeting the Minute students. Jay means nothing to the Grays. So when he walks away, Thyme doesn't try to stop him.

Then she realizes they've come all the way down into the city, standing still in a busy street, people all around them. She tries not to stare too hard at the hundreds of people all around her, because whenever there are enough people, someone always reminds her of Mom. She can't help it. Across the street, going into a clothing store, a woman wears a sunhat like the one Thyme bought for Mom last summer. Her heart bangs against the inside of her chest, trying to get out. But Thyme can see the woman through the plate glass window of the boutique, and the woman is Indian and certainly not Riko Mugen. Hope against all hope cracks and crashes once again.

Above, drones zip this way and that, small ones delivering coffee or meals to people in offices, or even right along the street. Others drop packages and envelopes at businesses. Like flies on a summer day, they flit about the air unnoticed by the 'morrows.

These are the first citizens of 2033 that the fobs have

encountered since crossing over from 1869. The style has changed a little since 2023 — Thyme can see the influences of her home era in the outfits of the young crowd. She can also see the gradual androgenization of attire that must eventually lead to the future fashion of 2118. Skirts are apparently favored by either sex. Makeup is flashy and seems to glow on its own, akin to Honor's incandescent tattoos. The guys have longer hair and the girls' shorter. With her pixie hairdo, Thyme fits right in.

Something is missing.

Thyme is distracted by the advanced attire, more conservative than 2023 in a reversal of societal trajectory. The girls cover up more than they show. The boys feature high collars and turtlenecks. There isn't a single citizen over the age of forty on the bustling sidewalks, not one out of a crowd of hundreds.

But that's not what's missing.

There's something else.

All eyes are on the four fobs standing still on the busy sidewalks. Jay has disappeared into the crowd. Everyone else seems particularly interested in the three girls and their baby. The look in the eye of the 2033ers is eerie. Like they are both studying Thyme and pondering something else simultaneously, like a person talking and texting at the same time.

A chill runs down Thyme's spine. She realizes what's missing. No cell phones. Not a single one.

***

They sit at a booth in a corner of a cafe that isn't so different from the eateries in Thyme's time. Jay is gone, so that leaves her to contend with the ramifications of her future destiny with Efren without the distraction of another male. Luckily, Efren is an infant and unable to woo, currently limited to coo and poo.

"What are you going to order?" Honor asks Candy.

"Pancakes," Candy says without needing to see a menu. "Extra maple syrup. And a soda. Do you think they have a Nehi Chocolate?"

"Imported," Honor confirms, as if she waitresses here part-time. Then she asks Thyme, always sounding as if she's accusing something. "And you?"

"I'll order a salad," Thyme mumbles absentmindedly, looking around the cafe. "With lemon water."

Honor nods. Like Thyme needs her approval.

Candy holds the tiny baby against her flat chest, Efren sleeping soundly, as he has done most of the time since they arrived in 2033. He is a good baby who hardly ever fusses or cries.

"What do you think happened to Jay?" Candy asks.

Thyme feels a pang of envy as Candy asks after the bad boy in the leather jacket. Why does Thyme feel jealous? She knows Jay couldn't stop ogling Candy, but is the interest mutual? Why does Thyme care if it is?

"What does it matter what Jay does?" Thyme asks. "He's better off being far away from this drama. The Chronfederates are after the four of us."

"Do you have a romantic interest in him?" Honor inquires.

"Me? No. No, he's not my type," Candy says. "My parents never approved of my type. Always wanted me to chase after someone other than who I was interested in. I'm not gonna play that game anymore."

"Good," Honor says. "Romantic entanglements are grody to the max."

Thyme glares at Honor and her anachronistic anecdotes.

"I'm worried about him, that's all," Candy says. "He's

kind of become one of us. I thought he'd come along all the way to New York."

Thyme wishes Jay would've come to New York, too. Maybe joined them at the school. After Ms. Norman learned what Jay did to help them escape 1960, she would've welcomed him into the Minute. But Jay is a breeze blowing in his own direction. Thyme wants some romantic option that isn't all wrapped up in predestination.

Thyme scans the patrons of the small restaurant, a dozen people all staring blankly off into the distance, not one of them engaged in conversation. There's a couple that certainly looks like they're married sitting silently across from one another. A family of four, including two kids neither older than six, sit still and mute in the opposite corner of the cafe. A ventilation fan in the ceiling brings air conditioning into the building to stave off the endless August afternoon, and it's louder than any other sound in the place.

"It's like a ghost town filled with living people," Candy says.

"What's wrong with them?" Thyme wonders aloud. "And where are all the phones?"

"In here," Honor answers, tapping her temple, the lights beneath her scalp moving and changing colors.

"The phones are in their heads?" Candy asks, aghast.

"Implanted," Thyme realizes. That's why everyone has that familiar phone-mesmerized look on their face without a physical screen in their hand—they're all seeing pictures in their heads. "The phones are internal. Integrated."

Honor nods. "Everything is recorded, all the time, in 2033. And everyone is networked. What one sees, they all see. Instant interconnectivity. You can look through the eyes of someone on the other side of the city. You can post video to social media accounts that can be shared with everyone else in 2033, instantly, with but a thought. Communication is constant and comprehensive. Like a hive mind."

"Where is privacy?" Thyme asks.

"What privacy?" Honor retorts.

A small drone brings out the food although no one has ordered anything yet. They'd just told Honor and she….

"You're jacked in to this hot mess?" Thyme guesses as a hovering robot drops off the platters, turns, and disappears.

Honor stares into the distance, seeing something that Thyme and Candy cannot. Seeing everything. "Absolutely ancient Wi-Fi interconnectivity. It is a constant stream of news, communications, picture sharing, holographic emoting. The unbearable avalanche of meaningless drivel makes me wonder how the human race survived the twenty-first century. The news is nonstop gossip."

Little different from 2023.

"So it's like Edward R. Murrow broadcast right into your head?" Candy asks.

"Maybe," Honor dismisses, obviously not knowing Edward R. Murrow from Eddie Murphy from Ed Sheeran. "Information is everything in 2033. The stream of data is nonstop."

"24/7 fake news," Thyme says with snark.

Honor rolls her eyes. Some expressions apparently become infamous. "That is so 2023. The news was widely panned as an unreliable source of information during your when, Thyme. Everyone distrusted every source out there. It was information anarchy. About the middle of the twenty-first century, the media rededicated to truth, which meant a resurgence in fact-finding and citation of sources and a renewed attempt at unbiased reportage. However, the news is always filtered through a human lens. And people always have an agenda. So as consumers started feeling like the media had figured it out and the lies were over, it actually made them willing participants in a greater fiction. It is exhausting fighting against overwhelming propaganda. It is easier to believe what you are told. So they do. They all do."

"From fake news to faker news?" Thyme asks.

Honor shrugs. "Things never get better before first getting worse."

The three girls pick at their plates, as silent as the customers surrounding them. This is the future—impersonal, interconnected, inhuman. For the first time since the clocks stopped, Thyme wonders if maybe it's better that tomorrow was canceled. This isn't a someday to look forward to.

Honor, advanced and almost robotic since they met in 2023, pauses between bites, her porridge half-masticated in her mouth. "Well, I'll be cow-kicked."

"What?" Candy asks.

"No one says that," Thyme says.

"We need to get out of here," Honor warns.

Thyme looks around. Menace has replaced the vacant stares. Even the small children in the family of four glare like Thyme has stolen their Christmas candy. The cook stands in the doorway to the kitchen, sneering like the fobs have shortchanged him on the tip. Something is wrong.

"Fake news," Honor whispers. "There is a news bulletin all over the feeds with our faces on it. They are calling us 'time terrorists.' They say we wrecked the train in 1869."

"Terrorists?" Candy exclaims, like she's announcing their intentions. Everyone flinches.

Thyme bolts, Honor on her heels, Candy scampering behind with Efren clutched against her chest. On the streets of Denver, automated cars zip along in a coordinated dance of merging and turning, the passengers paying no attention to the road and concentrating instead on the fobs standing along the street. Drones buzz above like an angry swarm of bees. Pedestrians up and down the sidewalk in front of the cafe stare at Thyme, Honor, and Candy.

"Thyme," says the closest citizen. "Thyme."

The rest of the population joins the chant. "Thyme. Thyme. Thyme."

"They are all relaying our location to authorities," Honor says. "There is nowhere to run."

"Maybe not 'run,'" comes a voice from the sky above.

It's Jay. He's riding a drone like it's the motorbike of the future. Beside him on a second drone is a middle-aged man with a flowing beard that is mostly gray, dressed in a manner that might've been from a far-flung future or long, long ago. They descend and hover over the sidewalk where a half-hundred 'morrows stare at the fobs and chant Thyme's name.

"Five e-minutes, Thyme Mugen," Jay quips as he floats alongside the fobs. "I leave you alone for five e-minutes and this is the trouble you get yourself into."

***

Thyme rides a drone behind Jay, looking like two kids sharing a bike. The other drone is piloted by a man Thyme has never seen before, with Honor cradling Efren in the rear and Candy wedged between them. The drones ascend and Jay banks the machine, following the other drone eastward.

"Who's your new friend?" Thyme asks as they follow a

roadway ten feet up in the air.

"His name is Shepherd," Jay says over the whoosh of wind. "He's a traveler."

"How did you find him?"

"I'll let him tell you the story."

"How did you get these drones?" Thyme asks instead.

"Shepherd has tech that can hijack the system. He spliced in these handlebars to a couple of borrowed Amazon drones." Jay points to a small circle of glass between the steering handles that looks like a touch screen. "That sets the altitude. Then it works like a motorcycle."

Beneath them, hundreds of Denver citizens chase through the streets in a stampede that looks like the beginning of a marathon when everyone starts all at once. The sound of thunder, feet on asphalt, rumbles from underneath instead of up above. It's a nightmare, one Thyme knows cannot be real, but she still can't wake up. She had watched the old black-and-white version of Frankenstein with Jiji one Halloween when she was ten, and that night she dreamed of an angry mob of villagers bearing torches and pitchforks surrounding her house shouting "Kill the monster!" Now the angry mob chases her through the streets of Denver wearing hipster sunglasses and expensive Christian Louboutins, shouting, "Thyme! Thyme! Thyme!"

"The traveler says we need to go that way," Jay says, pointing east. "Follow Lawrence Street. All the way to Oldtown. It's a part of historic Denver. Wi-Fi service is spotty over there. We need to get off the grid."

The buildings turn older. The signs announce a renaissance district. The mob following the drones starts to slow and scatter. The stream of information delivering the input to the Coloradans is interrupted. Thyme looks at Honor and Honor taps her temple, shakes her head. There's no signal here.

The drones pause and descend, landing along Lawrence Street. The traveler leads them on foot along Lawrence, turns, turns, twists, back again. Shepherd appears to be in his fifties in 2033. He could've come from any era across America. He wears a black mink parka that is entirely timeless. His leather moccasins might have been procured in 1841 or 2803. A wide-brimmed hat shadows his face, something Thyme has seen in pictures of the Old West and drawings of Ancient Greece, and featured as vintage in even the furthest futures. He doesn't seem like he belongs in 2033 because he looks like he could belong anywhere.

"Here," the traveler offers, stopping in front of a small bookshop.

Thyme wonders if it's a trap. "Why should we trust you?"

The traveler pushes the hat back, bright blue eyes gazing at the five fobs. "My name is Shepherd. I'm a traveler."

"Yeah," Thyme dismisses. "Jay already told us that. How do we know you're a friend?"

"Ms. Norman sent me."

Thyme stares. Does she have any choice? They cannot make it the rest of the way through Denver on their own. Shepherd goes inside. Jay follows him in. The rest of the fobs wait on her. She has to take a chance on Shepherd. Thyme finally nods, and they enter the small store.

This bookshop specializes in original editions, so the advent of the Freeze was an unexpected boon to the proprietor of the Book Nook. Thyme wonders how many of the authors are still alive in the fragmented world of jigsaw eras. Gazing across the shelves, Thyme sees first-run copies of Harry Potter and the Philosopher's Stone, Thinner by Richard Bachman, The Sound and the Fury from 1929, and an original quarto of King Lear.

Books have become a sort of currency in the post-Freeze world, where money is different between eras and minerals like silver and gold can be created alchemically in the futures. First editions have great value, as art is one of the rare items of timeless value. This place is more like a bank than a book shop. For the first time, Thyme notices the bars on the window and the deadbolts on the front door. It's less Barnes and Noble and more Bailey Building and Loan.

"An early edition Shakespeare," Thyme says. "Time takes, but time gives some back, huh?"

"So it has always been, young lady," agrees an elderly man who might belong nowhere or nowhen else. Small and bespectacled, he appears born to be a bookshop keeper. His ears appear so very small, as if hearing is unnecessary, while his eyes are large, as if designed for reading. "Time is both mother and reaper."

Thyme thinks of the propaganda pumped into the Wi-Fi-connected citizenry of Denver. "Sometimes fiction is truer than fact."

The old man nods. "I would trust William Shakespeare before Walter Cronkite. I'm looking forward to the Bard's upcoming sequel to Much Ado About Nothing. Appropriately, it's called Much Ado About Something."

Thyme smirks. What's next, The Bible 2?

"You don't...?" Thyme asks, tapping her temple.

"We prefer to get information a little more slowly here in Oldtown," the proprietor says. "The news comes around this neighborhood printed on actual paper. No Wi-Fi. Just words."

Thyme nods. "No fake news? No real fake news?"

The older man shrugs. "Facts are always up to

interpretation. Let's say putting it on paper at least requires a little more deliberation."

Thyme smiles. She likes the old man.

"My name is Orville Darwin," he says, holding out his hand.

"Thyme Mugen. I am from 2023."

"Those were simpler times," Mr. Darwin says wistfully, as if it was the Old West instead of ten years ago.

Shepherd hangs up a phone connected to a cord. Thyme hasn't seen one of those outside a museum. She wonders if it was imported from another era or simply a part of the bookshop's original ambiance. "I have arranged exodus from 2033," Shepherd says. "There's a hospital a few blocks away. Just outside Oldtown. We need to rendezvous with a helicopter to take you east. There's a helipad on the hospital's roof."

Thyme takes a last look around. She loves books, but she's no great student of history. Mrs. Hagar was her last social studies teacher before the Freeze, and she said once that Thyme "lives too much in the future. If you don't want to take some time out for yesterday, at least consider today. Today will soon be history, whereas tomorrow never seems to get here." Well, today is tomorrow. Thyme is living in 2033. And it got here a heckuva lot sooner than Thyme thought it would.

Mrs. Hagar also said that "history is like a wheel, and the spokes come 'round and 'round." That in particular strikes Thyme as she studies the bookshop. Thyme recalls the lesson that inspired Mrs. Hagar's thoughts. She was connecting the Underground Railroad to the story of Anne Frank, to illustrate that there are always good people to resist fascism and aid the oppressed. She was right about part of it—there are always good people, in every era. But she was wrong about the 'round and 'round. The spokes are not a wheel but a pincushion, all radiating out from a nucleus, sharp and apt to prick.

The traveler stands at the front door of the bookshop, checking the compass in his hand, an old-fashioned device in a shining silver case that could've been purchased brand new a century before Thyme was born, or might be an antique passed down for generations in Shepherd's family. Thyme notices the Bowie knife at his hip. Hanging from the back of his belt is a pouch that might've been made by Neanderthals or bought at Sacs in 2023. He could be from anywhen, a timeless traveler who doesn't fit in with Mrs. Hagar's past, present, or future. Maybe that's the perfect person to navigate this new world.

Shepherd exits the bookshop with baby Efren slung over his shoulder in a makeshift papoose, Honor on his heels, Candy in the middle, and Jay keeping a step in front of Thyme. Whether tomorrow or yesterday comes next, it's time to leave today.

***

"They are coming," Honor tells the traveler, two blocks from the bookshop, right across the border leaving Oldtown.

The fobs huddle under the cover of a marble statue of city founder William Larimer, Jr. A plaque details his history — Larimer settled in what was called Denver City in 1858. He has been dead for a hundred-and-fifty years, yet he might be still living just across the border in 1869 or maybe in 1841 Washington, DC. Dead doesn't mean what it used to, and what is mythic now might be the mundane over a border. Among his achievements, Mr. Larimer posthumously affords them cover from compromised Coloradans.

"The news streams are all reporting that we are attempting an escape from Denver. Based on our current location and direction, they have deduced our destination," Honor says. "There are hundreds of Coloradans gathering at Foster Medical Center to stop the terrorists."

"To stop the terrorists," Candy repeats, exasperated. She looks like the least likely terrorist of all time.

"I need to find us a way in," the traveler says. "Mr. Stone and I will scout ahead. The media is primarily concerned with the four students to the Institute. Wait here while we do reconnaissance. I'll take Mr. Cortez with me, just in case."

Just in case Thyme and the others are captured before Shepherd makes it back. He would save one fob instead of none if he at least gets Efren to New York. It would be easiest to smuggle an infant out of 2033.

Jay checks with Thyme. He seems unsure whether to leave her, like it might be the last time he ever sees the other three fobs. Thyme expects him to gaze longingly at Candy before they part, but ever since she turned only twelve, Jay hardly notices her anymore in the present. It's Thyme that he seems unable to quit. Finally, he looks away, scampering after Shepherd.

"It feels like a trap," Honor says in an ominous deadpan.

"Shepherd wouldn't do that to us," Candy disagrees. "Ms. Norman sent him to help us."

"Awfully convenient. He knew exactly where to find us?" Honor challenges. "How do we know he is on our side? Maybe the Chronfederacy sent him. What proof do we have that Shepherd is telling us the truth and not leading us straight to the enemy?"

Thyme has already considered the possibility. One person's truth is another person's baloney. But they don't have a choice but to trust someone else. They're up against a million

Coloradans that believe in the almighty media. And the press reports that these four fobs are terrorists. The teens don't have the resources to get across Denver on their own. They can't make it without a traveler.

But what if Honor is right?

"There is new news," Honor announces. "The latest headline. 'Traveler Caught with Two Terrorists. Assault on Hospital Thwarted.'"

"No," Candy cries.

"What kind of a traveler gets captured within a few e-minutes of the mission he was hired for?" Honor says. "Did Ms. Norman get his services at the dime-store?"

"Why do you have to talk like you stepped out of a gangster movie?" Thyme snaps.

"I am trying to make you feel more comfortable," Honor says. "Our language is so advanced from yours that I must use ridiculously simplistic terms. I suppose you would equate it to speaking baby-talk to an infant."

"Could you be any more condescending?"

"Of course. But Ms. Norman suggested that I tone down my blunt assessment of your primitive time zones if I wanted to fit in. You see, I do not really have friends back in my future."

"Surprise, surprise."

"This isn't your future," Candy says, taking Honor's hand. Thyme expects the 'morrow to flinch from human contact, but Honor stares dumbfounded as Candy holds her hand. Like a robotic android suffering its first human interaction.

"No, this really is not," Honor agrees, and for once Thyme can't tell if it's sarcasm or wonder. "So, what do we do next?" Honor asks, before Thyme can consider too long if the three of them just had a moment.

"We rescue the boys," Thyme says. "Then we get out of this zone."

The three remaining free fobs start moving cautiously along the avenue. Slowly, they make it safely to the corner around the avenue that leads to the hospital. Standing guard in front of the building before them are a thousand citizens from 2033, mass-media mannequins controlled by misinformation, forming a line that acts as a barrier between the fobs and Foster Medical Center.

"How are we ever gonna get through all of them?" Candy asks, exasperated. "We might as well give up right now."

"I am almost done with something that should cause a proper diversion," Honor says.

"Do you plan on scolding them until they scurry away?" Thyme challenges.

"If I thought it would be effective, my skills of disparagement are exemplary," Honor says, either not understanding sarcasm or choosing to ignore it. Thyme assumes it's the latter. "My plan involves manipulating the media. I can use information against them. I have spent the time since we were branded terrorists constructing a data bomb."

"Now we sound like terrorists," Thyme says.

"What's a 'data bomb'?" Candy asks.

Honor smiles. Thyme tries to remember if it's the first time she's seen the 'morrow with anything but a scowl or some indiscriminate expression. If she would smile a little more often, maybe she would find the friends in the past that she never found in her present. Perhaps she could even find a sweetheart.

"I have been constructing individual feeds of fictitious scandalizing headlines about celebrities and politicos. Hundreds. Backlogged and ready to release, I will flood the feeds with falsehoods, sensational clickbait that will make five fobs fleeing toward 13,411 BC seem downright boring by comparison."

"Really fake real fake news," Thyme says. "Genius."

"By your standards, my intellect is not even on the chart."

"How can I love you and hate you at the same time right now?" Thyme asks.

"Many mistake the two emotions as being on extreme ends on a sliding scale," Honor explains, like an instructor educating on electromagnetism. "Love and hate are actually intrinsically linked, opposite sides of a thin coin that can easily be flipped."

Thyme rolls her eyes. "Just drop the bomb."

Honor smiles again, even more endearing than the last expression, regurgitating a litany of fantastic falsehoods out of her mouth even as the same headlines scroll across 2033ers all over Denver —

"Scientists Discover the Secret to Restart Time.

"President Harrison Declares War on 2300 AD Arkansas.

"Elvis marries Madonna in 2311 BC Egypt.

"JFK Wins Special Election for U.S. Senate.

"Shakespeare's Reimagining of Romeo and Ryan Opens on Broadway.

"Sign of Progress: Maces Declared Illegal in 503 England."

And on and on and on, endless headlines one as tantalizing as the last. Dozens and dozens, demanding attention.

"Now," Honor announces between falsehoods. The three girls run toward Foster Medical Center, right through a crowd of a thousand, all standing and staring into space with the same vacant gaze that reminds Thyme of anyone with a smartphone in 2023 watching a cat video on YouTube. The screens could hypnotize her friends back in California, and now Thyme sees the same effect played across endless faces as Honor's deluge of data is impossible to ignore. Watching headline after headline scroll back in their own minds, the crowd doesn't notice three girls run by right in front of them.

Honor appears smug about her success. Thyme isn't surprised that the plan works. She has witnessed people walking into walls while texting, missing an entire parade while engrossed in a Netflix binge, ignoring an entire convo with their boyfriend while texting a girlfriend, and remaining oblivious while standing right next to Ariana Grande at the local Sephora because one was downloading the new Ariana Grande album from iTunes — that last one happened to Thyme Mugen herself, the last summer before the Freeze.

They get inside before the data bomb starts to lose steam. The mob surrounding Foster Medical Center starts to stir as the automatic doors close behind the three girls, some of the 'morrows already managing to muddle through the multitude of streaming headlines and discover the authentic updates about the "dangerous" fobs through the storm of misinformation. Behind them, a half dozen members of the mob burst in, giving chase. The three girls sprint across the main lobby of a generally deserted Foster Medical Center, the receptionists and smattering of patients all staring off into oblivion, still under the influence of Honor's data bomb. Chasing them down a long corridor, three burly men take the lead, any one of them big enough to put an end to the chase. At the end of the hall, an elevator opens. It's the only opportunity for escape from the fobs' pursuers. But there are already people inside, staring at the girls as they race toward the elevator.

It's Jay and Shepherd, with Efren slung over the traveler's shoulder.

The girls pile into the elevator with the boys as the doors close behind them. The pursuers were ten feet away and would have to wait for another car. It bought the fobs precious moments.

"You're free," Candy exclaims, giving the smaller Jay a big hug that would've made him swoon if either of them was past puberty. The big grin on her face offsets the unsettling circumstances.

"Whatever you did, it distracted the locals guarding us," Jay tells Thyme, wriggling away from Candy's embrace.

"It was Honor," Thyme says, and Honor explains about the data bomb.

"Brilliant," Shepherd compliments, and Thyme thinks that Honor might be blushing. Or maybe it's only her tattoo changing colors.

"Let's get out of 2033," Thyme says as the elevator reaches the top floor.

The elevator opens and the fobs race toward a door at the end of another corridor. It leads out to the roof, a helicopter already prepped and revving its propeller. Behind them, a second elevator dings and six pursuers from the first floor race toward them.

The exit door has a deadbolt that engages from the roofside, the interior needing a key so that the hospital can keep people off the roof except for authorized personnel. One of the brainwashed locals chasing them is a burly man wearing olive-drab overalls with "custodian" written on the breast and a jumble of keys jangling against his hip.

"Go," Thyme commands, closing the door on the pursuers and engaging the deadbolt. She keeps her hand on the turn, bracing against pressure from the inside as a key tries to open the lock. "I'll hold them off as long as I can."

"Okay," Honor agrees without hesitation, taking Efren from Shepherd and running toward the helicopter.

"No," Shepherd disagrees. "It should be me. I was hired to get you to 1980 safely."

"Then get the others to New York. Without you, none of us will make it."

"You made it this far," he says. By luck. They both know it. Shep finally nods, takes young Candy by the hand, and leads her toward the helicopter. She cries, but she doesn't put up a fight. She knows someone must stay behind.

"Let me," Jay says. "I wasn't invited to 1980 anyway. You go, Thyme."

"This isn't your fight."

"That's why they will probably let me go."

Inside, the key tries to turn the lock. Thyme holds fast. Even if she could consider Jay's offer, she worries that taking her hands away long enough for Jay to take over would be enough opportunity for the 'morrows to get through the door and stop Shepherd and the students. Besides, Jay is only seven in the present and can barely reach the deadbolt.

"No," Thyme tells. "The others will tell Ms. Norman what you did for us. She will let you enroll at the Institute. Go, Jay. Take my place at the Minute."

Jay turns. Thyme closes her eyes. What will this mob do to her once they get through the door? Will she be a prisoner, or has the war between the zones started taking casualties? She's lived for over a year in the infinite minute since her mother died, endless grieving at a life cut too short. Is Thyme now coming too soon to her own end?

She opens her eyes. Jay is still right beside her, waving off the traveler as the helicopter takes off.

"What are you doing, Jay?" Thyme cries.

"Fight or run away?" Jay says, a roguish grin that surely made some ladies swoon over the years. "I'm always ready for some fisticuffs, dolly."

And then the other fobs are safe, and the deadbolt slips through Thyme's fingers, and Thyme and Jay are caught.

CHAPTER SEVEN
07:47
5.09.1869 AD
Abilene, Kansas

Thyme wakes up and rolls over on a hardwood floor, facing a sleeping boy who is handsome and about seventeen again, looking much like he did when she first met him in 1960. Jay put up quite a fight on the rooftop back in 2033. Thyme watched the helicopter carrying Shepherd, Honor, Efren, and Candy fly away. Then the media-minced zombies from 2033 used something, contained in a tube so small it might have held Chapstick in 2023, to knock them both out.

Jay's eyes flutter open, brown and bright as aged, oiled leather, and he smiles when he sees her, a dazzling white grin. Wherever and whenever they are, the moment lasts for a while, a while that seems to equal eternity. Clocks or not, time stands still.

"I never noticed before, but you're very pretty," Jay says.

"Not so pretty as to distract your attention from Miss Candy Kane," Thyme teases, getting to her feet.

"She reminds me of the pinup girls that used to hang on my grandpa's wall," Jay says, standing up. "But I've never seen anyone who looks like you."

"I never know if you're complimenting me or insulting me."

"Take them all as compliments, Thyme Mugen. I'm not the kind of guy who ever insults a pretty bird."

"Whenever we are, I look like myself again." Thyme appraises herself in a large mirror covering nearly half of one wall. "Do you think they took us all the way back to 2023?"

Everyone reverts to their proper age when returned to their zone of origination, so if they were back in Hollywood then Thyme would be sixteen again. Of course, the borders dialed a random age across every zone, so they could really be anywhen. After all this effort, the worst thing would be California, right back when she started from.

The room is timeless. Painted the white of endless eras, it could be colonial America or a million years in the future. Curtained windows covered with nondescript drapes, a door made of stained oak, a light source, something behind a translucent glass, that could be an incandescent bulb or something futuristic, or simply an old-fashioned candle. A mirror hangs on one wall, but mirrors are probably the same in 1600 AD as 160,000 AD. Besides, this room may have been built after the Freeze with materials imported from across absolutely any state of time.

Thyme checks her wrist, the watch her mother gave her still there, still stuck at 7:30. What's that thing Jiji would say every so often, before the Freeze? "Even a broken clock is right twice a day." If they had extradited her back to Hollywood, it would be the one place in the United States of Time where her watch showed the correct time.

"I wonder who's watching us," Thyme says, and Jay, watching Thyme, suddenly turns suspicious, glaring at the mirror.

"What makes you think that?" he asks.

"Haven't you ever seen a spy movie with an interrogation room?"

"I went to North by Northwest at the passion pit when I was fifteen," Jay recounts. "You know Hitchcock in the future?"

"Sure we do. I saw Rear Window with my obaasan last month."

"The original with Jimmy Stewart or the one Hitchcock filmed in 2023 with George Clooney?"

"Clooney, of course," Thyme replies. "So does North by Northwest have spies that use two-way mirrors?"

"Crop dusters and Mt. Rushmore," Jay answers, shaking his head.

"Well, they're watching us. Through the mirror. Trust me."

"I do trust you, Thyme Mugen," Jay says.

Thyme turns. She has heard that tone of voice before. Bobby Vincent from across the street had had a crush on her since they were at Alvarez Elementary. Thyme always thought of him more as a brother than a boyfriend. When the world stopped taking measure of time, Bobby was out of the city and over the other side of the border, moving on in ways Thyme never could. Now Jay uses those same breathless expressions, and Thyme finds herself a great deal more interested than she ever was with Bobby Vincent.

"Be careful. I don't fall for bad boys."

"My kind of bad is probably practically a prude in the

future," Jay says. "I've seen enough of your kind of 'morrow. The backseat bingo of 1960 doesn't compete with your promiscuous pre-adults, and the worst we call someone is 'nosebleeds' and 'odd balls' instead of something with only four letters. Unless you're my color. There are always worse names for people of my color."

"There are always ugly names in every era for people who don't look like everyone else."

"There isn't an 'everyone else' now that all the clocks stopped," Jay says. "Maybe they won't have a use for ugly names anymore."

"They'll think of something," Thyme says. "We already call people from other zones 'morrows and démodés, fobs and fountaineers, trogs and time snobs. So don't worry, we'll come up with even more new ugly names that will fit a world where time stands still."

She realizes that Jay is so close. Too close. If Jay leaned forward, their lips would touch. This room is as big as her living room back in 2023, so why is Jay standing so near? Because he wants her to lean forward. And he's so handsome and earnest and interesting that she almost does. Time stands still. The moment draws on and on. For one infinite minute.

Then she remembers her mother again, that long moment after she was informed that Mom was dead, gone, an infant with no business behind the wheel of a vehicle wrapping the Escalade around a tree. The smile falters. Fades. Thyme doesn't have any right to be happy. Not when she's still so sad.

Instead of using her mouth for more pleasant things, Thyme says, "I thought it would be better, moving on. Getting away from the day my mother died. I thought about it all the time when I was in 2023. I still think about it all the time."

And instead of all the dumb things that everyone has said to her about her loss for all these e-months, Jay instead reaches out and takes her hand. It's the perfect gesture. And then after thoughts of kisses and making sad words, her mouth forms a smile instead as the tears fall down her face.

The door opens, and an old white man who looks like he stepped right out from colonial America stands in the doorway. Thyme wipes away her wet face. His scowl belittles Thyme without having to use a single ugly word. There are certainly all sorts of terrible terminology to refer to people like Thyme and Jay from this man's zone. Thyme can think of at least a dozen four letters words that are worse than "nosebleed" to call this guy.

"I take it we're in the past," Thyme guesses.

"You don't recognize me?" the white guy grumbles. "I'm in all your history books, both in 1960 and 2023. Apparently, Mallory Norman isn't taking recruits to her Institute based upon scholastic aptitude."

"Jefferson Davis," Thyme says, like his name contains just four letters.

Davis raises one bushy, unkempt eyebrow and gives Thyme a smug smirk. "You can call me 'Mr. President.'"

"Lofty ambitions," Thyme says.

"It's only a matter of time," he says. "You're invited to dinner. My associates will arrive shortly to escort you to private quarters where you may prepare for the evening. We will meet in the formal dining room in one equivalent hour."

***

Sixty e-minutes later, Thyme walks alone into a resplendent dining room wearing a dress perhaps borrowed from a stage production of Gone with the Wind. The pale blue skirt covers a cage that is about as wide as it is long. They had to make doorways wider in the past to fit these things from room to room. It is tight, itchy, heavy, and yet Thyme feels like a Disney princess in one of the old cartoons from before computers took over animation. Sometimes things were better in the past.

Jefferson Davis sits alone at the head of a ten-foot table crowded with dishes and food. With graying windswept hair and a short tail growing out of his chin, he looks like the antagonist in any number of Bruce Willis action movies that Thyme's mother used to watch on Saturday nights. He wears charcoal-colored clothes authentic to his zone, like some figure stepped out of a Lincoln biopic and right into this dining room. His eyes flicker over Thyme like she's a bug that he's deciding whether to squash or ignore.

Nearly everything about the room is authentic to 1869, from the sideboard displaying a set of fine dining-ware to the ingrain rug and black walnut trim. A gas pendant hangs over a large table to aid candles around the room flickering against the gloom. Beautiful blue curtains with gold fringes and pediments as opulent as Thyme's dress cover two large windows. In other zones, it seems that elements of the future have crept into design and entertainment, but there's nothing here to indicate import from another era except the flat-screen television mounted between the two windows. It looks as out of place as an Asian girl in the company of a Confederate councilman. Or a teen of color from 1960 wearing a ditto suit in charcoal gray with a matching bow tie escorted in by two white gentlemen.

Rhett to Thyme's Scarlett.

"Please, have a seat," Jefferson Davis offers with a wave of his hand. "Eat."

Thyme sits. Jay takes the seat beside her. On the television, one of the 24/7 news channels plays a live interview from Salem, Massachusetts in 1692. CNN correspondent Isha Sesay holds a microphone up to a young woman in white and black frocks, asking her about today's trial. A girl named Elizabeth Freely is being tried for engaging supernatural forces to stop the clocks. "Lizzy has nothing to do with the Freeze," the young woman protests. "This is a witch hunt." Across the bottom of the screen scrolls headlines. "President Harrison's European trip to include 1942 Germany"; "Stock market of 1980 continues streak of gains to two-hundred eighty-three e-days"; "Cher announces her 'Turn Back Time' World Tour"; "Clean air trade talks stalled between 2504 BC Egypt and the floating international cities over the Mediterranean in 3627 AD."

Waitstaff appears from the wings, some the color of Thyme and mostly Jay, with eyes cast down and shoulders slumped. The concept of personal freedom has never been something Thyme considered much beyond cheating curfew or an answer on a civics test, but now the history lesson is dishing steaming stew into a bowl before her and arranging breads and butter and savory side dishes around the table. The servants scurry out as if they've avoided a scolding.

Neither Thyme nor Jay takes a bite. "Why does this feel like a scene from a horror movie, where Hannibal the Cannibal sits the protagonist down for breakfast?" Thyme wonders aloud.

"You seem to think I am the villain of this piece," Davis says.

"I don't recall shooting you out of the sky or kidnapping you from the future," Thyme snaps.

"I'm sure we can sort this all out if you present the proper paperwork for crossing several borders between zones," Davis says. "Certainly, you must have official visas to permit interstate travel."

"You know perfectly well that Ms. Norman has all our papers. You're the one who had her detained in 1960 and told your lackey great-granddaughter to hold us prisoner, you ruthless sack of—"

Jay grabs her hand under the table and squeezes. Thyme stops.

"Tut tut, little scrapper." Davis takes a slow sip of hot stew, making a dramatic slurp. "I assure you that the detention of Mallory Norman in 1960 was a mere formality to get some bureaucratic red tape unraveled. It certainly is no excuse to flee across five time zones without proper clearance in hand. Your only visa allowed travel between the west coast and 1980. You weren't authorized to be in 68,437,912 BC or 2033 AD. This is what happens when you break the law, Miss Mugen."

"This is a mutiny against President Harrison."

"This is imposing order in a chaotic situation. Without rule and regulation, it would be anarchy. The world is already broken and confusing. Borders exist for a reason. To retain reason. They keep things contained so bedlam doesn't leak out everywhere. So things make sense. Something as fluid as multiple eras coexisting within the confines of a single continent needs walls to keep everything in, or else the citizens of each zone will spill out everywhen. A spill makes a mess. We need to enforce laws to keep things from descending into insanity."

"Is that why you once fought a war to keep an entire population enslaved?" Thyme challenges. "Yeah, I might've cracked open a history book once or twice. They didn't bother with a picture of you because you ended up just a footnote to history. Nothing more than an asterisk at the end."

"You have your facts wrong, Ms. Mugen, although this time the blame can be assumed by your educational system. It seems propaganda passes for fact in the public school systems of tomorrow." Thyme considers the zombies of 2033 downloading Honor's data bomb and hypnotized by the stream of false headlines. Was Davis entirely incorrect? "The conflict between the Confederacy and the Union was predicated on states' rights. I presided over the seceded states because we believed that individuals ought not to bow to central control. Washington, DC, wanted to dictate the laws of the south, against our will. We were the men fighting for freedom."

"Freedom," Thyme scoffs. "As long as you were white and a man."

"Such hubris to think you can judge all history by skimming skewed passages in an institutionalized instruction book, Ms. Mugen. I cannot presume to understand a world where women can vote and people of color become president, but I won't judge the future on the precedent of my present. That's why we ought to keep our times to ourselves, rather than mashing disparate centuries together. I want to follow your rules no more than you want to follow mine. That's what I wanted to discuss with Ms. Norman when she was detained in 1960."

"Where is she now?" Thyme asks. "Or should I say when?"

"Not now," Davis says, and Thyme isn't sure whether he means he won't answer her at the moment, or that Ms. Norman isn't in this present.

Thyme can finally resist the smells no longer. Jay has already given up his hunger strike and gobbled most of the stew and two helpings of bread. He isn't dead yet, so Thyme assumes the food isn't poisoned. She takes a bite of stew, then fifty more. Buttered beans that somehow taste better a hundred-and-fifty years ago disappear like minutes and moments and all of her somedays. Coffee brewed from beans indentured servants surely harvested tastes better than any espresso in 2023 (sorry, Starbucks). Apparently, flavor had suffered the gradual blandness of evolution over the course of the last century. Darwin's theory of the survival of the fittest obviously doesn't pertain to tastiness.

"Fine coffee," Davis declares with a smile, as if he knows Thyme's rejoicing tastebuds are conflicted by her guilt as she imagines hundreds of slaves working on a coffee plantation.

"Your Chronfederacy is as destined to fail as your Confederate States of America," Thyme says.

Davis wrinkles his nose, as if he smells something bad or speaking with minorities so long is affecting his allergies. "Chronfederacy. I detest puns." Jay glares at Davis like he believes that "puns" is some archaic racial slur. It's Thyme's turn to squeeze Jay's hand, still entwined together under the table, to tamp his torqued temper. "As to our success, it matters less that we win and more that we try. President Harrison wants to impose federal rule on all the time zones without proper discretion to the powers of the states. It's politics, Ms. Mugen. Freedom. I see us as united individual states, and the president and his cronies believe we are one homogenized America. I don't want a man who is dead and gone in 1869 telling everyone in the future what to do. Do you?"

"He's the president," Thyme says.

"He is one president. John F. Kennedy is alive in 1963 Dallas and has graciously stepped aside to allow Harrison to govern. President N'thdn in the 2248 Northeast rules over an America that looks very different from today's. Other leaders will come forth, others that will run to succeed Harrison if the Freeze lasts. The president is just a man. What if the next man and the old white men of 1841 decide that zones before 1776 shouldn't be allowed in the Union because they haven't ratified a state constitution? What if they apply the laws of 1841 and disallow women and minorities the right to vote? Slavery was allowed by states in 1841, so is that the law we follow, Ms. Mugen? Do we all obey laws dictated by a bunch of nineteenth-century bureaucrats, or do we want each of our time zones to find their own future, freely?"

"The waitstaff didn't look free," Jay says. "And I don't feel very free."

"Because you're not in your time zone, Mr. Stone," Davis declares, answering the last part of Jay's statement and ignoring the first.

Thyme is quiet. The United States of Time depends on leaders elected a hundred-and-fifty years before Thyme was even born. She has spent so many e-months in mourning, the present passed her by. She didn't think about what it means to have a world struggling to stay together when each piece is made so differently.

Thyme is done arguing politics.

"What are you going to do with us?" Thyme asks.

"You'll be extradited back to your homes. Regardless of intent, you crossed zones without proper visas. Your personal belongings are there beneath the sideboard. Take them with you. I don't want to be responsible for tomorrow items showing up on the 1869 black market," Davis says. "The federal government will deny further approvals now that you have a record as an illegal immigrant. You won't be attending the Mallory Norman Institute of Time, Ms. Mugen."

"You tried to kill us," Thyme accuses.

"My, my. You young people have such grand hyperbole in the future. How do they say in 2023? You should have sheltered in place. The authorities of 1960 could have straightened it out. Instead, you ran. You broke about a dozen federal laws."

"We ran because you were chasing us," Thyme says.

Davis shrugs. Confesses nothing. He dabs the corners of his mouth and stands. "Making it this far was an impressive feat. I had to meet the young woman with such diligence. In your own time, I'm sure you will make a formidable leader. But this isn't your time, Ms. Mugen."

"You're going to let us go home?" Jay asks, surprised.

"This is a free country, after all," Jefferson Davis says as he exits. "And I'm trying to keep it that way."

***

"What're we going to do?" Jay asks, still nibbling at the bread that's like manna from Heaven. They sip coffee so good it would make Thyme's java-aficionado obaasan weep with pleasure. "You think we should give up and go home?"

Back to 2023. Thyme had been stuck in one place for a long time before Ms. Norman finally gave her an opportunity to move forward. Now Jefferson Davis wants her to return to the beginning. Quit the game. All the way back to start. Thyme still carries her grief wherever she goes, but it seems lighter ever since she's been away from California. Because she isn't carrying it alone. She has Honor and Candy and Jay and Efren.

"I don't want to go back," Thyme tells.

Jay stares at the television, surely different from the 1960 piece of furniture that would look more like that sideboard placed against the far wall. His gaze is dark and mysterious, something deeper than the boy who ogled Candy for the last different decades. He said his dad died in the war before Jay ever had the chance to meet him, but Thyme sees a little soldier in Jay's eyes. The way he fought the truth zombies in 2033 was impressive. He had broken the custodian's nose when he came through the door of the roof and had brought a man who outweighed him twofold to his knees. Jay is a fighter.

"It was hard in 1960. Before the Freeze," Jay says. "My mom worked at a casino on the Strip, trying to make ends meet. But there were some tough months. She was hungry, and I was hungry. She wasn't the right color to get a promotion no matter how hard she worked. That was all before time stopped. After that, things got better. We saw the future, and things are different. Mom got a better job at a new casino built by some rich woman from 2023 that didn't care if Mom was black or green. But before the Freeze, before things got better—well, I did some things that maybe I'm not proud of. I got really good at breaking into places. Sometimes I could be as subtle as a shadow. Other times, I needed to be as blunt as a hammer. I was good at either one."

"That's all in the past, Jay."

They are still holding hands after all these moments. There's something haunted in his gaze. A darkness swims beneath the surface, like a shark beneath a sheet of ice.

"The past is all around us, Thyme," Jay says.

Jay lets go of her hand. Stands. His bomber jacket hangs on a coat tree near the door that Davis exited. Jay takes off his ditto jacket and pulls the leather coat back on, looking like Marty McFly from 1955 from the waist up, and Marty McFly circa 1885 in the pants and shoes. Jay picks up the leather satchel tucked under the sideboard that contains the rest of their belongings, putting the strap over his shoulder. He looks like a dashing adventurer perfect for an inclusive Indiana Jones reboot. Jay's eyes smolder. Thyme is supposed to be Mrs. Efren Cortez sometime in the future, but she doesn't feel very married in 1869.

"Get ready," he says. "We don't know what will happen next."

"We never do," Thyme agrees.

Jay sprints forward like a runner out of the blocks, rocketing no slower than a missile off a launchpad. He throws himself forward, upper body padded by the bomber jacket, arms covering his head, into the beautifully draped window. He flies right through the pane. SMASH! Jay crashes, rolls, and stands up outside in a field of shattered glass. The wind sucks the drapes out of the window, flapping in the spring breeze.

Guards dressed in the rebel gray of Confederate soldiers come charging around the perimeter of the house, rifles that would be in a museum in Thyme's day now loaded and ready to shoot an illegal immigrant without bothering with a warning shot. White men with guns and authority—a couple of minority kids in danger of getting shot. The future is the past is the present.

But this is the past and the future, and Jay has a present. He pulls an object out of the pocket of his bomber jacket and rolls it out in front of him, toward the soldiers bringing their rifles to bear. Small and silver and looking like a pinball pellet, the orb stops right between the 1869ers as they take aim at Jay. With a blue crackle of electricity in a diameter of ten feet, the globe gives the two men a jolt that singes their cuffs and blows off their caps and makes their hair stand on end. Wiry beards extend out of their faces, making them look like two humans eating a porcupine whole. They topple like felled trees in opposite directions, guns clattering and bodies giving a thump.

"Something I picked up on our way through 2033," Jay

says with a smirk. "We've been in enough tight spots since I met you to grab a couple of 'get out of jail free' cards when I saw them. I have a hidden pocket in my jacket, where I used to sneak due backs so my mom wouldn't see 'em."

"How did you know how to use that thing?"

"Honor knew what it was." Jay nudged one unresponsive soldier with a toe. "She said it could get me out of some hot water."

Thyme looks in both directions, then turns to check the open prairie behind her. "Out of the kettle and into the fire."

"We need to move," Jay says. More soldiers could come around the perimeter of the house or burst through the broken window. "Where to?"

"Anywhen but here. 1869 extends west and east for miles and miles. South isn't an option because there are certainly more soldiers around the front of the house. So that leaves due north. Across the pasturelands. Either back to 2033 or whenever else is north of here."

Jay nods. Thyme leads. The woods give way to open plains where cattle roam by the thousands. A train off in the distance chugs into a stockyard the diameter of a sports stadium. A muddy creek wends its way around the border of the pasturelands. Reproduction is as suspended as time itself after the Freeze, so the supply of beef in America is limited, making the cattle here in Abilene very valuable. Guard towers rise over the pastureland to deter cattle thieves who might try to hustle the herd out to other zones.

"I don't suppose you have a Holographic Overlay Device with Omni-Sound in that hidden pocket of yours?" Thyme asks.

"Nope." Jay peeks at a small shed with a door cracked open

enough to see inside. "But I'm not the only one with something secret from the future. I have an idea."

***

When Thyme was sixteen (she has started to think of herself as seventeen now, more than a year gone from when the calendar pages stopped turning and she should've passed another birthday if December had ever come again), she was entirely in love. Her next-door neighbor, Joaquín Herrer, had been off for college for the last three and a half years and came back the January before the Freeze, after he finished the fall semester. He had a degree in statistical science, wore glasses, and had the fashion sense of someone from when Thyme stands now. He wasn't anything like the cool kids she chilled with at school, with their four-letter words and their focus on fashion and boys that only considered females as conquests rather than complex creatures. Joaquín was logical and quiet and thoughtful, and he had a motorcycle.

Joaquín told Thyme it was simply prudent that a college student on a budget would ride a motorbike instead of driving a car. He owned a Genuine Scooter Co. Stella that Joaquín claimed would get "ten times the mpg of an Escalade," which Thyme took to be an actual mathematical ratio rather than rhetorical. Mom forbade her to ever, ever, ever get on a motorcycle, so from the moment Joaquín pulled up in January of 2023, Thyme had a new conquest. She would ride that bike before Joaquín found a job and moved on.

Thyme had a super-crush on Stella.

The weeks worked against her, with school taking ever more effort as she made her way through her sophomore year, and Joaquín zipping here and there all over SoCal for job interviews. Yet when an opportunity appeared, Thyme was ready.

It was a Saturday. Mom was shopping with her girlfriends on Melrose Avenue. Joaquín returned from a morning meeting with a movie studio for a position as a data analyst. Not sexy. He pulled up on his scooter, recently shined and full of gas. Stella was certainly sexy.

It was a warm end to March, and Thyme put on her shortest shorts and skimpiest tank top and timed her appearance exactly as Joaquín pulled Stella up to the curb in front of his house. Thyme might not think twice about Joaquín other than as access to Stella, but Joaquín did a double take as Thyme came striding down the sidewalk toward him in an outfit that featured the first hint of the long, long summer to come.

"I want to ride her," Thyme said. She leaned across the handlebars with lips close enough that Joaquín could have stolen a kiss.

"I—" he stammered. "I suppose I could take you for a short spin."

"No," Thyme said. "I want to ride her. Can I take her out for a little bit?"

"Do you know how to use a manual transmission? Are you licensed? Are you even old enough to ride a motorcycle?"

Thyme stood up, stepped back so he could see her from head to toe, and asked him, "Don't I look old enough?"

"A manual transmission is, uh, a bit tricky."

"I'm a fast learner," Thyme said with a confident smirk.

And it was over. Joaquín was a boy, and boys were pushovers for a girl showing skin. He showed her how to work the clutch, handle the controls, this and that, and in ten minutes she was off.

That was a hundred-and-fifty years from now.

An e-year plus a regular four months after her brief fling with Stella, Thyme is racing again. Jay spotted the imported motorcycle in the shed behind the house where they had supped with Jefferson Davis. Someone had it smuggled in from the future. Jay said his mother had a picture of his dad on the same bike from when Abraham Stone was his son's age, an original 1931 Royal Enfield Bullet. Jay thought he was going to drive and Thyme would have her arms wrapped around him as they raced across the pastureland toward whenever lay next. Thyme set him straight with a short series of very salty syllables.

The Bullet is even more beautiful than Stella, fast and powerful and absolutely perfect. Thyme rockets out of the shed and toward the open pastureland, gaining speed and feeling the wind against her face. She's still wearing the dress from the nineteenth century (sans the cumbersome metal hoop cage), a great deal more covered than she was when she zoomed around Hollywood with Stella, but if Jay and Joaquín had compared notes she looks even more alluring in 1869 than in 2023.

Jay rides behind her, his arms wrapped around her waist as they accelerate toward a herd of cattle. The men in the towers guarding the valuable beef watch the Bullet as it revs from zero to sixty in six e-seconds. The ground is relatively even and chewed smoothly down to the surface, so Thyme only must avoid an occasional rock and the sporadic slick cow-pies and the periodic pockmarks of gopher holes. The men in the towers take aim, but it's exceedingly difficult to hit a Bullet with a bullet. Not one of the guards can get a bead on the fobs.

Thyme and Jay must pass between two towers situated close to each other, sentries posted along the shimmering scarlet border to another time zone. Cattle thieves could most conveniently sneak across the closest border to make a hasty escape, so the point of easiest exit is most heavily guarded. Thyme and Jay may be a tough target rocketing along the open plains at a hundred yards out, but coming within sixty feet of the towers to navigate to the next state would bring them too close to trigger-happy trogs from 1869.

Thyme swerves near a small group of cows chewing cud. The oblivious bovines look off in the other direction as if clocks never meant anything to them in the first place, and are thusly unaffected by the change in timekeeping. Thyme gets as close as she can and revs the engine, a predatory growl that startles the cattle and sends a dozen old girls running and bellowing. Thyme starts a stampede.

The sound of thunder accompanies Thyme's lightning sprint across the plains, hundreds and hundreds of hooves clamoring against the hardpan. Jay yanks Thyme to the side, narrowly avoiding a pointed horn from an antagonistic cow. Two large beasts squeeze together in front of the Bullet, almost smashing the bike between them. Thyme yields to a dozen steers cutting diagonally across the herd and slows enough that the fobs almost fall victim to a group of massive bulls behind them.

Close enough to the two towers guarding the border to the next zone, Thyme spots an opening between cattle. The animals start to slow and turn as they approach the glowing red curtain that indicates another era. Instinctually, the beasts know that racing pell-mell across the border is like jumping over a cliff. They stop and stand, but leave enough of a weaving way to get through. Thyme swerves and darts forward, startling a couple of cows nearest the next zone to stumble across the border as the Bullet starts to enter the next time zone.

In the split e-second before she escapes 1869, Thyme has

time to pray that she won't turn into an infant and crash into a tree.

CHAPTER EIGHT
23:02
8.14.13,411 BC
Missouri River, Missouri

Thyme came across from 1869 at age twelve, and Jay crossed over closer to thirty years old. The dress she had filled impressively in the nineteenth century was practically falling off as she barely managed to bring the Royal Enfield Bullet to a safe stop. Two sprinting cows had come across as calves, one wobbling like a newborn on unsure legs. As Thyme ruffles through the leather satchel where Jefferson Davis had packed their clothes back in 1869, Jay rustles the small bovines back over the border, keeping close to the priceless beef so none of the guards in the towers try to take one last shot across the border between zones. Once the two cows return to their own time, the guards put away their guns. Thyme and Jay are someone else's problem.

Thyme pulls on her jeans and T-shirt from 2023 right under the nineteenth-century dress. Then she stands up and the velvet gown sloughs off. Her clothes from home are loose after losing six years of adolescent development, but she cinches her belt tight around boyish hips and lets her shirt flap loose, almost more like a skirt.

Jay is a handsome adult with a strong jawline, his dark complexion accenting the dangerous look in his eyes. His bomber jacket makes him look more gang member than geometry instructor, but Thyme feels like a grade-schooler with a crush on the teacher. He stands by the Bullet with a triumphant smirk on his face.

"I suppose it's my turn to drive now, huh?" he says. "A little thing like you could hardly manage a Pacemaker scooter."

Thyme doesn't have a choice. They need to get as far away from 1869 as possible, as fast as they can. Davis will send someone after them. Thyme looks over her shoulder, through the red curtain between time zones, ready for a battalion of Grays to erupt from the herd of cattle.

She nods, refusing to voice defeat. Jay grins wider, and instead of a crush, she wants to punch him. He mounts the motorbike. Thyme swings her leg over behind him, wraps her arms around his middle, and breathes in the leather smell of his father's bomber jacket. Thyme is secretly glad she has to be the passenger—until he starts driving. Cool and dangerous, Jay nevertheless stutters and stammers the Bullet along like a two-year-old on training wheels.

"Where to?" he asks as they wobble and weave away from 1869.

"East," Thyme says, her hands balled into fists across his chest as they seem constantly in danger of tipping this way or that.

It's night in the new zone. Thyme doesn't know exactly when they are, but the world is deserted and dark. As the sunlight of 1869 slowly disappears behind them, they are left with only the single headlamp of the Bullet to stab a path through the night. The world is full of deep shadows concealing a world unblemished by man.

Eventually they come to a river that cuts through the zone. "Whether we are far in the future or back in the past, the best chance of finding civilization is by following a major waterway," Thyme says.

And it turns out, great minds think alike. Or at least two people destined to be married do. Thyme shakes her head as she sees the first page of Fahrenheit 451.

Thyme's mom would read to her from a volume as thick as the King James Bible every night from when Thyme was a toddler until she finally stated, rather haughtily, at age eight, "I think I'm too old for this, Mother." Thyme thought about that a lot on the three-hundred-and-sixty-five e-nights she was stuck on July 16th, 2023 — how she would do about anything for one more night of hearing her mother tell a story.

The book was Tiffany's Tall Tales, modern retellings of retooled classic stories. Thyme thinks about one now as she and Jay meander down the Missouri like some Huck and Jim adventuring in an America before anyone settled the area. The short story called "Handy and Ghetto" was meant as an update of "Hansel and Gretel." The tale featured a couple of blue-collar youths, the kids of a carpenter from the wrong side of the tracks, who get lost on the seedy side of town when they get off at the wrong bus stop. They snap pictures of signposts with their smartphones on their way so they do not get lost, but then they get mugged and someone takes their phones. A tweaked-out meth-head invites them into an abandoned warehouse with promises of taking them away from all their mundane modernity, and the kids end up baked, homeless addicts living on the streets for the rest of their lives.

In the original "Hansel and Gretel" tale, the kids left breadcrumbs, certainly no more reliable than marking the way with iPhone photos. Instead of methods susceptible to a data breach or mastication, someone has left a trail by marking trees along the river with pages from Ray Bradbury's Fahrenheit 451, one page every so often poked onto a branch facing the river.

Efren Cortez had come this way, and he left Thyme a trail.

It seems they think alike.

Thyme doesn't want to consider that. In some other someday, she marries Efren Cortez. They start a family. But that's in a world with ticks and tocks. A world that may never come to pass. She doesn't want to think about having to fall in love with Efren. Especially here and now, alone with Jay. Thyme is too busy avoiding her past to make the effort to avoid the future, too.

***

They look down at a meandering waterway seemingly unspoiled by man. There are no signs of civilization. Thyme doesn't know if they are in the far future or the distant past, but the world seems fresh and uncorrupted. Mankind has either never come to this section of the river or left this place a long time ago. If this was the case, Thyme wonders what happened and if global disaster still poses a danger, nightmare creatures creeping in the lush vegetation that follows the winding waterway.

"We need to follow the river," Thyme says, pointing to a page poked on a branch. "Shepherd brought the rest through this zone. He knows the river is the constant. This must be the Missouri River. We can move generally east if we follow it."

"I wasn't very good at geography. I was more interested

in history."

"At least geography still makes sense. History doesn't mean anything anymore."

"Maybe it means more than ever. What was once in books is now all around us. Living and breathing."

Thyme whirls around on him and points her finger in his face. "This isn't some stupid adventure, Jay. This is life and death. This isn't the way it's supposed to be."

"Life never seems to turn out the way it's supposed to."

"My mom isn't supposed to be dead."

"And it's okay because my dad died before the Freeze? It doesn't make it any easier, Thyme."

Thyme stops. There is plenty of heartache to go around. She doesn't have a monopoly on grief.

"The Bullet is about on empty," Jay suggests, changing the subject. "I can make a raft, and we can float down the river."

Thyme looks at him like he suddenly spoke Japanese. "Make?"

Jay shrugs. "I took woodshop and mechanics in school. I like to see how things are put together."

He builds a raft from fallen trees undisturbed for a hundred years, tied together with cordwood that Jay harvests from the cores of weeds he finds in the forest along the river. He rigs the headlight of the Bullet directly to the battery, and they take it with them to find their way on the water. Pages of Fahrenheit 451 are poked onto boughs overhanging the Missouri River at regular intervals.

Miles and many e-minutes later, they've found dozens of pages, around every bend along the stream. The two of them are lulled into a somnolent expedition, like they're the only two people left in the world. Thyme remembers watching The African Queen with her obaasan, starring Kate Hepburn as the spitfire sassy-pants that became her idol, sailing down the Ulanga River with Humphrey Bogart. Jay doesn't look like a Bogart. He looks more like a bae.

Kate was abrasive and commanding and tough as nails, and she still fell for the flinty captain of The African Queen. Thyme tries to be as independent and churlish as the magnificent Ms. Hepburn, and she still falls for the bad-boy sailor of this little Huck Finn raft. Thyme thinks about Efren. Her future husband. Another Thyme's future. She isn't going to follow the footsteps to any set someday.

Jay aims the headlamp at yet another Ray Bradbury page. Then he flashes the light to the side, eye-shine catching in the beam before disappearing.

"We're not alone," Jay warns.

Have those words ever been uttered to inspire anything except dread?

Terrible biological monstrosities populate Thyme's imagination, the most nightmarish renditions from Tiffany's Tall Tales stalking the two of them from the shores — Rumpleskeleton, Jack and the Murderous Giant, Serial-killer Sammy, Little Dead Riding Hood. Horrors come to life, following them along the snaking river in a never-ending night. It's worse than anything Thyme ever dreamed of when she was younger and prone to fear. That was before her mother turned three months old and drove into a tree, and Thyme learned what real nightmares are made of. Terror is the unknown stalking you at the edges of what happens next.

Time may have stopped long ago, but experience has entropy, moving forward in consecutive moments. There are infinite minutes like the aftermath of her mother's death that stretch on for eternity. Now is another occasion for perpetual pause, fear freezing even the increments of instances. Thyme stares out into the darkness and dreads what will happen next.

Glowing lights appear on the water between the raft and shore, first far away and then growing nearer, floating illumination on a trajectory to intercept their position. Like UFOs observed unexplained in the midnight sky, these unidentified swimming objects torpedo toward their raft, three white incandescent balls brighter than the starlight sprinkled here and there on the surface of the Missouri. Thyme imagines all sorts of extraterrestrial predators of some far-flung future where humans are extinct.

The trio of lights grow close enough for Thyme to see them clearly. They are beyoncés, the inflatable spheres that saved them from jumping out of the upper-floor window of the Stardust back in 1960 and from the sinking submarine in the Mesozoic Sea. Three air-filled orbs roll along the surface until they surround the raft, normal everyday Americans inside looking as insidious as any aliens.

Within the beyoncés are two women and a man, all dressed in the timeless apparel of Shepherd, beholden to no era.

"More travelers?" Jay asks.

"No," Thyme says, noting the menace and greed in their eyes. "Raiders."

Some of her friends back home in 2023 followed the exploits of raiders like they were the celebs of the new world without clocks. Her friends had adapted quickly to the post-Freeze, but Thyme stayed stuck. Left behind. They had all looked up their individual futures, the way of tomorrow, obsessed over what happens next, while Thyme had been stuck in the now, entangled in infinite sorrow.

Rather than travelers who ferry immigrants from era to era, raiders are bounty hunters who cross the borders between states for profit. They plunder time zones for treasure. Usually, raiders are searching for lost gold or rare art or mythical artifacts. Today, the prize is a girl named Thyme Mugen.

"Jefferson Davis sent you?" Thyme asks, although she already knows the answer.

"Come ashore," says one of the women. "We're taking you home."

"And if we put up a fight?"

The woman indicates a pistol on her hip as she tilts the holster in the teenagers' direction for emphasis. Apparently, Calamity Jane here believes Thyme can be returned to 2023 either dead or alive. Jefferson Davis wouldn't have been pleased when he learned his captives escaped 1869.

Thyme checks with Jay to see if he has another trick up his sleeve like he used in the past/future, but he shrugs. They're out of options. The three beyoncés move as if by magic along the surface of the Missouri, and they nudge the small raft toward the leeward bank. Until a soft explosion sounds, like the cork popping from a champagne bottle, then a flatulent noise like Thyme's obaasan after an evening at Enrique Escobar's Enchilada Emporium. Two more pops, two more deflating beyoncés.

The raiders work to shed their bouncy inflatables before they become engulfed in the futuristic polymers and sink. Thyme and Jay float away as the three bounty hunters struggle in the surf. Some ten yards separate the raft from the raiders by the time they extricate themselves from the sagging balloons. Thyme spots Calamity Jane drawing a gun, the other two bounty hunters following suit.

"Freeze," comes a command from behind Thyme and Jay.

Thyme turns to see a large ship that is certainly not from this time period gliding toward them almost silently across the surface of the river. At the helm is Shepherd, standing astern like Washington crossing the Delaware, just as commanding and twice as timeless. Efren is his shadow, old and gnarled like a withered tree. Honor huddles in the dark, holding a cooing, giggly infant hidden by the night. The traveler wields an orb crackling with electricity.

"Holster your weapons and swim for the shore," Shepherd says, "or I will zap all three of you and leave you floating in the past like dead fish."

The traveler saves them. Just in time.

***

"Friends of yours?" Thyme asks the traveler as the modern boat zooms quickly down the length of the Missouri, many times faster than the floating log raft, more hydrofoil than Huckleberry Finn.

"Raiders." Shepherd shakes his head, like he had a taste of something foul. "They're the opposite of travelers. We believe in open borders and that free folk should be able to roam across the United States of Time without ridiculous visas controlled by the federal government. Raiders are greedy treasure-hunters who cross borders purely for personal gain. To get the prize. They are without principles."

"They were going to shoot us," Jay says.

"There's a bounty on Miss Mugen's head that makes her very valuable," Shepherd says. "They don't care if you end up dead or alive, Mr. Stone."

"That's completely uncivilized." Thyme fidgets with her

watch, exasperated. "What is this? The stone age?"

"It's 13,411 BC," Shep says. "But man hasn't really evolved much since we invented the wheel."

Honor steps forward, a wiggly Candy in her arms, all smiles and drool. "Maybe you peaked too early as a species." As if she isn't Homo sapiens herself, but something else. Then again, maybe the 'morrow is something else.

"How did you know how to find us?" Thyme asks.

"I was keeping tabs on the raiders," Shep says. "I knew if anyone would try to collect the bounty, it'd be those soulless bandits."

"What happened to you?" Efren croaks in an old man voice. He casts a jealous look at Jay.

"We got caught," Thyme says. "Then we got away."

Efren winces at her use of "we."

"When did you get the boat?" Thyme asks Shep. It's obviously not from 13,411 BC.

"You'll see soon enough," Shep says.

Thyme traces their progress on a holographic map hovering over the navigation screen. They travel east along the river for another forty miles. Near a bend in the Missouri, still several miles before where the river runs into the Mississippi, the boat steers to the side and Shep moors the hydrofoil to the riverbank. The traveler is off first, disappearing into the darkness along the shore. Honor hops off carrying baby Candy, who giggles at something no one else can see, the two of them following the traveler. Jay waits for Thyme, watching an ancient Efren as the elderly fob struggles to get off the boat. Awkward. Left alone with her future husband and the guy she has a crush on.

"Give me your hand," Jay finally snaps at Efren, unable to bear the fumbling slowness of the nonagenarian 'morrow even a moment longer.

"I've got it," Efren grumbles like a curmudgeonly old man. Older than ever, he looks like a lanky skeleton covered in loose leather, ears like shrimp tempura, eyes tiny glimmers folded in tangled layers of wrinkled flesh, fingers featuring more knobs than the dashboard of Jay's Ford Mustang back in 1960.

He doesn't, in fact, "got it," prevented from tumbling overboard only by Jay grabbing his bony elbow at the last e-second.

"Get your hands off me!"

"You couldn't swim long enough in that old body for me to even dive in after you before you'd sink, you old grump. Whatever you've got against me, is it worth tumbling into the drink and dying?"

"Maybe," Efren huffs. "I'm not going to owe you anything."

Efren stubbornly struggles, but eventually manages to make it over the edge of the boat and put a foot on dry land. Thyme could've offered her hand, but she refuses to encourage their fated romance. That was another Thyme, one without a dead mother, and another Efren, one much younger than his nineties.

The boys follow the others, Thyme bringing up the rear. She can hear everything, despite trying mightily to ignore them.

"Stay away from her, you hear?"

"She's not your wife, Efren."

"She will be!"

"Not now. Not here. This isn't 2023."

"Do you think love is determined by location, Jay Stone?" Efren asks. "It transcends the moment. It exists beyond the ticking of a clock. Love isn't dictated by a zone or an era or a certain set of circumstances. If two people are truly meant to be together, then they'll find their way to each other no matter what."

"Unless an irresistible greaser with a crazy bomber jacket swoops in and makes her swoon."

"It won't matter," Efren says.

"Then what're you worried about?" Jay counters before pressing faster ahead, as if proving he's confident enough to leave Thyme and Efren alone together.

The night is doubly dark under the canopy of trees that radiate out from the shores of the Missouri. Sounds of nature chirp and croak in the distance, something unique to a girl who grew up in the inner city. The scent of fresh air is almost too much, like the time Jiji was on an oxygen tank after a nasty bout of pneumonia and Thyme took a pull off the little tubes that fed the air. Dizzying.

Thyme and Efren walk beside each other, like a married couple who has had to endure appearances for the family long after love fizzled out. Another time, another river, and this might have been a romantic getaway to celebrate the anniversary of something special. Now the hour never turns and there are no anniversaries of anything, with romance as far away as all their tomorrows.

"I'm not a prize to fight over, Efren," Thyme finally says. "I'm not the chapter at the end of your book, either. Whatever this world is, whatever happened after the Freeze, it isn't our destiny to be together anymore. My story is still being written. And I don't even know where it will lead."

"I do," Efren whispers. "I can feel it."

"Well, feel something else," Thyme snaps.

Efren flinches, like he was stung by some prehistoric wasp.

"We're here," Shepherd announces, waiting for them at the edge of a clearing. "This is where we borrowed the hydrofoil."

Thyme notices the lights, the first signs of industrialization outside the accessories used by the raiders and the boat brought by Shep. It isn't like the natural light from the stars above, but the soft glow of incandescence nonnative to this time. Imported illumination brightens the little clearing in the trees. Honor is talking to a stranger. Now Jay carries Candy. As Thyme arrives side-by-side with Efren, she notices an envious glance from Jay.

A small village like nothing Thyme has ever seen stands before her. The buildings are constructed of a space-age material, each one glowing a different color of light rather than featuring a different flavor of siding. Yet the style is nothing out of science fiction, but rather ripped from a history book, two-story colonial styles with steep roofs, diamond-shaped casement windows, and chimneys emitting thin smoke that looks like iridescent mist.

It's always near midnight in 13,411 BC, but the town bustles with activity. Even though it's always night, that doesn't make everyone sleep all the time. The bright homes give the community a glow that mimics morning, as if their world is always at the precipice of dawn. The villagers fascinate Thyme even more so than the architecture—half of the citizens wear primarily colonial attire with Puritan dresses and suits like something out of a Thanksgiving pilgrim decoration. But instead of old-fashioned clogs, the women wear futuristic tennis shoes that glow like the houses, and the men sport hats with animated logos on the fronts advertising football teams in three-dimensional holograms. The other half are citizens of some future, wearing fashion with bright colors and changing patterns, yet several women wear colonial coifs and archaic capes, as if the 'morrows were merged with a Puritan. Several of the démodés walk around with floating holographic screens before their eyes, and Thyme spots a 'morrow hanging clothes on a line here and another chopping wood over there.

"This is," Honor whispers, "something new."

"This is the future after the Freeze," Shepherd says.

***

A crowd gathers along a bend in the Missouri River, representatives from the future and past all present to welcome the newest visitors to this amalgamated community. Thyme notes the similarities between this place and Ms. Norman's school that is gathering students from across America. Both locations intended to illustrate that people from disparate timelines can coexist peacefully. Has Ms. Norman ever visited Missouri? Maybe this village was the inspiration for her idea.

The fobs stand among the immigrants to 13,411 BC, pioneers who decided to make their home in this unoccupied time zone that predates even the earliest North American settlements. Half of the citizens of this new settlement are 'morrows emigrated from Honor's home zone on the west coast, all the way here from 2803. The other settlers voyaged from 1692 Salem, leaving Puritanical Massachusetts for a fresh start in Missouri. Together, they've created a commune of conflicting chronologies, and after six e-months of experimentation have deemed the new society a success.

Honor seems aghast at the unprecedented undertaking. Her fellow 'morrows voluntarily journeyed halfway across the continent to set up a new civilization with démodés from more than a millennium in the past, an upstart village they call Oasis. Thyme supposes that would be something like John Conner choosing to coexist with Cleopatra. Honor appears apoplectic at the very idea.

Thyme looks at Jay, standing on the other side of Efren.

The last time they'd gathered with ghosts, they were sitting down to supper with Jefferson Davis in 1869 and close enough to touch. And they did touch. Thyme and Jay held hands. A connection across half a century. Now Efren is between them. Jay fights against the future while Efren is stymied by the past.

Two women stand at the forefront of the group at the edge of the river, one from tomorrow and the other from yesterday. Shepherd explains, as he introduces the fobs to the pioneers, that these women serve as equal leaders of Oasis. Truth Morrison and Sarah Prynne. One from 2803 and the other from 1692. Side by side, Thyme realizes they're also holding hands, as she did with Jay in 1869. Romance across the ages.

The women perform a ceremony unique to this time and these people. Sarah cups her hands and bends down to the edge of the river, scooping water into her palms. She stands, holding the water over Truth's open hands, and spills the water over the 'morrow's fingers. Then Truth repeats the same action.

"The Missouri represents time," Sarah says. "The origin of the river starts somewhen else and moves to another someday, meandering along the way, shifting direction and filling space. Now it is still, unmoving, and only when we disturb its surface do we see change."

Honor asks, "What happens if the clocks start ticking? Aren't you afraid of getting trapped in this past?"

"Whatever comes next will be something other than what we have always expected. We are pioneers of a new tomorrow. That is why we divorced ourselves from our home zones. We mean to make our own future," explains Truth. "Destiny is dead, Honor Fitzgerald."

Thyme observes other couples along the shore. All

shapes and sizes. She expects acceptance in the future, 'morrows like Truth and Honor unfazed by couples of different colors, genders, and creeds. Now Salem couples of the same sex are also finally free to express a love formerly forbidden. Partners from different zones pair up, Puritan pilgrims in love with anachronistic agnostics, white Anglos from Salem coupling with the amorphous ethnicity of the Californians of the future. This is the new American melting pot.

"We've imposed upon your hospitality enough, Ms. Morrison," Shepherd says, stepping forward. "The raiders will report back to their Chronfederate cronies. The Grays will send a more substantial force to deal with us next time."

"Our technology is more advanced than Civil War veterans from 1869," Truth assures. "We are cloaked from conventional means of surveillance, and we can defend ourselves from the nuisance of nineteenth-century soldiers if necessary."

"Jefferson Davis has resources beyond 1869 at his disposal. He has allies even in 2803 and beyond." Shepherd looks at his feet, as if already imagining them moving forward, moving on. He is a traveler not only by name, but by nature. "I'm afraid if he wants to find us, he can mount an attack that even Oasis cannot repel. Davis means to start a war."

Sarah Prynne looks at Truth, worry writ across her face. Folks from Salem, Massachusetts, know a little something about persecution and living in fear. They thought Oasis might be a place exempt from such concerns, but violence and conflict are as universal as love and hope. Thyme studies the river. Some prefer to consider time as a lake, self-contained and without venture, still and staid and remaining unchanged. But it must move on, flow forward, ever-changing.

Shep walks with Truth and Sarah, carrying baby Candy

and making arrangements for the fobs' impending exit. Jay glances back at Thyme, their eyes meeting along the shore of the Missouri, across the river of time. He would be eighty years old in 2023, but he's still young in 13,411 BC. Yet there's more than just a stack of decades between them. Jay turns and walks off after Shep. Efren waits until Jay takes leave of Thyme, then shuffles off after the rest of them.

Honor stands at the edge of the Missouri, watching the water that's going neither here nor there. Thyme steps forward until they both have toes touching the edge of the river. The girls are alone under the starlit sky. Honor appears in her twenties in this zone. Bald and exotic, she looks almost alien bathed in moonlight. The LED tattoos under her skin pulse to the tune of her heartbeat.

"We do not perform rites of passage or ceremonial claptrap when I come from," Honor says. "It is considered archaic and an improper use of time."

"No claptrap," Thyme says. "Got it."

Honor doesn't reply. No withering insult. No superior snark.

Honor bends, scoops up a handful of water, and stands. Thyme holds open her palms, and Honor lets the water run over Thyme's fingers. Then Thyme repeats the gesture. The girls look at each other. For once, Honor doesn't say a word. They gaze out at the Missouri again for a while, the ripples from them touching the river radiating out until they touch the opposite shore.

Eventually, the water stills again.

After a while, the girls turn away and follow the other fobs.

CHAPTER NINE

14:29

8.28.1929 AD

Chicago, Illinois

The Untouchables drive a 1928 Cadillac Town Sedan, chasing the fobs up Michigan Boulevard in Chicago, Illinois. Shepherd takes a hard turn onto Madison Street and nearly tips the imported 2019 Toyota RAV4 as it corners on two wheels. Thyme is in the back with Efren, unbuckled, the turn sliding her hard against the man she would eventually marry. Right now, she's eight and her betrothed is only ten.

Another time. Another place. A maybe romance that might be never ever instead of ever after.

A pair of black and white Dodge Chargers with flashing red and blue lights appears in front of them, speeding up Madison on a collision course with the fobs. Thyme isn't sure anymore if the CPD would be an ally or an enemy in 1929. Already they've made a foe of Elliot Ness and befriended Al Capone.

"Are they going to help us or shoot us?" Candy asks from the front seat, fingernails digging into the dashboard. She's back to being a young adult and gorgeous as a goddess. Maybe in her early twenties, she's the oldest of the fobs in 1929, looking like the young mother of an unruly brood.

"Fifty-fifty chance either way," grumbles Shepherd, about twelve and still cantankerous. Short for his age, he can barely see over the steering wheel. He ought to be sitting in his daddy's lap to practice driving, but the other boys are even younger than the traveler. Efren is a tween, and Jay can't be more than two.

A Hudson Super-six speeds from the north and sideswipes the two Chargers in a scream of crunching metal and the peal of shattering glass. Airbags inflate, obstructing the Chicago police officers coming for either rescue or arrest. The man behind the wheel of the Hudson could either be an Untouchable or a mobster. They all look the same in 1929.

"Wheeee," Jay squeals.

Shepherd could easily lose the federal agent following him through the historical streets of Chicago but for the pesky drone overhead that matches every twist and turn the Toyota takes. As Shepherd accelerates past a Walgreens and a Woolworths and a Marshall Fields, the drone keeps pace to relay their position to FBI démodés with access to futuristic technology.

"We need to get to New Chicago," Efren whines in the same tone of voice as are-we-there-yet.

"That's where I'm heading, kid." Shepherd sounds like he might not be opposed to pulling over and slapping the kid silly, even though he is only maybe two years older than Efren.

The RAV4 revs west toward Tri-Taylor, where large skyscrapers loom like the future on the horizon. Many are under construction, development in the Chicagoland area betting on the Freeze lasting a long time. Modern architecture erected in a bygone neighborhood, the fobs are betting New Chicago will be more welcoming to six passersby trying to get to 1980. Because in Old Chicago, the fobs are being chased by federal agents and assisted by Al Capone.

In the overcast sky, a massive German blimp floats between a pair of hundred-story skyscrapers, the Graf Zeppelin stuck in 1929 on its voyage around the world. When they first limped into Chicago an e-day ago and Thyme gazed upon the floating dirigible, she was as awestruck by the airship as anything she had seen since she left 2023. It was no less impressive than being rescued by a WWII submarine or seeing Tyrannosauruses raze a train in 1869.

Shepherd races along Chicago's side-streets, cresting a hill at sixty miles per hour and catching air for a long few e-seconds before crashing back down to the boulevard. Thyme spies a Starbucks wedged between a J.C. Penney and a barbershop, and she knows they are getting closer to New Chicago. The streets become paved with modern materials embedded with incandescent lights right in the roadway. There are suddenly businesses that are further in the future than even 2023, interspersed with Apple Stores and Walmarts.

Chicago is more progressive than previous time zones, and the fobs know that Al Capone is central to the modernization of 1929. When Prohibition ended as the new federal rules of the after-Freeze took effect, Capone started bootlegging modern contrivances instead of alcohol. The mob always finds supply to fill a demand. Capone's vision of a new city that reflects an amalgamation of eras may be visionary, but his overlooking of trade laws between timelines and smuggling between millennia to avoid tariffs and taxes has made him a continued enemy of the federal authorities.

Capone's dream is grandiose, but his methods are unsavory.

And now the fobs are on the run as accomplices to Capone's indiscretions.

Shep zooms along new storefronts that advertise Imax movies, hologames, and things like mantalcakes and sinscrubs that Thyme has never heard of. At the intersection of Obama Avenue and Winfrey Lane, Shep stomps the brakes and the adolescent fobs fly around the inside of the Toyota. More Untouchables flank them and now blockade every avenue, Cadillac Sedans barricading the futuristic roadways in three directions.

"Carcarcarcar." Jay claps happily.

Above the Cadillac, floating gyroscopes arrive with a beyoncé at the center of each, spinning blades somehow allowing the bouncies to fly, made from some polymer that appears a lot tougher than the inflatables the fobs have used for escape in other time zones. Inside the bubbles are more Untouchables. In each Cadillac are two local démodés with guns trained on the fobs, and there are weapons mounted to the sides of the floating gyroscopes also aimed at the RAV4. Behind them, three more Cadillac Sedans approach on the fourth leg of the intersection.

Thyme and her companions are surrounded.

Just how had it all come to this?

***

The Oasis settlers in 13,411 BC had let them use the hydrofoil to make their way farther east along the waterway and stay ahead of the raiders and any Grays on their trail. The fobs continued along the Missouri River, then over to the Mississippi River, and made their way up the Illinois River close to Peoria, where the water supply ended in a shift of landscape that differed from Shep's maps.

"Eventually this will connect to the Des Plaines and could have taken us all the way to Chicago," Shepherd said. "Looks like geology fifteen-thousand-years ago had other ideas."

They walked the last few miles to 1929 and crossed the border back into a civilized world. Peoria was a booming town in the Roaring Twenties, almost a hundred-thousand people in the city. The theme to Thyme's last prom had been centered around The Great Gatsby, and she had gone with Reggie Tam as a flapper. There was a great difference between the costume she had worn to the prom and the authentic dress of the time. Nothing compares to the real deal.

"We need to wear something a little less conspicuous," Shepherd announced before they were sighted by any locals. "Anyone who sees us will remember a group of fobs hitchhiking across Illinois if the raiders or any Chronfederate soldiers come asking."

The fobs had come over mostly miniature — only Candy presented as an adult. That ended up being their one bit of fortune in this bad-luck zone. Anyone else would've had trouble procuring disguises in 1929, but Candy had the benefit of being only twenty years removed from this timeline and as pretty as a pinup girl. She walked into a local shop in Peoria and purchased six sets of period clothing, a size for each of the fobs. The young male clerk had been too busy drooling to ask how, why, or what for.

They made their way along rough roads all the way up to Chicago. Honor, six and short for her age, pressed the twelve-year-old traveler about contacting another time zone. "We must request assistance from federal authorities," Honor said. "Washington, DC, set up the Institute in the first place. Surely, they can be trusted. We need to call for reinforcements."

"Ms. Norman hired me to take you all to New York. She said the Grays have infiltrated the highest echelons of government. No one can be trusted, kid."

Honor persisted. Shepherd resisted. Honor insisted. Shepherd hissed, "Drop it. Or I'll let them take you back to the future." Honor quit.

Every time Jay, just a toddler, saw an antique car go by on brand-new, very old roads, he squealed and pointed, "Carcarcarcarcar."

"Why are we going to Chicago?" Efren asked as the skyline of the city loomed before them.

"When you realize anyone among your allies can be a traitor, the only person you can trust is your enemy," Shepherd said. "At least you know what you're getting when you deal with a criminal."

"Who's the enemy in Chicago?" Thyme asked.

"The same now as it has always been," Shep replied. "Al Capone."

Al Capone still runs an import business not unlike the one he had managed before the Freeze. Instead of bootlegging alcohol during Prohibition, now he smuggles in futuristic technologies and valuable artifacts from other zones. 1929 is not so different now than it was then.

So Shep and Candy went off to meet with Capone and appropriate the accessories the fobs would need to avoid the raiders and the Grays and finish the final leg of their trip across America—fake IDs, indigenous attire to alternate eras, transportation arrangements across antagonistic zones. Thyme and the others waited behind at an F.W. Woolworth that would be preserved on a historical registry in Thyme's 2023.

Honor was uninterested in ancient lore and remained outside, sitting on a bench beside Jay, watching passing vehicles, "Carcarcarcarcar" a mantra that went on and on. Inside, Efren took a seat at the counter beside Thyme and ordered a Nehi Peach from the soda fountain. He fidgeted like a schoolboy on his first date, although neither of them looked old enough even to hold hands.

"Want one?" he asked about the drink.

"I already ordered a chocolate egg cream."

Efren nodded. "I found a picture," he blurted out. "Online."

He had a phone from 2023 still. On the screen, a picture of himself and Thyme, some twenty years in their future. Two children stood in front of them, smiling bright and big. The boy looked no older than Efren in 1929, the spitting image of his father, tall with ears as wide as sails. But the boy had Thyme's mother's eyes, brown and narrow and burning with intelligence. The girl reminded Thyme of the picture from her first day at kindergarten, only taller than Thyme had been by at least a head and missing her two front teeth. They were all standing in front of Rikona Mugen's house, the same one Thyme left behind in LA Squinting, Thyme was sure she saw a shadow in one window looking out at the central scene of the picture. Was it her mother watching her family stand for a photo? Superficial evidence she still lives in the future, like the grainy photograph of a UFO or a blurry image of Bigfoot.

"Why are you showing me this?" Thyme felt her face turn red.

"Because you need to see it," Efren snapped. "This is what happens with us. We're together, Thyme. We have a family."

"That isn't me."

"It will be."

"We'll see," Thyme said, and it wasn't because she agreed with Efren. Yet he nodded decisively, as if she had conceded his point.

Thyme didn't want to be told what tomorrow would be. Her mother should still be alive past 2023 according to Thyme's grandson from 2118. Eventually Alzheimer's may claim her mother's mind, but Rikona Mugen was still alive when this picture was taken. Thyme stared a little longer at the photograph on his screen. Her mother. Her children.

"Their names are Liam and Lori," Efren revealed.

"It might as well be Hansel and Gretel," Thyme seethed. "It's a fairy tale."

"Not to me. I believe it's real."

Thyme handed back the phone. "That's because your mother is still alive in 2023. And mine is dead. That's real. Not some photo of a someday that can never happen, Efren. My mom is dead. As dead in 2023 as 2118 as she is now. Whatever you think is in our future, that picture is a fantasy that will never come to pass. It can't. It's a dream that we woke up from when the world fell into the Freeze."

Shepherd and Candy pulled up in front of the F.W. Woolworth's in an imported 2019 Toyota RAV4. Thyme and Efren exited the store as Shep leaned out. "Get in." Thyme slid in the back with Efren, trying to sit as far away from him as possible. On the floor by her feet was a rucksack full of illegally imported contraband.

"We got what we came for," Shepherd said. "Now let's get out of 1929 before they show up."

"Before who shows up?" Thyme asked.

Shepherd frowned, a little boy pouting because he couldn't have another piece of candy. He pointed out the windshield at an approaching 1928 Cadillac Town Sedan. "Them. The Untouchables."

That's when the world had turned topsy-turvy.

***

Now, the federal agents surround the RAV4, standing alongside their sedans with era-appropriate guns pointing at the fobs. The gyro-beyoncés in the air above the sedans hover like helium balloons accessorized for airborne assault. In all, Thyme estimates there are some sixteen weapons trained on them.

"Are they working for the Chronfederacy?" Candy asks.

"No," Shep says, sitting so low behind the wheel of the RAV4 that he can barely see over the steering wheel. "They're feds. FBI. Working for Washington, DC."

"Aren't they supposed to be our allies?" Efren is eternally optimistic and annoyingly naive.

"Not today." Shep wears a grimace like a kid doing a Clint Eastwood impression. Thyme's obasaan loved old Eastwood westerns. "They don't know who we are, and we ought to keep it that way."

"We should be able to go to them for help," Honor says. "The Institute is approved by the federal government."

"My transaction with Capone probably broke ten different laws," Shep says. "And the five of you have snuck across a half dozen borders illegally. We have too much explaining to do and not enough time to do it."

"Get out of the Toyota with your hands up," calls out one of the Untouchables.

"I think I prefer prison over getting perforated," Candy says.

"I'm saying they won't give us a chance to explain it, kid," the preteen traveler points out to the twenty-something blonde. "It's too late."

Too late in a world without ticktocks.

This isn't the hugs-and-feels law enforcement of 2023. These guys might fill this RAV4 with bullets Bonnie-and-Clyde style in a hail of gunfire even if the fobs do come out with their hands up. After surviving brainwashing 'morrow grandsons and Tyrannosauruses and train wrecks and prehistoric sea monsters and Confederate soldiers and timeless bounty hunters, at the end of the day the kids face capricious execution by a bunch of local good guys.

"They're serious," Shep says.

"We need to surrender," Thyme concedes. She has to at least try to save them from a hail of bullets.

Thyme reaches for the latch to the backdoor before the Untouchables start firing on the SUV, but as she touches the handle, something happens to give her pause. Beams like lasers erupt from a storefront on the corner where the fobs are cordoned off. The lasers originate beneath a rotating holographic logo consisting of a small circle with tick-marks arranged like a simple clock face. Under the icon, the words "RAMtech" float in glowing green. The store may be selling electronics or locally sourced energy boosters, or even information about the future.

The lasers target the tarmac near the RAV4. The lasers seem to stitch images out of nothing. Scarlet red and as large as sasquatch, like Iron Man armor made of solid light, the fobs watch several holographic forms flank the Toyota on all sides, facing the Untouchables in defensive postures as if they are imaginary protectors with futuristic ideals of chivalry.

"Robotrobotrobotrobot," Jay repeats.

"HaLiCons," Honor says.

"What the HaLi…?" Candy asks.

"Hard Light Constructs," Honor explains. "In the future, RAMtech develops machines made of solid light, able to be beamed into harsh conditions containing hazardous elements and survive unscathed. Light can resonate at a frequency to make solid constructs, able to dig and lift and carry. They are primarily used for construction and salvage in 2803, but it appears someone repurposed them for defense."

"To defend us?" Thyme cannot fathom who would come to their rescue. Ms. Norman?

"It seems we have a mysterious ally," Shep says.

"Divine intervention," Candy declares.

"God is stuck between the seconds," Honor says. "This is deus ex machina. Truly."

The Untouchables beside the sedans and the ones in the gyro-beyoncés fire on the RAV4 and Thyme flinches, but the HaLiCons are solid and block the bullets. Then the six scarlet constructs advance on the Untouchables, the massive machines made of light lifting the Cadillacs off the street and plucking the gyros out of the air. Like cans crushed in a vice, the futuristic defenders smash the sedans and rip the gyro-beyoncés in two. One HaLiCon snags a rifle away from an Untouchable and snaps the weapon in two. The federal agents scurry away on foot in four directions, outmatched but unscathed.

One of the HaLiCons turns toward the fobs and electronic sound issues from the construct, as if light can vibrate at a frequency to make a voice. "Head for the edge of town. The Graf Zeppelin has been appropriated to facilitate escape from 1929. The captain will provide safe passage to another time zone."

Shep stares out the windshield.

"Why are we waiting?" Candy cries out. "It saved us. We need to get out of Chicago before more of those Untouchables arrive."

Shep doesn't move his foot off the brake.

"What's the matter with you?" Candy screeches.

"He isn't sure whether we can trust this mysterious benefactor or if this is just a trap," Efren says. "The Untouchables aren't affiliated with the Chronfederacy. This might be a trick by the real enemy to get us back into Jefferson Davis's clutches."

The fobs sit still. The clocks aren't moving, but moments pass. The Untouchables will return. The question is where to go — follow the HaLiCons, or take a chance on their own?

"We have to trust somebody sometime, Shepherd," Thyme says.

The traveler closes his eyes, as if checking some inner compass that might guide him in the right direction. Whether he finally decides to take Thyme's advice or simply follows his own instinct, he changes his foot from brake to gas and they move forward. Move along. Toward the Zeppelin tied to the radio mast atop a brand-new shining skyscraper in the distance. Maybe not to the future, but surely away from the present.

Chapter Ten

13:25

10.10.3627 AD

Olympus

Thyme comes across into 3627 AD feeling like she has awoken from a glorious dream. Better than the nightmares that have plagued her life ever since her mother died in 2023. The last few e-days were a fuzzy blur that makes her wonder if that's what it's like to remember a previous drunken night. She looks out the window of the Graf Zeppelin as it glides across a sky that's no longer 1929, and nowhen near Chicago.

"You were a newborn and slept through most of the last time zone," Honor says. "Candy had to change your diaper."

"I see," Thyme tells.

"A lot," Honor adds, aged to eighty with a sour attitude to match.

"All right. Thanks, Candy. Sorry about that, I guess."

Candy smiles brightly, looking close to her real age, blonde and bubbly and beautiful. "That's okay. I love babies."

"You didn't miss anything. It was the Triassic period."

Efren is in his twenties, so very tall and clean-cut and handsome in his gangling way. "Apparently that part of the world was super-boring two-hundred-and-fifty million years ago."

"The Chronfederates didn't try to attack us in the past?" Thyme asks.

"The Triassic was cloudy and rainy, an endless electrical storm from one end to the other," Efren says. "The past at least afforded us stormy sanctuary from any satellite spies."

Thyme peeks out the window. The sky is blue with big cumulus clouds all around them, the zeppelin gliding between the white mounds like a whale paddling languidly among puffy islands. It could've been anytime from the far future to the ancient past. Below, the Earth is masked by a dirty carpet of gray stratus clouds obscuring the ground. The sun may be Thyme's own from 2023, but it hasn't changed for billions of years, and will probably not change for billions more.

"When are we?" she asks.

"The future." Honor looks curiously out of a round porthole. "Even for me."

"The year is 3627 AD," Efren says.

"We're at the fringes of future civilization," Shepherd says, entering the stateroom with Jay at his side.

Shep is as old as Honor, bent over with an octogenarian bow. Jay is the same age as Efren, both of them in the prime of their youth. There's something happening between Thyme and Jay. Something she wants to explore. The look Jay gives Efren is antagonism—the gaze Efren returns is full of antipathy. If the boys brawl over her here in the future, it would be fairer than in most zones, since at least they are currently the same age.

"What's the plan?" Thyme asks Shep.

"The edge of this time zone is as far as we can safely travel in the zeppelin. Davis wouldn't dare offend the future by attacking us in 3627. They are technologically advanced enough that a counterstrike on the Chronfederacy would be devastating. The states farther east, however, are too dangerous for us to chance the Grays having access to a jet or a gyro or even a satellite in space that can blast us out of the air." Thyme remembers the airship being shot down over the Mesozoic Sea. "There's a city at the edge of 3627 where we dock. Then we'll cross into the next zone on foot."

"There's a city somewhere down there?" Thyme asks, trying to peer through the steely stratus.

"Not down there." Efren startles her, suddenly right beside her, so close. Too close. He points out the window of the zeppelin toward the distant east, his arm brushing hers. "Up here."

Thyme sees the city in the sky, defying gravity, a group of individual suspended orbs like balloons let loose of their strings and risen into the bright blue sky. Some are the diameter of an average family home, while others are as big around as a stadium. Perfectly circular, they hover in place like miniature planets suspended in time and motion. As they grow closer, the orbs resolve into space-age structures, transparent domes surrounding inhabited domiciles. The largest are commercial districts, spherical collections of stores and entertainment venues and service industries. A whole galaxy of individual establishments, the future's version of a city, floating in the sky. Someone has applied the technology of the bouncies to make an entire metropolis among the clouds. Beyoncé City.

Below, the cover of stratus clouds opens enough to reveal the world. Niagara Falls is directly below them, the waters cascading over the precipice turned an iridescent green, as if every neon glow-stick ever made broke open and caused a flood. Something happened to the world below, and civilization fled to the skies.

As suddenly as the gray revealed a glimpse of the world on the ground, the hole in the clouds closes and covers the scene again.

"You can't cross this zone on foot," Shepherd says.

"What happened down there?" Thyme asks.

"Progress," Shepherd spits, like it's a swear word instead of merely the momentum of time.

"So they made cities in the clouds," Thyme marvels.

"They call it Olympus," Shepherd says as they approach one of the larger spheres. "A kingdom fit for gods."

The zeppelin docks with a sphere the size of Epcot as the cabin of the dirigible aligns and interlocks with a portal in the shell of the city. The fobs all gather at the entrance to Olympus. Even Honor looks curious. They're about to visit the far-flung future.

Thyme fidgets nervously and Jay notices, taking her left hand. Not to be outplayed, Efren takes her right. It seems the future is going to be very awkward indeed.

***

The androgyny that had begun in Thyme's grandson's 2118 and epitomized Honor's 2803 is replaced by more traditional gender identification by 3627. Shepherd said that the 'morrows named this place after Mt. Olympus, home of the Greek gods of myth, and the first people they meet might be Zeus and Hera in the flesh. The woman who greets them at the point where the zeppelin docks the great floating sphere features platinum hair that flows like the legendary Niagara Falls far below the city in the sky, with a white gossamer gown so thin and ephemeral it's as if she's draped in cloud. The man beside her steps out of Michelangelo's painting on the ceiling of the Sistine Chapel, hair and beard white as God's, a toga made of the same wispy immaterial alabaster. Their outfits make shadows of the perfect forms beneath their clothing.

The woman points to herself and says, "Aaia." and then indicates the man and says, "Eooi." She speaks in a way that reminds Thyme of a movie she had seen once where a zoologist is trying to teach a chimpanzee to communicate.

Honor steps forward. "I will have you know I am from 2803. I am not like these other Neanderthals."

"We assumed your origins by your appearance." Aaia slowly appraises Honor's style from tip to toes, taking particular note of her lack of hair and eyebrows.

"You do not have to speak to me as if I am primate," Honor says.

"Using this simplistic form of information exchange is indeed like talking to a monkey," Eooi declares.

"I can speak Esperanza if you would rather use a higher form of language," Honor suggests.

Aaia smirks. Apparently sanctimonious expressions are timeless. "No one has used Esperanza in centuries."

Thyme has had enough of the attitude, even if she is enjoying Honor getting a little of her own medicine. The 'morrow triggers Thyme's volatile temper. She steps forward, the two boys clasped onto each of her hands dragged along with her. "Obviously, one thing that stays intact across the centuries is the innate ability of some women to always be a royal bi—"

"Royal, indeed," Shepherd interrupts, stepping between Thyme and Aaia. "We appreciate the royal court granting us passage to the next zone."

Aaia and Eooi turn their attention toward the traveler. For all Thyme knows, Shep could come from 3627. She has no idea of his original timeline. He seems to fit in anywhen, and yet belong to nowhen.

"I trust you have brought πληρωμή," Eooi says.

Shepherd nods, patting his rucksack that contains the contraband Shep procured from Capone in 1929.

"We will move the enclave into position. You will be able to descend to the surface and cross to the next zone in approximately twenty-four e-hours," Aaia announces like it's some sort of royal decree. "In the meantime, anyone interested may join me on a tour of the future." Thyme swears the 'morrow glances at Honor as she says that last part, as if rubbing it in that the pair from 3627 think the fobs are all démodés.

Thyme examines their surroundings as Aaia and Eooi start leading everyone out of the room where they docked with the Graf Zeppelin. The sphere is encased in a clear barrier that resembles a bubble and reminds her again of the beyoncés they have used across America. Outside, the dirigible detaches and departs back the way it had come, the pilots returning to 1929. Shepherd said that the land below them is inhospitable. Now the fobs have no choice but to rely on the 'morrows to take them east.

Thyme follows the group, catching up as Aaia declares that the citizens of 3627 have answered every question ever posed. "We have unlocked all the secrets of the universe. Gravity is mastered, and we now occupy the skies. Science is just history to us, as we solved every equation several centuries ago. There is no more disease, no violence, no death. The unknown has been eradicated."

"You are truly gods," Candy gushes in awe.

"Faith was a failed hypothesis, and God was an excuse for an inability to understand," Eooi says. "We are simply enlightened."

"Yet you call this place Olympus and dress like Greek deities," Honor points out.

"Do not mistake confidence for divinity," Eooi says.

"Do you know the nature of time?" Efren asks.

Aaia glances at Eooi. He stares back at his fellow 'morrow.

"We know what time is," he carefully confesses.

"Then you know what happened at the Freeze?" Efren presses. "You know how the clocks stopped?"

Again the 'morrows check with each other. They seem reluctant to say anything further. Finally, as if confessing a great sin, Aaia admits, "We do not know how this happened. How it is even conceivable to stop time. We understand the nature of time, and it should theoretically be impossible to stop the clocks."

"That means you cannot fix it?" Honor asks, more than a hint of smugness in her tone.

"It is not broken so much as it is on pause," Eooi says. "There is nothing to fix. It is more accurate to say it is stuck and needs a push."

Like a car caught in the muck. Like Pooh wedged in the honey-hole. Thyme had always pictured in her mind a shattered clock face, broken and smashed like the Escalade that her mother crashed into a tree, but it wasn't like that. It is like an Escalade stuck in a bank of snow. It is like the frozen hands on her wristwatch.

"You said something about death," Thyme says softly. "Did you figure out what happens after someone dies?"

Aaia smiles, softer than she has before, as if she somehow understands even the depths of grief in her knowledge of all.

"Not only did we solve the mystery of death," Aaia reveals, "but we also know how to bring people back to life."

***

The Olympians call it the "rejuvenation room," as if it's a place at a spa featuring massages and pedicures instead of a laboratory for resurrecting the dead. They are upside down, the world below them obscured by gray clouds. Inside, the mood is nervous and suspicious. Honor and Efren don't believe it's possible. Thyme and Candy stand closest to the 'morrows, wide-eyed and open-minded. Shepherd and Jay wait in the wings, curious and noncommittal.

"About two centuries ago, we discovered one's spirit is made up of a unique collection of energies," Aaia explains. "Radiant emanations called 'genesis particles' collect in unique signatures to make up a person's soul. When someone dies, the genesis particles disperse into the universe. When someone is born anew, random genesis particles gather and recombine in new signatures, particles from a million billion different past persons, making up a new soul, so everyone is always something different, but also something the same. Constant."

"Our souls are made up of the reconstituted remnants of dead souls?" Honor asks.

"Recycled energy repurposed into the unique being that is you," Eooi rephrases.

Aaia continues. "Resurrecting the dead is a matter of reconnecting energy into the same unique pattern that originally made up an individual. That energy contains information stored in the genesis particles — the dispersed remnants of the person's memories are recorded within as bioelectric data. Medical science had advanced eons ago to allow for cloning new bodies. So now we can make new people and put their souls back in. Resurrection as effective as Jesus raising Lazarus."

Before Thyme can ask more questions about her mother and what it might mean to bring her back, Candy steps forward. "Can you bring back my twin brother?"

Thyme blinks. The bubbly blonde who seemed not to have a care in the world has a twin who died? Thyme checks with Efren and he shrugs. Honor looks unconcerned.

Jay comes closer to the Olympians. He may no longer look at Candy like he thinks she's Marilyn Monroe reincarnated, but he still cares about her. The five of them have become close. Friends.

Jay stands beside Candy. "What happened to your brother?"

Tears stand in Candy's eyes, and she's pretty even when she's crying. "It was an accident. We were at the beach. Billy and I were only six, but our mother kept a close eye on us. She let us play in the surf, staying in the shallows. It should've been safe as houses. But it was what someone called a 'rogue wave.' Swept him off his feet and out to sea. We found his body —"

Candy's words catch in her throat and her mouth crumples.

Honor moves her eyes from the 'morrows, who appear ready to resurrect the dead like it's just a matter of pouring a guest lemonade from a carafe, to Candy. The girl from 1948 wipes her eyes with the back of her hand.

"You pretend you are happy instead of dealing with the pain?" Honor challenges.

"It's all I can do," Candy says.

"You're weak," Honor accuses.

Candy nods. "Most of us are."

Honor's eyelids flutter, as if she had been shown a terrible truth.

Thyme misses her mother terribly. She wants her back more than anything in the whole world. But at least her mother had forty years to live. Candy's brother only had six. She has to let Candy go first.

"Death is merely a state of being, Candy Kane," Eooi says. "Like water can be changed to ice or steam, the genesis particles that made up your brother can be reconstituted into the boy you knew as Billy Kane. Our devices will tap into the fabric of the universe and borrow back the particles that made up your brother."

"Are you sure about this, Candy?" Jay has a concerned expression on his face. He doesn't quite trust this.

"He didn't get a chance," Candy says. "Maybe this is how it's supposed to be."

Aaia and Eooi nod. They approach a wall where lights move under the surface. A sphere the size of a beach ball rises out of the floor. It's filled with white mist not unlike the opaque material of Eooi and Aaia's clothing. The ball grows, expanding to three times the size. Then it opens, and a six-year-old boy steps out.

He yawns like a napping cat, as if he's a wee Rip Van Winkle waking in a new era. Naked as the day he was first born into a world some seventeen-hundred years ago, Billy Kane returns to life. He looks around, blinks like he was roused from a long dream, and then focuses on Candy. "Sis?"

Candy rushes forward, sweeping the boy into her arms, and the two embrace for a long, long time.

"So this is it? This is all there is?" Efren has his arms straight out, slowly turning in a circle. "No God. No Heaven. Just science and energy."

"This is Heaven, Efren Cortez," Aaia says. "We know everything there is to know. We can bring souls here to live for all eternity. There is no more hate or violence or ignorance. Is that not what you understand to be Heaven?"

Thyme gazes at Jay, then Efren. Her path forward with Efren is destiny. In the world when time ticks forward, where they get married and have kids and live a life together. Like Aaia and Eooi and their absolute knowledge, Thyme knows what her tomorrow is supposed to be. But even though she knows the truth, she looks from Efren to Jay. Fate and future have faded, and she can make tomorrow whatever she wants it to be.

"Get some rest," Eooi says to the fobs. "We have prepared chambers where you may comfortably await arrival to the edge of the next zone."

The fobs file out, Candy leading Billy along, the boy wrapped in gossamer swaddling like a figure from one of the paintings in the big Bible Thyme used to page through at Jiji's house when she was younger—Jesus come back after three days dead, the rock rolled away from his tomb. Billy is alive again.

Thyme could do the same with her mother.

As she exits last from the rejuvenation room, Aaia offers, "Let us know, Thyme Mugen, if there is anything we can do for you." As if the 'morrow knows exactly what Thyme is thinking.

***

Thyme stares out the clear ceiling as the sphere revolves in a slow, lazy turn. West becomes east, around and around. The people of Olympus have mastered gravity as they conquered death, nothing left to reach for in 3627. Except tomorrow. Yet Thyme stands in the future, yearning for the past.

She has only a short time left to decide if she should ask

Aaia to bring her mother back from the dead. They're an e-hour away from the next zone, when Thyme will either have to move forward and make her life into something else or reach back to make things the way they used to be. All this time racing across America, she thought she was running away from the terrible thing that had happened in 2023. But maybe she had really been running toward this future where she could fix all the things that went wrong.

"I didn't know about your brother," Thyme whispers. "I'm sorry."

Candy stands in the doorway of the room empty of everyone besides Thyme. "It happened a long time ago."

"I wondered why you would leave home. 1948 California is a perfect fit for a girl like you, but you're trying to find sometime new. Sometime else," Thyme tells. "Yet you put on a happy face every day. How can you do that?"

"I'm from Hollywood, my dear. It's called acting," Candy emphasizes with a dramatic flip of her hand. "Honor said I'm weak. She's right, you know. I fake being strong. I pretend every day. That's how I got through the last ten years without Billy."

"And now he's alive again."

Candy is quiet. She doesn't give Thyme an answer to that.

"They tell you a lot of things when someone you love dies," Candy says. "Empty words like 'Time heals all wounds.' We've put a million years between now and then, and does it feel like it cuts any less deep?"

"No." The hole in Thyme's heart where her mother used to be is as big and black as it was more than an e-year ago. "It feels the same. I thought if I ran away from that day, it might get better. But it never does."

"It never does," Candy agrees, peering back over her shoulder down the corridor to where the rest of the fobs wait.

"But now you have your brother back."

Candy shakes her head. "That might be a kid named Billy Kane, but it's not the same boy that drowned in the sea."

Thyme frowns. "Aaia said they could reconstitute the soul."

Candy shrugs. "Maybe they can. Maybe they did. Billy said he remembers breathing water, salty and thick. He remembers drowning. Then darkness. Nothing. Then there was a light at the end of a long tunnel, and suddenly he stepped out of that egg that they used to resurrect him. But my brother was found two days later along a seashore, half-eaten by a sea-scavengers and tangled and bloated in a clump of seaweed. That little boy is not my brother."

"It will take some getting used to, Candy."

Candy sighed, shaky and long. "You can't get used to living in a dream, Thyme. This isn't real. We live in a fantasyland. The real world is one with clocks and time and tomorrows. The real world is the one where your mother is still alive and my brother is still dead. And when the minutes move, we will all wake up."

"Then why did you bring him back at all?"

"It wasn't for me. He only got six short years, Thyme. Not enough. Nowhere near enough. I wanted to give him some time, even if it is just a dream. At least he has a future here."

"So you aren't staying? And you won't take him with?"

"He belongs here," Candy says, as cold as anything she has said since Thyme met her. "And I belong somewhen else."

Tears roll down Thyme's face. "I miss her so much. I want to see her again."

"And you will," Candy assures her. "When the clocks start and this is over, you'll wake up and your mother will be waiting for you. Like Dorothy at the end of the Wizard of Oz."

"You really believe that?" Thyme asks.

"I do."

Thyme cannot tell if Candy is just acting.

Then the sphere turns and Thyme faces east. To the next zone. Toward tomorrow.

Aaia steps into the room with Thyme and Candy. "The hour grows short, Thyme Mugen. Do you have something you want from us?"

The 'morrows could bring her mother back to life. It's everything she ever wanted since that terrible moment when time stopped and everything changed. But this is 3627, and the mother who returned would be one who lived longer than 2023. Thyme learned in 2118 that her mother is supposed to live until 2061. If Thyme agrees to resurrect her mother, she would come back as a woman who had lived to be almost eighty instead of the baby who wrapped her Escalade around a tree. The Rikona Mugen who came back would not be her mother.

To move on, Thyme must move forward. Her mother is in the past. Maybe Candy is right and this is all a dream, and her mother will be waiting when Thyme wakes. Perhaps this is a new reality and her mother is gone forever. Either way, her mother lived a long enough life in a world with birthdays and anniversaries and holidays.

Candy brought her brother back for the sake of a little boy who hadn't had enough time—Thyme would be bringing her mother into this world with stopped clocks and stilled seasons for her own selfish reasons.

"No," Thyme tells. "I'm ready to get back to a world with more questions than answers."

CHAPTER ELEVEN
21:19
9.30.2057 AD
Wilkes-Barre, Pennsylvania

For once, Thyme is relieved to be a different age than she's supposed to be. She came across from 3627 only about ten years old, prepubescent, which is a mercy considering the affections of two boys always directed her way. At least her hormones wouldn't contribute to the contest between fate and free will.

Honor crossed into 2057 in her twenties, and Shepherd refuses to sneak to the other side of the zone with the 'morrow looking like an advertisement for illegal immigration. "That tattoo glowing on your bald head shouts 'I am from the future!' We'll all end up in a perennial colony before we get within an e-hour of 1980. We're too close to get caught in a zone that's entirely intolerant of illegal immigration."

"I am not wearing that." Honor stares at the wig and the dress in the traveler's outstretched hands intended to make Honor blend in to 2057.

"Then you're never going to make it to the Minute," Shep says.

Honor glares. Shep glowers. Thyme rolls her eyes and offers a compromise.

"You brought outfits for everyone?" Thyme asks.

"Of course," Shepherd says.

"Including something appropriate for geriatric assimilation?"

"I'm a professional. I had Eooi replicate a selection of outfits for every eventuality."

Ten e-minutes later, Shep has changed out of the clothes he's worn since they met in 2033. In his eighties, his outfit features a bow tie and a cardigan that makes him someone's grampa. Honor is outfitted in the traveler's timeless duster, wearing his wide-brimmed petasos to cover her tattoos, moccasins slapping asphalt as they finally start east again. She sports the rare smile. Shep grumbles under his breath like an ornery octogenarian.

"You sure know how to get under people's skin, over and over and over," Thyme tells Honor.

The 'morrow must take it as a compliment. She smirks and says, "I think it was Maya Angelou who said, 'Oops, I did it again.'"

"Britney Spears," Thyme corrects.

"Same difference," Honor says.

Some things never change. Maybe some things never should. The past is the present is the future. And once in a while, that's okay.

The fobs keep to side-roads and safe throughways. Shep nervously watches the roadway as cars drive themselves by, as if he expects enemies at any time. The fobs make it halfway across the zone without being apprehended, consciously staying off the major routes.

Shep explains that the CIA at Langley here in 2057 were charged by President Harrison himself with crafting enforcement policy for immigration across the whole United States of Time. They formed a Task Force T to test methods of incarceration that Shep deems "extreme." He acts nervous about being in this zone, but 1980 is just on the other side of Pennsylvania. The only alternative would've been a long way around. With Jefferson Davis sending raiders after the fobs, any delay is as dangerous as the chance of being caught by Task Force T.

The fobs walk into Wilkes-Barre, Pennsylvania on foot. Honor the traveler takes the lead beside the elderly Shepherd, now walking with a cane out of necessity rather than authenticity. Efren is old again, on Candy's arm as he fights exhaustion after all these many, many miles on foot. Thyme and Jay are both about ten and watch vehicles pass them by that change color at will, gliding silently and safely as super-speeds.

"We'll get rooms here," Shepherd says, stopping in front of a hotel and leaning on his willow cane. Efren, almost as old, leans against another kind of Kane. Thyme expects a pang of jealousy as her future husband cozies with a bombshell blonde, but there's nothing. Nothing at all. "I need to arrange passage the rest of the way across to 1980. The border is heavily guarded between now and New York."

"Why do we not turn ourselves in?" Honor pushes back the petasos like a professional, revealing a steely gaze. "We might not have papers, but we do have approval to travel to 1980."

"That's fine for you and Candy and Efren and me," Thyme says. "But what would happen to Shepherd and Jay?"

"Ms. Norman will take care of it once we get to 1980."

"We don't even know if Ms. Norman is free or if she has run afoul of Jefferson Davis and the Chronfederacy again," Thyme says. "We can't risk Jay and Shepherd's freedom. We wouldn't have made it this far without them."

"Besides, your passports are only valid for travel between 1960 and 1980," the traveler reminds Honor. "You're not supposed to be in 2057. You, too, are here illegally. If Ms. Norman is unavailable, you all would be incarcerated along with Jay and me."

"Fine," Honor says. "Give me the money, Shepherd. I will rent the rooms."

Shep thumbs through his current currency and pulls out a wad of 2057 bills with Obama on the face. Some establishments verify travel papers, and some don't. Shepherd picked a place that believes business is business, whenever it comes from. The front desk attendant takes the money and rents the group two rooms, no questions asked.

The girls gather in one suite and the boys take the other. Candy and Honor turn in early, exhausted. The two elderly men also are snoring in moments. After trekking halfway across 2057, Thyme is grateful for a break. The women sleep behind her as she sits outside on the fourth-story balcony, gazing up at a moon suspended indefinitely in its place in the sky.

This is 2057. 1980 is near. Her tomorrow is finally coming.

"Wanna check out the future?" comes a voice from the next balcony over.

Jay balances on the railing, walking along with arms stretched out to each side like it's a tightrope, five feet from where Thyme enjoys the starry twilight. He's her age, a roguish ten-year-old boy. His bomber jacket is three sizes too big, a kid dressing up like his daddy. His smile is almost as bright as the shining moon.

Her future is coming. She's supposed to be with Efren. Her fate is out there, available online. Marriage, kids, grandkids. A whole life. Efren believes she's his destiny.

Thyme wants to make her own fate.

"Yeah," she says.

***

It's a timeless truth among every zone they've visited, from one ocean almost to the other, that whenever they find themselves, kids mostly go unnoticed. However, in some periods across this new America, even a young Asian girl with a boy of color might garner a suspicious glare. In 2057, racial tolerance is at least on an upward trajectory. Here and now, they're more apt to be prosecuted for when they're originally from rather than where.

"Where are we going?" Thyme asks as Jay leads her out into the streets of 2057, entirely unnoticed by the native population crowding the streets.

"A date," Jay says.

"I didn't agree to that," Thyme replies.

"Not that kind of date," Jay assures her.

The hotel where the rest of the fobs are still sleeping is in a business district. There are still McDonald's in 2057, with a menu more health food than fast food. Future Starbucks have been rebranded "Retros," the coffee shops remodeled to match their decor in 2023 but meant to be nostalgic in 2057. There are kiosks called "Applets" that provide tech in vending machines and virtual storefronts called "6els," and something that reminds Thyme of an old-fashioned cinema with a marquee featuring titles like Dawn of the Sun and The End of the Day.

"What is this place?"

"It's called The Sun Day."

"You're taking me out for ice cream?"

"No," Jay answers. "You'll see."

Jay takes her hand and leads her inside.

"This feels like a date," Thyme says.

"Not that kind of date," Jay reiterates as he buys them a ticket with some current currency he lifted from Shep, a coin featuring a woman Thyme thinks might be a New York City politician from 2023.

They walk inside and it's another world entirely. Timeless. Like a ship unmoored by day and month.

"This kind of date," Jay says, "doesn't use a clock or a calendar."

At the entrance to the hall, someone stands taking tickets. He accepts Thyme's and Jay's and lets them pass. "Down at the end on the right." They walk along a corridor with doors on each side, passing by one labeled A Long, Lazy Afternoon and another signed Morning Passes. Jay pauses between two doors, one that reads Twilight to Midnight and the other The End of the Day.

"Is this a movie theater?" Thyme wonders.

"It isn't any place you've ever been before, Thyme Mugen."

"You're just full of new adventures, aren't you, Jay Stone?"

"I'm not the tale that's already written, Thyme. This isn't the story you know."

"That's good," Thyme says. "I don't like it when someone spoils the ending."

"In here," Jay says, opening the door to The End of the Day.

"How did you know about this place?" Thyme asks.

"The rest of you have been running through zone after

zone with your head down and your eyes closed. You only see when you are going and when you have been, but you don't stop and look around at right now. This whole adventure seems to be all about the past and the future. What about the present?" Jay stops talking and looks through the door he's holding open. He smiles. "I take time to talk to people in all these different eras. And you know what? People aren't so different. You'll see, when you get to that special school in 1980. Things aren't so different from the beginning to the end."

"And what's in here?" Thyme asks. "The beginning or the end?"

"Only beginnings with you, Thyme Mugen."

They enter a world more end than beginning. It's late evening and the sun is suspended over the ocean, a big orange ball hanging in the sky like a loosed balloon. The beach stretches out to either side of them on and on and on, romantic pairs of people strolling along in the surf and couples sitting close in the sand. Thyme and Jay hold hands, walking up to the edge of the beach. Thyme slips off her shoes and the sand is real. The Sun Day uses holograms and physical props to recreate the moment. To mimic movement. The holographic sun descends, slowly lowering toward the horizon.

"A sunset," Thyme whispers. "I haven't watched the sun set in more than a year."

"I've never been to an oceanside beach before," Jay says, staring out into a distance that seems to go on forever, recreated to perfection. "So beautiful."

"You should see the real thing," Thyme says.

"I'm looking at the real thing."

Thyme turns and Jay isn't ogling the ocean anymore. He's

looking at Thyme. He smiles. His grin could light up a room. Thyme's mom is dead and she can only rarely find her own smile. Jay's dad is dead. Killed in a war. He never even knew the man. Yet Jay still finds occasion to be happy in this life. He seeks out fun. Humor. He's not bogged down by the loss of his parent.

"I wish I could be more like you," Thyme tells, watching the sun touch the sea, watching him watch her.

"I wish you would stay just the way you are," he replies.

They're kids. Ten years old and playing as adults. But ten is sixteen is seventeen is thirty in a timeless world. The future is the past is the present.

The sun is swallowed by the sea, and even Jay must watch at it as the colors bleed into the ocean. Twilight falls softly on the shore, gray cooling what had been bright and bold. Night arrives in a replicated scenario that Thyme had taken for granted sixteen years of her life.

For the first time, she watches until the last light of day goes out.

"Candy doesn't believe any of this is real," Thyme says. "She thinks it's a dream that will all go away."

He still has her hand in his. Jay appraises her like no boy ever has. Not even Efren. Efren's gaze is filled with arduous expectations, and Jay's eyes hint at endless possibilities. "I'm not going anywhere."

"Are you one of the Minute fobs?" interrupts a middle-aged person approaching from the entrance, androgynous in the way that can only be 2118. He's flanked by two others from the same zone. Thyme recognizes them. They're the three brothers who came across from her grandson's time zone and boarded the train with them in 1869. Honor said they were an envoy to the president. They had been carrying a silver case at the time, and now they carry nothing.

"It isn't wise to admit to being a fob around these parts," Thyme says.

The 2118er takes it as confirmation. "We've been looking for you. We need your help."

***

Thyme and Jay sit in twin chairs facing the rest of the fobs, looking like two children that got in trouble for sneaking out after curfew. Shep and Efren shuffle back and forth in front of them with puckered faces, old men with frustration manifest in wrinkles. Honor is on the other side of her teens, waving her fingers in the air, pointing at a hologram of dancing light floating over where she reclines on the bed. Music issues from the pulsing ball of light, an Elvis Presley/Madonna duet changing to Roy Orbison covering a Taylor Swift song instead. Candy stares into the mirror, reapplying lipstick redder than any sunset ever recreated in The Sun Day.

"Why did they come to you?" Efren asks.

"They know we had contact with Jefferson Davis in 1869," Thyme says. "They hoped we might have insight to any insidious plans."

"Well, do you?" Honor presses, sitting upright with the hologram playing music floating right by her head.

"Are you asking me if I know something you don't, Honor?" Thyme snaps.

"They tracked you down all the way to 2057. I guess they seem to think so."

"And how did they know when to find you, anyway? How did they know you were sneaking around the future, out on a date with the wrong boy?" Efren asks.

"Don't take that tone with me, mister." Young Thyme wags a finger at the old man eight times her age. "You're the one who's been speaking with Theodore. You told your grandson we were at this hotel."

"Our grandson," Efren corrects, pouting defensively.

"Not yet," warns Thyme, as if not yet might mean not ever. "Theodore told his 2118 minions where to find us. They followed Jay and me from the hotel to The Sun Day."

"It was foolish to sneak out on your own," Shep says. "They could've turned you in to the authorities in 2057."

"They're desperate," Thyme says. "They lost the case they were transporting to 1841. The three of them were supposed to personally deliver something special to the president. Something that would help against Jefferson Davis. After the train crashed in 1869, they were taken into custody by Davis's men. They eventually escaped, but the case they were carrying had been confiscated."

"Did they say what's in that case?" Shep asks as Honor changes Orbison to some synthetic sound from the future, mashing Katy Perry's California Gurls with the Beach Boys' California Girls.

"Yeah," Jay says. "And you ain't gonna like it."

"Our grandson sent that case to 1841," Efren adds. "I'm sure he had every good reason to do so."

Thyme scowls at Efren. "You keep pushing destiny and fate, Efren Cortez. That we're supposed to fall in love and have this family in the future. Descendants like Theodore in 2118. Well, he's the one that sent that case to President Harrison. He's the one who inadvertently put everyone in 1841 in grave danger. How is that fate? It sounds more like folly."

"What did they do?" Shepherd asks. "How were they

planning to stop Davis?"

"They call it a 'fugue-bomb,'" Thyme reveals. "The device can wipe everyone's memory in a hundred-and-fifty-mile radius. Theodore weaponized his brainwashing technology from 2118. Instead of curing dementia, he's willing to trigger it. Our illustrious grandson was smuggling a weapon of mass deconstruction to Washington, DC, so that President Harrison could use it as a deterrent against Jefferson Davis's insurrection. Harrison could've made everyone in Jefferson Davis's 1869 forget who they are and what they're doing."

"What kind of a lunatic thinks that inducing mass amnesia is a viable weapon?" Honor sneers.

"Theodore would think of it as a humane option against untold bloodshed between zones if war breaks out between eras," Efren says. "He believes that healing through the erasure of the precipitating cause of pain is a cure for an ailment. The disease of bad experience. If the Chronfederates don't know why they are fighting, maybe they can find peace in forgetfulness."

"It was supposed to prevent a second Civil War," Thyme says. "Davis could either give up and remember defeat or continue fighting and forget every last memory, right down to his own name."

"Instead, it's now in the hands of Chronfederate forces." Jay looks from one fob to the next, one by one. "They plan to detonate the f-bomb in 1841."

Thyme sniggers despite the dire circumstances. Efren smirks.

"What is so funny about the potential first strike in some terrible sequel to the War Between the States?" Honor snaps.

"No, it's just…." Efren explains. "In 2023, an f-bomb is

something very different."

"Maybe let's call it something else, Jay," Thyme requests.

"I don't really like to say 'fugue,'" Jay says.

"Enough," Shepherd interjects. "If you two didn't learn anything about this fugue-bomb while captive in 1869, then there's nothing we can do about it. We need to leave the situation to the proper agencies and keep moving on to 1980."

"The proper agencies?" Thyme is tired of chasing tomorrow and running from yesterday. What about right now? "The proper agencies already know. President Harrison deported the 2118 trio from 1841 because of their failure, and they came here and now to find us. To try to fix their mistake. The 'proper' agencies don't know tomorrow from yesterday, Shepherd."

"More the reason to get to 1980," Shep says. "These are dangerous times."

"What if we can help?" Thyme counters. "We've seen associates of Davis in 1869. Or maybe the raiders that have been tracking us across the last time zones know something, if we can turn the tables on them. And you want us to simply run away?"

Run away. Isn't that what Thyme has been doing since she left 2023? She fled from the infinite minute of her mother's death, the unending day that she relived repeatedly. She avoids the destiny that Efren constantly reminds her of. For the entire trip across America, Thyme has been closing her eyes to what happens next and trying not to think about what happened before. She wants to forget both the past and the future. And as Jay said, she has been ignoring every present. She's running with her eyes closed. But that doesn't mean she will turn a blind eye and let innocent citizens from 1841 suffer involuntary amnesia.

"I was contracted by Ms. Mallory Norman to keep you safe, Thyme," Shep says. "I was not drafted into some timeless

War Between the States."

"We didn't ask for any of this, Shepherd," Thyme whispers, thinking of the beach and the sunset and Jay's hand in hers. "But life has never been about everything working out the way you think it will. Time has never been a friend to anyone. It's a test, one that features twists and turns that you can never prepare for. Things haven't changed so much since the Freeze. We just no longer mark the moments with minutes as they pass through one unpredictable occurrence after the other. Somebody told me lately that things aren't so different from the beginning to the end. There's always a curveball. So do we swing and play the game, or stand there and wait to see if we walk or strike out?"

"I hate baseball metaphors," Honor grumbles.

Shepherd looks at Thyme. Thyme stares defiantly back. She's going to try and stop the f-bomb. Shep knows he can't stop her.

"My mission is to get you safely to the Institute," the traveler says. "I mean to fulfill my promise to Ms. Norman. I leave for 1980 in an e-hour. It's time to get you when you're supposed to be. I can't make you go, but I can get you there."

Thyme looks from Shep to Jay to Efren to Candy to Honor. It is time. It's time to either keep running away or stop and make a stand.

***

The fork in the road. The choice that can change everything. Thyme can think of previous moments like this—the time her mother almost decided to move them to the Midwest because she was getting serious with a guy—that relationship fizzled when the guy was surprised Thyme was coming with instead of being left behind with Jiji; the time the cool girls in middle school told Thyme her initiation into the popular clique required her to help them shoplift a diamond bracelet and Thyme refused — the Princess Posse got caught and ended up in juvie for the next two years; the time she paused on her bicycle in front of the dark woods between school and home one cool autumn evening, debating whether to ride through or go around, finally deciding to face her fears and take the shortcut — a gas main exploded under the street on the alternate route, and Thyme will never know if she would've been blown to bits if she had succumbed to her nerves.

This is a moment like those, where some e-day Thyme will look back and see this as either a good choice or the worst one. It's the point where the fork leads down two very different paths. Thyme wonders, occasionally, whether someone made a choice that resulted in the Freeze. Was there a fork in the road that led to a different destination than cracked clocks and a world of patchwork time periods?

North of Wilkes-Barre is a time zone that has never been clocked. Thyme sits at the edge, staring out at the stars. The universe looks different, whether it's the vast past or a far future. Fewer stars pepper the sky, where one could pick out each individual pinpoint of light and name it if they took some time to do so. Earth hasn't been born or it's long gone, giving Thyme the effect of sitting on the edge of a high cliff and gazing out into a canyon containing the entire cosmos.

The scarlet sheen of the curtain between zones is almost invisible against the black backdrop. The only evidence of its existence is the stars shimmering with a pale pink light. Thyme examines across, from side to side, and then up and down, the vastness of nothingness too big to comprehend. It's like staring into her future and every errant star is a possible tomorrow, each point of light a plausible destination. A fork in the road multiplied a hundred times.

"Shepherd is about to leave."

Efren sits beside Thyme in the grass at the edge of sometime a billion years hence or thence. His old bones creak as if he's a billion years old himself. Efren manages to bring his arthritic knees up to his chest and sits there next to Thyme, as if they're young lovers on a date, connecting the dots in the sky to draw a mutual future.

There are two routes out of town, one that continues east along this border in the direction of 1980 and the other south to 1841. Thyme means to take the latter, and Shepherd is still aiming for the former.

"We'll be heading out ourselves soon enough," Thyme says. "Jay is double-checking the routes."

"He's going with you?"

"He wasn't invited to the Institute. He has nowhen else to go."

"Maybe I should go help him plot a course," Efren offers.

"You aren't coming with us," Thyme says.

Efren opens his mouth to say something. Closes it. Opens it again and only wordless breath expires. Closes it again. He stares out at the empty universe.

"There's something you need to know, Thyme."

"Simply because you needed to know doesn't mean I do. I don't want to know what else you found out about the future."

"It's about Liam and Lori," Efren says. The names of their children.

"Those are characters in a story, Efren. And it isn't our story."

"They are here in 2057," Efren reveals to her anyway. "They live in Pittsburgh."

Thyme simmers. He won't listen. He refuses to understand. They are like two teens on a first date—where one looks preteen and the other octogenarian—sitting in front of a fortune teller who predicts they're destined to be together forever. Thyme isn't going to bet her whole life on a crystal ball. Efren seems ready to get engaged.

"Candy thinks this is all a dream. Although some people would call it a nightmare," Thyme tells. "But what if this isn't a dream or a nightmare? What if it just is? This is the new real world, forever and ever. Do you want to do everything we were supposed to do because fate tells us it's so? Do you want your life planned out by some unavoidable future? Do you want to live in the now, or live for tomorrow?"

"You can't run from the future, Thyme," Efren says, as if he's reciting a scientific fact. "We belong together."

"Why don't you let me figure that out for myself?" Thyme argues. "And maybe you should find it out for yourself, too, instead of letting the Internet tell you who you should love."

Thyme really looks at Efren. He's about eighty in this zone, and it seems appropriate. Obsessed with how his life turns out in the future, Efren appears like an old man reminiscing about days already lived. It's as if tomorrow already happened for him and he's strolling through the memories. Trying to carefully follow preexisting footsteps in the sand so perfectly, print for print. Thyme wants to forge her own path. Blaze her own trail. Make new memories instead of reliving old ones.

"We should go to 1980 and get to the Institute," Efren sighs.

"That is when you are going. You've been all about the

end since the very beginning," Thyme says. "But I need to try and save the past."

"I'm going whenever you go."

"If you want there to be any chance for...for us, you need to quit holding on so tightly. Get to 1980. You follow your path, and I will follow mine," Thyme says. "If you believe in fate so much, Efren Cortez, then you need to give me room to breathe. If it is destiny, then I will find my way back, won't I?"

"How can I let you go?"

"If you don't let me go, then you're never going to get the chance to have me," Thyme replies.

Efren sits there for a while longer. Tears stand in his eyes, twinkling in a magical mixture of moonshine behind them and starlight before them, but Thyme cannot stand to look at him. She might not love him like he wants to be loved, but there's a piece of him in her heart, beside Candy and Jay and even Honor. The moment seems to draw on and on, and eventually he gets up and gets gone, slipping away while Thyme isn't looking.

"They are leaving," Honor announces, appearing beside Thyme in the field out back of their hotel, in the spot where Efren had been.

"You're coming with us?" Thyme asks, surprised.

"The rule of three," Honor advises. "We needed to split the whole group exactly in half to safely cross into two different zones."

"I assumed you were going to 1980," Thyme tells. "I thought Candy would come with us."

"I hate it when people assume," Honor huffs.

Thyme smiles. Nods. "All right, then. The timely trio it is."

"I hate puns," Honor snaps as Thyme stands up and they

start southeast.

Jay waits for Thyme along the road. She peers out into an endless distance, a map of maybes that stretches on forever.

"Efren thinks that tomorrow is already set," Thyme says. "He keeps going on about accepting my fate."

"Fate is what people talk about when they fear the unknown. Efren studies the stars and thinks he knows which one is his. He believes the universe picked his point and he's trying to get there. He needs someone to tell him where to go," Jay says. "I don't think you need anyone to tell you where to go, Thyme Mugen."

She takes one last look back at the stars behind her. They might be the past or the future, but they are pretty things to appreciate rather than ponder. If it's tomorrow, it is not her tomorrow.

CHAPTER TWELVE
16:52
3.29.1841 AD
Quad-City, Delaware

Thyme feels like herself again. Sixteen in 1841, she fits into familiar skin for the first time in years. Jay is in his twenties and as handsome as any movie star from 2023. Honor looks forty and fit, like a professor who cultivates the mind yet doesn't ignore the body, maybe taking a daily morning jog before her eight a.m. class.

Thyme's mother took a trip to Washington, DC, with Jiji four years ago to attend a ceremony that honored Thyme's grandfather's brave sacrifice in the Korean War. Now, here's Thyme in the same city where her mother had taken pictures of herself standing in front of the Washington Monument—not built yet—and the Lincoln Memorial—Abe would be a thirty-two year-old lawyer in Springfield, Illinois in 1841—and the Vietnam Veterans Memorial—Vietnam is currently in 1945, and not one man is dead from the conflict—and the Martin Luther

King, Jr. Memorial—technically, 1841 is still about thirty years from giving blacks the right to vote, which means it's still almost eighty years until women can vote, even though one of the first acts after the Freeze had been equal suffrage, insisted upon by the American 'morrows.

It's like Thyme stepped into a section of her history book from back at East Valley High. Now she's been to 1960 and 1869 and 1929, but those had been like visiting movie sets rather than traveling in time. This is the place of legend, a world chronicled in textbooks and tested on during semester finals. Thyme observes from an open field, studying a White House without the veil of a camera lens or a hundred-and-eighty years of history. It stands in an undeveloped expanse without a city as a backdrop, no multistory structures looming in the distance, just a mansion as iconic as any house ever built. Horse-drawn carriages pass on the dirt road, and pedestrians of the era meander along without pausing to appreciate the view.

A limousine rolls up, jarring Thyme like being violently woke from a pleasant dream. A couple steps out, a man in his thirties holding hands with a woman in her eighties. They both wear identification that designates them as official tourists from another era. The man takes out an iPhone like the one Thyme left in California, suggesting he's from 2023. The couple takes a selfie in front of the 1841 White House. Then they pile back into the limo and it takes off down an unpaved Pennsylvania Avenue.

"That was weird," Jay says.

"Everything you démodés do is weird," Honor opines.

"The trio from 2118 had e-week old information. Now we need to know if the authorities have any leads that are more current on where to find the Chronfederate terrorists," Thyme says. "We need to get past the guards and talk to President

Harrison himself about the fugue-bomb."

"What guards?" Honor asks. "There was no security at the White House in 1841."

Indeed, there's no one at the gates monitoring who comes and goes into the White House. Coming from an era of intense security, where metal detectors are featured at even her own school, Thyme cannot believe her eyes as she sees regular citizens stroll right up to the White House and enter the front doors.

"They've had a full e-year to adjust security measures to the post-Freeze world, but they still allow people to walk right in?" Thyme asks.

"The savage terrorism and unchecked violence that permeates your present have not yet infected the past," Honor says. "Outside the occasional tourist, it seems that there is no reason for increased caution in 1841."

"Except there's an f-bomb floating around history," Jay points out.

"A Gray can use the bomb to obliviate everyone in a hundred-and-fifty-mile radius. There is no reason to walk into the West Wing and detonate it right in front of President Harrison."

"'Obliviate' isn't a real word," Thyme says.

"We do not live in the real world," Honor argues. "And by the way, many Tolkienisms were added to the Oxford dictionary in the middle of the twenty-first century."

"That would be a Potterism," Thyme corrects. Honor stares like she just doesn't care. Thyme changes the subject, examining the White House. "We need information. If we can find out what they know, maybe we can help."

"We stroll in there, the president is going to call for the police and we're going to get arrested," Jay says. "Maybe they send you and Honor on to 1980. Or back to California and your own times. But they will probably put me in a perennial colony."

1841 strictly enforces immigration policy. If they get caught without a green card, the feds might sentence them all to a perennial colony. The perennial colony is a prison where the inmates get stuck in time. Built right between two time zones, the prisoner gets transferred back and forth across a border until the convict is a baby, then left as a perpetual newborn. A drooling, unaware mess. That would truly be an infinite minute. Infantile for all eternity.

Maybe President Harrison would understand the fobs' predicament. Probably he would. But Thyme can't be sure. All she knows about Henry Harrison from history books is that he didn't even live much past his inauguration. There wasn't enough information to make a judgment on his character. And Thyme hasn't been following politics since the Freeze. She's been too busy grieving.

"We need a disguise," Thyme says. "What kind of professions exist in this time zone?"

"My great-grandmother was a match-maker in the 1800s," Jay says. "Is President Harrison married in 1841?"

"The First Lady is Anna Harrison," Honor informs.

"That's good," Jay sighs. "I really don't know what a match-maker wears."

"We do not need to get information right from President Harrison. We need someone with connections to the president." Honor looks southeast to the highest hill in the city, where the Capitol Building rises in the distance. "Luckily, Thyme, you have an ancestor serving as the senator from North Carolina."

***

Instead of a hundred senators in 1841, there are only fifty-two seats. Thyme finds this fact harder to accept than some of the more fantastical things she has seen these last few e-weeks. It feels like a basic number she's always believed as some core kind of truth has been manipulated, like someone changed the value of pi or two plus two now equals five. Such a nice, round number like one hundred seems almost a shame to break up into fifty-two.

"They're going to hold a special election to fill the senate chamber up to a hundred members again," Senator Willie Mangum says. "Many senators and representatives in Congress have already resigned, their constituencies lost to time or changed so completely that they no longer know how to represent their home state. I mean, there were politicians serving in the legislature that history tells us would go on to serve the south in the War Between the States, and yet they were representing future populations that are predominately minorities. The new membership will be represented chronologically rather than geographically. Each senator will represent an era instead of an anachronistic state."

Senator Willie Mangum wears dark trousers and a dark tailcoat that make him look like an extra from a 2023 special on the History Channel. His hat is a stovepipe and looks ridiculous, like steampunk cosplay gone too far. He has long black sideburns that connect to a black mustache. He is Thyme's father's ancestor. He is white.

Thyme didn't even know she's part white. She doesn't know her father's ancestry. Thyme doesn't even know who her father is. She never much considered it before now. Mom was all she ever really needed. A dad was a myth that she never much minded being missing. Mom didn't talk about him, and Thyme never bothered to ask. In 2023, being from a single-family home was commonplace, and Thyme had no reason to know more.

Thyme tries to recognize some part of the girl she sees in the mirror every day in the man who stands before her. She always knew her ethnicity was watered down by some other color, but she couldn't see the features of her great-great-great-great grandfather that contributed to her present. Perhaps in the nose? Maybe it isn't important. What does the past matter if Thyme stays stuck in the present? How can she be curious about the life of her father when she's so obsessed with the death of her mother?

The Capitol Building is much smaller than Thyme pictured from the photographs she remembers from her mother's trip to DC. The dome is made of tarnished copper instead of the iconic bubble topped with the Statue of Freedom. The overall proportion of the building is currently being revised, scaffolding surrounding the structure as renovation occurs on all sides.

"The intent is to expand until the site more closely matches the historical accord, something nearly approximating what you might be familiar with in the future," Senator Mangum informs.

"The Capitol is in a museum in my future," Honor says, "under the same roof as the Empire State Building and Wrigley Field."

"Do you keep Mount Rushmore in there, too?" Thyme quips.

"Ridiculous," Honor replies. "There would never be room for eight mountainous heads in there. How big do you think Artifact Hall is?"

Thyme blinks. Shrugs. Turns back to the Capitol being renovated in 1841with massive earthmovers working on three sides and big yellow cranes lifting pieces into place. Construction workers that might've been at home on an LA freeway in 2023 survey the project in hardhats and tool-belts, among skid steer loaders and diggers. Modernity manipulating antiquity.

Thyme wears long sleeves and a dress tight at the waist and shaped in a bell that almost drags on the ground, a layered muslin pelerine draped over her shoulders. Her black boyish hair is mostly covered by a sugar scoop bonnet the color of daisies. Honor uses a broad-brimmed hat to disguise her bald head and glowing tattoo, a blue gown covered by a brown cape that makes her look more Elizabeth Bennet than Katniss Everdeen. At the equivalent age of forty, she looks like she's three cats away from being a spinster. Jay wears a dark coat over a white cotton shirt with a cravat and tan trousers, as handsome as Thyme has seen him in all these years. She can't help but steal sidelong glances at Jay every few moments ever since they came across from 2057.

In the old 1841, the small group standing on the Capitol Mall would have drawn stares. An Asian teenager, an African American man, and a bald woman of indiscriminate descent mingling with a prominent white United States Senator would have been unprecedented. Now, passersby walk past with nary a glance. Plenty of tourists have come through town this last e-year.

Senator Mangum examines Thyme with a tilted head, as if he can't quite believe what he's being told. "You're my descendent from 2023. My great-granddaughter."

"Add about three 'great's to that and you might be close," Thyme says.

"Times certainly change," he comments, probably referring to Thyme's ethnicity. "I'm glad you came to me for help. If you had approached President Harrison, he would've been duty-bound by law to detain you."

"And you're not?" Thyme asks.

"I'm a lame-duck senator. My days in the Congress of the United States, I am afraid, are numbered. Every politician on the Hill will be running to represent 1841 in the new Congress. I don't stand a chance. Besides, this is about family."

Thyme tells him that it was her own grandson, another of the senator's descendants, that sent the fugue-bomb to DC. The connections stretch across generations and geography.

Then sound erupts from the breast pocket of his suit coat, Johnny Cash's "Man in Black." Senator Mangum pulls out a modern device even more futuristic than Thyme's iPhone from 2023. "These things are a marvel. Sending letters over great distances without taking pen to paper."

"Do you have news?" Thyme asks, impatient to get information before the fugue-bomb detonates and she forgets everything.

Everything.

Efren thought she so easily rushed headlong into action because she wanted to rescue 1841 from amnesia and protect the United States of Time from the Chronfederacy. But even as Thyme stepped across from 2057, she wasn't so sure whether she meant to stop the bomb or embrace its effects. Maybe she wasn't here to save the day but to bask in the shockwave. She could forget her mother, her home, this topsy-turvy world. She decided in 2118 that she didn't want to lose those memories, but would she mind losing those memories? She could start anew with Jay without the memory of the infinite minute of her mother's death, or of a future where she married a boy she barely knew.

"Intelligence from 2057 suggests that the fugue-bomb was smuggled into Quad-City," Senator Mangum says.

"Oh," Honor sighs. "I believe Langston Hughes wrote,

'And the whole world has to answer right now just to tell you once again, 'Who's bad?'"

"That was Michael Jackson," Thyme corrects. "And I don't know what you're even talking about."

"It means that it is not good news."

"What's Quad-City?" Jay asks.

"It was renamed after the Freeze. The city sits in the location formerly known as Wilmington, Delaware," Honor answers. "If the bomb goes off there, it would wipe memories from 1841 Washington, DC, all the way up to 1980 New York City."

Thyme looks at Jay and Honor. The rest of the fobs were supposed to be safe. But Shep and Efren and Candy are still in danger of involuntary amnesia. And they don't even know it.

***

They spend the night at a hotel on the outskirts of Quad-City, in a place called the Darragh Tavern in New Castle, Delaware. It is 4:52 p.m. at the end of March in 1841, the sun suspended some two-and-a-half standard hours from setting. Yet certain circadian rhythms have been habit for life, and call to the fobs as they make their way north. Despite afternoon appearances, everyone in the small town is asleep as they stroll into New Castle.

"We'll get into Quad-City in two e-hours on foot," Thyme tells. "Let's get some rest until Senator Mangum calls with an update on the f-bomb situation."

Jay and Honor nod wearily. In a world without seconds and hours and days, one might not need to eat or sleep or use the restroom for anything besides actually powdering one's nose, but the absence of any of those regularities takes a toll. Rest and recuperation are still requirements for being active lest the mind devolves into a sort of exhausted dementia. And food is still a guilty pleasure, with the biological byproducts of ingestion a fair price to pay.

Honor checks them in using a set of forged papers provided by Shepherd before they had gone their separate ways in 2057. No one dared give the gruff girl guff about the specifics of their fake IDs, no one eager to elongate the excruciating experience of being excoriated by the unpleasant 'morrow. Honor's abrasiveness, once an irritant, has become an asset.

Jay is asleep in moments, snoring like a lumberjack on the floor in the corner of the room that looks like some historical recreation of a colonial bed-and-breakfast. Modern conveniences like a digital clock placed on the nightstand and a small mini bar stacked with flasks of futuristic alcohol recall somedays rather than yesteryears. There's one bed, big and frilly, and the girls are tucked in side by side.

"Do you think we can change the future, Honor?"

"This is not going to turn into one of those pathetic heart-to-heart conversations where we do each other's makeup and share our feelings and become best friends forever, is it?"

"It would take both of us having a heart," Thyme snaps, wondering why she even bothers. "Or feelings."

"Good," Honor sighs. "I hate makeup."

"Never mind, Honor."

There's silence for some time. Thyme assumes the 'morrow has fallen asleep. Jay sounds like a bear grumbling in its cave, discontent with hibernation. Outside, instead of the familiar sounds of traffic and sirens and an occasional airplane, there's the whinny of a passing horse and the clangor of the blacksmith across the road and the melody of drunken locals walking home from Darragh Tavern singing, "I'm bringin' sexy back."

"You cannot change the future, Thyme. It is already happening. Tomorrow is today is yesterday. But we can stop the fugue from affecting our friends. We can make a difference right here in the present. In all the presents."

"Our friends," Thyme repeats. Honor Fitzgerald has come a long way since 2803. Jay. Efren. Candy. Shepherd. They're everything Thyme has left. She ran away from 2023 to escape being stuck in an infinite minute where nothing ever changed, and now she runs toward a situation in motion, a crisis that can change everything.

"Efren believes he and I are destined to fall in love," Thyme whispers in the dim interior, afternoon light leaking in a little around the draperies.

"Are we going to talk about boys?"

"We don't have to talk about anything, Honor."

"I hate talking about boys."

Thyme really wishes Candy would've come along instead. Candy understands that the way things are isn't the same as the way things were. And she likes boys just fine.

"Efren Cortez still thinks of time as a tower that you build from the foundation up, but the tower is already here," Honor explains. "Each level of the tower already exists. You can remodel it, gut it, and build it anew, but what you do on the 2023rd floor will not affect what happens on the levels above or below it. The tower stands outside todays and tomorrows."

"That makes sense," Thyme tells.

"Of course it does," Honor says, "or I would not have said it."

Honor has a computer in her brain. Since she's from the future, she knows a lot. She thinks she knows everything. Maybe she knows enough....

Some questions are easier in the dark.

"Do you know who my father is?" Thyme asks.

"You do not?"

"No."

"Well, this is neither the time nor the place."

"I want to know," Thyme says.

"Then let us get the fugue-bomb disarmed and make our way to the Minute. You can look it up yourself online when we get to the Institute. It is a school, after all, and schools are meant for learning."

And with that, Honor promptly falls asleep, as if she has a switch and she flipped it. Thyme lays there for a long time, thinking about the past and the identity of her father, the piece of the puzzle that connects her to the Caucasian Senator Willie Mangum. She ponders the future and the son she has with Efren that will connect her to Dr. Thomas Cortez in 2118. She considers the present, when she has feelings for a boy born before her grandmother, and lies beside a girl from the future who is her new best friend.

After a while, Thyme falls asleep, and morning comes too soon — 4:52 p.m. and the start of a brand new day.

***

The marketplace in Quad-City was formerly known as Wilmington circa 1841. The population of the city in the mid-nineteenth century was less than ten-thousand citizens. A quiet colonial town along the Christina River, it wasn't due for a population explosion for another twenty years. Now fifty-thousand people move through the marketplace every day.

"Quad-City is unique in all of Post-Freeze America," Honor explains as the trio of fobs meander among booths selling wares consisting of anything from virtual simulators advertised as "The Newest Gadget from 4807!" to a first edition Dracula signed by Bram Stroker to a stack of Rubik's Cubes featuring LED lights. "The Freeze divided the former city of Wilmington, Delaware into fourths. The marketplace is on the 1841 side and features a vast operation where peddlers offer their imported and vintage colonial goods to shoppers from all over time. It is a duty-free town where the laws of commerce and trade are suspended in an experimental setting. It is the test for things to come, or a cautionary tale of the excesses of sharing across eras."

"This is black market stuff in 1960," Jay says, eyeing a merchant offering saber-toothed tiger whelps mewling in a box in exchange for a hoverboard made after 2050. "What if we get caught here by a customs agent?"

"These dealers are entirely legitimate," Honor says. "We are far more likely to be spotted by border patrol than a customs agent."

That didn't seem to put Jay at ease. Thyme reaches out and takes his hand. He appears too old for her by ten years, so she doesn't do anything more to draw attention. The gesture is as chaste as a mother holding her toddler's hand while they cross the street. But Jay's eyes quit darting around like he's some little kid in an old-school candy store mesmerized by pulled taffy and licorice whips and brightly colored lollipops.

"The city is split four ways?" Thyme asks Honor. "When are the other three zones?"

"1980 is to the north in the most populous part of the city, which they renamed Brat Town. It is mostly a residential area, suburbs expanding to the north as citizens from the other three quadrants relocate to the outskirts."

"The 'burbs are getting filled up by people from 1841?"

Honor nods as she pauses, examining a table full of bobbleheads in the style of each of the hundred-and-fifteen American presidents. "Not only from this zone. The suburbs are the trendy destination for Quad-City folks going retro from 3214 AD and Homo neanderthalensis moving in from 215,138 BC."

"So Tami Tomorrow and Nancy Neanderthal are next-door neighbors in suburbia?"

"Quad-City is given great leeway by the federal government. Just as they approved the Mallory Norman Institute of Time, they also granted thousands and thousands of permits to the citizens of Quad-City to allow relocation from zone to zone." Honor pauses and holds out her hands, as if presenting a memorial at a staid ceremony. "It is a trial for the new America, to see if disparate eras can coexist without devolving into predictable violence."

"Noble intentions," Thyme says. "And Jefferson Davis and his Chronfederate goons are trying to ruin it all."

"We'll stop them," Jay says.

"Can we find them in time?" she asks. "It's like looking for a needle in a haystack made of years instead of straw. The terrorists could be hiding anywhere."

"The trio from 2118 came to us because they thought we might be able to help," Jay reminds Thyme. "They thought we knew more than we do. Or maybe they were on to something. Maybe we can learn more than a bunch of the president's stuffy men asking questions."

Jay surveys the vendors lining the streets of the marketplace. The palette of their skin is rarely white, usually one color or another in shades of earth. All the colors of the world. In 1841 as in 1960 and even in 2023, these are the people who don't trust the authorities. The past is the present. Minorities in all these time zones have been betrayed too many times by white people in power to be forthcoming to 19th Century Caucasian interrogators.

Jay approaches a young man of color hawking holodots, some sort of wearable tech from 2057. The black entrepreneur is maybe thirty in 1841, but he has a gravitas behind his dazzling smile that indicates he was an old man back in the future. Old enough to have seen his share of inequality. His expression turns from professional as he thanks a local white couple purchasing a pair of holodots to genuine as Jay steps up. The merchant's crisp suit is as prim and proper as his pitch. "You ready to get jacked in and ride the information highway, sir?"

"If I ride the highway, it's going to be in a Mustang with the windows down and my foot on the floor," Jay answers. "I am looking for information, though. Not the kind you get from a dot, either, big daddy."

Thyme rolls her eyes in the dramatic fashion of someone sixteen.

"We're looking for someone," Thyme tells the holodot vendor. He seems more receptive to answering questions from a pretty girl than someone awkward and anachronistic. "Have you seen anyone come through town in the last few e-days that might be…odd?"

"I've sold my merchandise to anyone, from a 'morrow who called these magical buttons 'vintage' and 'quaint,' to a Neanderthal who bowed to the dot like it was a god and managed the only words I think he knew. 'How much?'" the vendor replies. "Odd is all the time."

Thyme pauses. Thinks. Quad-City allows the best location for affecting everywhen from New York to Washington, DC, with the f-bomb, but the Grays would know someone might be searching for them. They had to have a place to hide.

"Has border patrol come through asking the same questions?" Thyme inquires.

"They're always asking questions," the vendor says. "We get a lot of illegal immigrants that come through the marketplace."

"What did you tell them?"

"I told them that I sell holodots. If they want information, they can buy a holodot and surf the ether."

"You don't sell out potential clients to the feds," Thyme suggests.

"Bad for business," the holodot hawker confirms.

"How about a good customer who wants to know where folks who don't want to be found might find a place for rest?"

"How good of a customer?"

Thyme considers her wristwatch stuck at 7:30. She got it from her mother for her birthday when she turned ten. It's the last reminder. If the fugue-bomb goes off, it will be all that's left of Rikona Mugen. If the fugue-bomb goes off…. We will stop it.

"A 2023 original," Thyme offers, handing over the wristwatch.

The holodot dealer examines it. Runs his thumb across the face. Scrutinizes it front and back. Nods.

"Try the Nexus Hotel at the very center of Quad-City. Tell them Ben Ross sent you."

***

Current America is a fractured republic composed of fifty individual time zones. Quad-City is located on a fault-line of four disparate eras. And in the middle of a split city in a broken nation is a building erected with a wing spanning each chronological quadrant. The structure in 1841 is a three-story brick building reminiscent of the time period. To all appearances, the brownstone built at the edge of the nucleus of four zones acts as the terminal point of 1841, but in fact the masonry façade masks construction that extends into the other three zones, attached rather than adjacent, all four quadrants secretly connected within one building that spans centuries.

Thyme tells the front desk clerk that Ben Ross sent her. The clerk takes them directly to a drawing room off the lobby, where they meet an illegal immigrant from 1960 who calls himself QT and acts like he's known Jay since forever simply because they come from the same zone.

"Which one of you is the traveler?" QT eventually asks after some old-school handshaking and a bunch of banter that might make sense to a Greaser or a Soc. He's eyeing Honor's attire like he already knows the answer, as she's been dressed in Shepherd's anachronistic clothes since she switched back in the twenty-first century.

"We left our traveler in 2057," Thyme says. "We're students enrolled at the Minute and en route to the Eighties."

"You're just kids?" QT sweeps his eyes back and forth as if suspicious he's being set up in a sting operation. "This is no place for children."

"We've done more time than any of your locals," Thyme says. "And we're here trying to stop 1869er terrorists from detonating a fugue-bomb that will make everyone from New York to DC forget everything they ever knew. They have a weapon from the future that can induce mass amnesia."

"Grays?"

"They mean to start another Civil War," Honor says. "Jefferson Davis wants to keep federal overreach out of the time zones at any cost. He does not want 1841 or 1980 or 1960 or anywhen else imposing its will on the rest of America."

"War," QT whispers. "The past is the present is the future. It always comes to war."

"Not if we can stop it," Thyme says.

"Is there anyone from 1869 staying at the Nexus?" Honor asks.

QT looks around the room. Thyme follows his gaze. The Nexus was built after the Freeze, but everything about the space is designed to fit the time period. No modern conveniences to convince customers that this is anywhen besides 1841. Gaslights illuminate the windowless room. The furnishings are turned wood and sourced from local lumber. Era-appropriate wallpaper decorates the walls. Seats covered in red leather look like they belong in the nineteenth century.

The primary purpose of the Nexus is to keep secrets. Protect clientele. QT is the caretaker of confidentiality.

"If I tell you where to find the '69ers, it'll mean my job," QT says.

"If you do not tell us where to find the Chronfederates, you will not remember what your job is anyway. Or your own name. Or if you have a wife and kids," Honor says. "So close to the detonation site, I do not know if you will even remember how to properly use the bathroom."

Jay looks at Thyme worriedly. He was never really warned how much he might forget if the f-bomb goes off in his face.

QT nods. He leads them over to a grandfather clock where the hands have been stopped at eight till five for months and months. He takes a last look back at the three fobs who are offering rescue from forgetfulness. Everyone has already lost their future—no one wants to lose their past. He turns the minute hand forward until it touches the twelve and something clicks inside a gearbox. The grandfather clock swings outward on hinges, revealing a passageway behind it.

"Batman?" Jay asks.

"Of course Batman," QT replies with a wide smile.

The corridor leads them back to where the Nexus Hotel appears from the exterior to have ended, but actually extends toward the next zone over, enclosed all the way across the border into three other time zones. Doors on either side are labeled with room numbers — 1841 AD on the first row and a room number below. 102, 103, 104, and so on. This is the secret part of the Nexus, the place where people pay extra to remain anonymous.

Where terrorists would go to hide.

"There are eleven rooms at the Nexus currently rented by '69ers," QT reveals, checking a device in his hand certainly beyond 1841 or 1960. "Odds are that the first few choices will end up being innocent patrons. By betraying their tenancy, it will mean my imminent termination. You kids better be right about this f-bomb."

Indeed, the first try reveals a woman from 1869 having a tryst with a 'morrow from 2803. The next room is occupied by a reporter from The Commercial Appeal writing an exposé on the misrepresentation of the forty-nine zones outside DC, currently governed by a congress elected before the Freeze. The third strike is a young man bartering passage to a future zone to undergo gender reassignment surgery.

Then they meet Gustavus Henry, a Confederate politician who served as the senator from Tennessee in the South's Congress during the first Civil War, in town to convince locals to support Jefferson Davis and secession from the Union all over again. The past is the present is the future indeed. The fobs sack the room while QT restrains the separatist stooge. There's no fugue-bomb among his possessions. Gustavus Henry might be a turd, but he isn't a terrorist.

"We need to find it before hotel security comes to relieve me of my duties," QT warns as they ascend the steps to the second floor. It won't be long before Gustavus Henry is discovered tied up in his room and reports them to the authorities.

They're running out of time.

Thyme pauses. She stands on the top step, the other two fobs and QT behind her. Down the hall, two démodés that were walking toward them suddenly halt in their tracks. One of them is carrying the case that Thyme last saw aboard the train in the possession of the trio of androgynous 'morrows.

These two terrorists have the f-bomb.

They run. Thyme chases.

CHAPTER THIRTEEN
06:46
7.09.215,138 BC
Quad-City, Delaware

Thyme pursues the two terrorists right through the border between zones, changing from sixteen to seven in the blink of an eye. The transformation in the length of her legs makes her stumble, even as both démodés cross over in their twenties and sprint fast, widening the gap between the fleeing 1869ers and the fobs.

Jay becomes elderly and Honor stalls as a toddler with even shorter legs than Thyme. QT turns from a man in his forties to an adolescent who looks like he ought to be headed to the Minute with the rest of the fobs. He should've been faster than any of them, but he purposely stays at the rear, jogging slowly behind a scampering Honor.

"Is this the stone age?" Jay asks QT.

"We call it Bedrock," QT says. "It's like hanging out with dozens of Bam-Bams."

The terrorists are already down the hall and through the door at the far end before Thyme barely gets halfway down the corridor. The doors on either side of the hallway now read 215,138 BC on the first row and 260, 259, 258 on the second row. She feels stuck in amber as she pumps her knees as hard as she can down the hall and still moves at half speed. Thyme, only fifty pounds and thin as a sapling, hits the exit doors at the end of the corridor and bounces off a closed exit-way constructed of imported steel. Jay, panting like a winded dog, arrives and helps her shove the door open.

The other side is something entirely different from the hall behind her. Thyme steps into a rocky hollow with paintings decorating the walls, stick figures of cavemen fighting saber-toothed tigers and making fire. There are openings along the rocky wall all down the craggy corridor, hotel rooms marked with slash marks instead of actual numbers. As QT and Honor step into the quartz cavern with Thyme and Jay, the door closes behind them. From this side, the door mimics a slab of stone set against a granite wall.

"The Nexus is set up the same in all four sections of Quad-City," QT explains as he jogs down the corridor carved from solid earth, bringing up the rear of the group of fobs. "The innermost rooms of the hotel act as the secret intersecting place where fobs complete their illicit business. The outermost rooms facing each of the four time zones serve as a façade of sorts, a normal local hotel serving law-abiding citizens."

Neanderthals poke their heads out of cave openings on either side of the narrow gorge, cavemen looking quizzical, more confounded than even their normal expression of perpetual perplexity. Thyme wonders if the Freeze and all its illogical ramifications is impossible to comprehend by the rudimentary intelligence of early homo sapiens. She can't understand it herself with an extra 200,000 years of evolution.

"Wha?" chirps one Neanderthal. Then another, "Wha?" Soon, like a flock of birds start chirping in a chorus, dozens of confused cavemen repeat, "Wha? Wha? Wha? Wha?"

Thyme ignores them. Jay tries to keep pace with the dashing six-year-old. Honor follows unsteadily. QT stops and tries to calm the panicky Paleolithic crowd.

Down a steep incline to the first-level cave system, they race past the lobby where a front desk is carved from limestone. The clerk on duty looks like a bamboozled Barney Rubble, standing entirely erect with a tie around a beefy neckline and wearing a name tag with a picture of a stick figure that might have been a self-portrait. A hominid who is either a hairy man or a balding ape stands sentry as a bellhop, aged and stooped, his wait for new tenants interrupted by scampering fobs. The free coffee bar features swill standing in a stone bowl, more swamp water than arabica. Granite tablets with hieroglyphics stacked at the entrance act as the free morning edition of the stone age news, and a warning of a strict "no smoking" policy is posted in hysterical hieroglyphics carved right into the cave wall — a painting of fire with an "X" through it.

The foursome stumbles out the open mouth of a grotto and into a land of lush vegetation as thick as an African jungle. Thyme plunges through the thick fronds without hesitation despite Honor's small squeaky voice crying out for caution. Thyme is determined to catch the terrorists and not about to wait for the toddling 'morrow, but she swears Honor said something about a "saber-toothed tiger."

"Just leave me alone, Honor," Thyme mumbles under her

breath, running and running.

Alone.

Thyme stops and looks around. She's in the middle of a clearing about the size of a Starbucks. Green is everywhere, vibrant and alive and endless. Fronds mask direction every which way she turns, so north-south-east-west means as much as minutes, her internal compass as inert as the clocks. Which way did the terrorists go? Where are Jay and Honor? What direction does she go where she won't be lost forever in this prehistoric past?

She is alone for the first time since she left 2023. Really alone. She can hear her own breathing, whistling loudly through gritted teeth. It's not the only breathing. There's something else. She's not alone after all.

A saber-toothed tiger creeps out of the underbrush, crouched as if its every step might be to pounce. It circles Thyme, a low growl in its throat like a powerful engine revving for top speed. Tusks like razors gleam in the cascade of sunbeams coming through the canopy of trees. More powerful than the great cats she visited at the Los Angeles Zoo with her mother when she was a kid, this creature appears designed for the sole purpose of killing.

The saber-toothed tiger crouches, opening its mouth to reveal rows of weapons dripping with saliva. It pounces, and the cat hangs in the air for an infinite minute, something beautiful and terrifying and definite in every twitch of muscle and gnash of teeth. Thyme looks into its eyes and sees death. Past. Present. Future. Death is everything and all things. Eras might be turvy and curvy, lost in a loop. Tomorrow is trapped, somedays on perpetual pause. But there's still always an end. Everything eventually dies. Even time.

Even Thyme.

A spear punctures the saber-toothed tiger's throat, driving the animal down with a sickening thump, cracking jaw and breaking legs. The cat is already dead before it hits the ground. A Neanderthal stands at the perimeter of the clearing, watching Thyme like she's an alien in a sci-fi flick. He looks different from the caveman in the lobby back in the Bedrock section of the Nexus Hotel. Unruly hair covers his body, a mane that recalls the lions from the exhibit at the Los Angeles Zoo framing his face. His forehead is more sloped than the clerk at the hotel, his face rangy and shaped like a cinderblock.

"'Mo?" he asks.

Thyme points to herself. "I'm a 'morrow, yes," she says. "You live out here?" No reply. "Home?"

The Neanderthal must understand rudimentary English. He points to an opening in the earth several yards away, a cavern that leads underground. Below. Away from the rest of civilization. There is separation even in these times. This caveman is of lower social stature than the desk clerk and the hotel patrons. Someone always finds a reason to separate society into classes.

"Which way to the hotel?" Thyme asks.

"This way." Honor stands at the edge of the clearing beside Jay, who is huffing and puffing so hard he can't catch his breath.

"Thank you," Thyme calls over her shoulder as she sprints after Honor, no time to waste. The Neanderthal stares after her with a vacant expression. Her clueless hero.

Through thick undergrowth, the three fobs exit at the edge of the next zone. A scarlet curtain of light separates 215,138 BC from the future. A wall of water rises a hundred yards into the sky, suspended in place by a breakdown of gravity. The next zone is undersea. Stations have been placed along the border between time zones, steel cubicles with metal wheels locking massive iron doors.

"Pressure chambers," Honor explains. "You must acclimate the body to the submersibles in 3214. The démodés are already through. Acclimation takes sixty-six e-seconds."

"Then let's get to the future," Thyme says, running toward an empty pod.

Chapter Fourteen

17:07

9.27.3214 AD

Quad-City, Delaware

Back to the future. Surrounded by an ocean, Thyme is twelve. Honor aged to look twelve also. Jay got younger, the same age as the girls. A trio of tweens.

Honor points to the metal wheel once the three fobs are inside the pressurization chamber that extends underwater farther into the future. Thyme turns it until the entire structure glows green and softly pulsates. There are vents in the ceiling that activate. The room pressurizes, although Thyme doesn't feel a thing.

"What happened to the future?" Jay asks as they wait, sixty-six e-seconds like an eternity.

"Global warming?" Thyme guesses.

Honor frowns, glares. "I suppose you believe in plagues of locusts and natural selection as well. Do any of you study the future in school?" Honor pauses and takes a deep breath.

"Nature has its surprises. Tectonic shifts will lead to a global event. The rich flee to great seafaring constructs like The Bubble here. The poor gather in the ten percent of dry land that remains after the oceans rise. They have to fight for every acre against a population that counts some fifty billion at the time of the flood. Compounding the plight of the common folk is the ferocity of futuristic predators trying to survive on the scant soil left above sea level. The creatures were originally genetically engineered to reduce the overpopulation of woodland prey, and instead the beasts pick off the last remnants of stranded mankind."

"My God, it sounds brutal."

"It is fascinating," Honor says. "The sanctimonious 'morrows of 3214 purport strict pacifism, yet when it came to sink or swim, they left behind ninety-nine percent of the population to fend for themselves."

"The cream always rises to the top," Jay says.

"The future is the past is the present," Thyme observes yet again.

"I hate that humankind can never learn from what has gone before," Honor says.

"Maybe they'll learn from the past and the present and the future all existing simultaneously," Jay suggests. "Three lessons simultaneously."

Thyme gazes behind her out a portal in the decompression tank, thinking back to the zones she has seen since she left 2023. She shakes her head. Maybe humankind is incapable of learning some things.

The green pulses pick up tempo. Almost acclimated.

"Yet now these rich 'morrows are docked on dry land," Thyme points out, looking ahead at the future. The part of Quad-City in 3214 is a massive translucent structure that contains affluent survivors of a future flood like some AD ark. The Bubble is as big as a biodome, housing thousands of 'morrows and anchored to the past.

"Indeed. There are invaluable natural resources in the past that have been drowned and washed away by the future floods or used up by a so-called altruistic aristocracy. The patrician pacifists could never trade with the savage survivors on the scant islands remaining in 3214. For these 'morrows, the Freeze is a miracle. The Bubble was running out of food and supplies. Without the intervention of broken time, time would have run out for these idgits." Honor wears a smug expression regarding the fate of the 'morrows some four-hundred years in her future.

"Really, Honor, no one says 'idjit.'"

"Sounds like these 'morrows were served some cold karma," Jay says. "They leave the less fortunate to fend for themselves on scraps of dry land while they float above it all, and then fate turns the tables on them. Maybe they're getting what they deserve for being so selfish."

"I don't know who's more uncivilized," Thyme wonders. "The Neanderthals behind us or the 'morrows in front of us."

"What makes us the same is more eternal than the things that make us different, Thyme," Honor says.

"So we find enemies in every era, over and over and over?"

"It is not all bad. There is some good. A mix," Honor says as the blinking stops and the doorway forward begins to open. Unexpected optimism from the 'morrow. "I believe it was Barack Obama who once said, 'You—'"

Thyme interrupts, "This isn't going to be Obama."

"I think it is," Honor says.

"Who's Obama?" Jay asks.

Thyme blinks, aghast at the black tween boy. "President Obama? The black president?"

"The black president? I thought there were all kinds of presidents of color."

"There are," Honor says. "Thyme is just so 2023."

"Say it, Honor. So I can tell you it isn't Obama."

"You take the good. You take the bad. You take them both and there you have the facts of life."

"That's a sitcom theme song," Thyme says with a drawl. "Not a presidential speech."

"Well, it should be," Honor says in defense. "It means there is good and bad. And if we take them both—accept them both—maybe then we can find friends."

Thyme blinks, staring at Honor and wondering if she's really hearing what she's hearing. She moves her eyes toward Jay and then back to Honor. Friends.

Now the door is ajar and they race onward, a preteen trio careening down the hallway at full speed, a light-footed sprint unique to twelve-year-olds. Thyme takes point, Jay easily keeping pace, Honor's enhanced physicality in a reduced gear so she won't overtake the démodés. The corridors are transparent tubes surrounded by water, strange lifeforms passing in the deep water, exterior lights illuminating genetically modified creatures that appear like they came from outer space.

"They have a pretty good head start," Thyme says, nearly out of breath.

"They need time to set up. It will take a significant power source to boost the signal to reach a hundred-and-fifty-mile radius. Assembly and set-up will take time. They need to lose us so they can properly prepare the fugue-bomb," Honor says. "If we can keep them running, they will not have a single moment to finalize."

The maze of passageways leads back to the Nexus Hotel (a tunnel that reminds Thyme of her friend Carmen's clear plexiglass hamster tubes). The corridor opens on a vast central atrium converted to a lobby area. A humanoid, looking no closer to anyone in 2023 than the Neanderthal who saved Thyme from the saber-toothed tiger in the Stone Age, stands behind a translucent desk that glows like the pressurization chamber back on the border with BC. More robot than receptionist, the clerk stands perfectly still and expressionless, watching the fobs chase across the lobby like they are skittering cockroaches.

Signs embedded in the walls are like rainbows that flicker and fade as they fly through the lobby. The words are a mixture of letters and images, another language. One must be a sign that says, "No smoking," holographic flames snuffed by animated rainfall. Pneumatic tubes that appear to serve as transport for baggage intersect in an area near the front desk. Thyme feels like she's running through a video game.

Thyme skids to a stop at the other end of the lobby. There's water outside in every direction, clear walls a dozen stories straight up with water all around. To all appearances, it's a dead end. But the other branches of the Nexus Hotel had hidden passageways near the nexus of the four timelines where illicit clients may take lodging. There must be a secret doorway.

Thyme stalks to the front desk and the bio-mechanical attendant. "Which way did those démodés go?" Thyme slaps the countertop authoritatively.

The clerk doesn't blink. No change in facial arrangement. Not even a flinch. The future has created a customer service attendant who cannot be intimidated.

"Allow me." Honor sniffs haughtily and starts speaking Esperanza. The clerk listens intently.

Thyme is mesmerized by the sea surrounding them. The Bubble is hundreds of fathoms under the surface. Outside in the dark waters of the ocean depths, more strange things swim by — creatures out of Jules Verne, monsters from Loch Ness, glowing things that remind her of a movie she saw with Jiji when she was younger called The Abyss, and something that even looks mostly humanoid. She stands at the transparent wall that separates her from certain crushing death. Jay stands beside her.

"The future. The past. The present where my mother died," Thyme tells Jay. "None of it makes sense. I keep waiting to figure it out. To understand why. I think if I only have enough time that maybe I can come to terms with it. But we never get it. People never learn. How many examples of that do I need to see? We get over one way to hate and we find another. People discover endless new ways to oppress. Geniuses solve one mystery and create a dozen more. We claim to know it all, but we simply ignore our own ignorance, like those fools from 3627. Humanity declares pacifism here in 3214 and then these insufferable 'morrows let billions of people suffer. I keep waiting for answers, but there are only more questions."

Thyme leans forward, forehead against the surface of the Bubble. A single tear tracks her cheek and touches the interior surface of the barrier, a thin border between a single salty tear and an endless amount of saltwater.

Behind Thyme and Jay, Honor starts yelling. The clerk stares ahead without expression. It reminds Thyme of the look on Jay's face when the Neanderthals in the Bedrock wing were saying, "Wha-wha-wha-wha." Or the expression Honor has had in reaction to everything Thyme has ever said. Now Honor is getting a taste of her own magniloquence.

"You are ridiculous," Honor says in plain old-fashioned 2023 lingo.

The 'morrow answers in something from another language that is short and emotionless.

"Nothing," Honor says through gritted teeth. "This attendant will not direct us to the démodés because he thinks we will hurt them. He makes a claim of pacifism. I told the fool that no one is going to know violence from peacefulness once we forget everything, but apparently pompous 'morrows like this one believe they are immune to primitive technology from 2118. This coming from people who flooded their own future and were gasping and dying at the edge of extinction until the Freeze saved them. To embrace nonviolence rather than fight for what is right is not wisdom. It is weakness."

"We need to know where the Chronfederates went," Thyme says. "We're running out of time."

Honor spins around in a circle, searching for some secret passageway like the granite slab concealed in Bedrock or the grandfather clock in 1841. She's the closest of the three fobs to thinking like someone from 3214, but she can't figure out where the two terrorists went from here.

The attendant at the front desk stares at Thyme and Thyme gazes back, the tear still standing on her cheek. Their eyes meet, and something passes between them beyond years or language or social status. There is heart, and heart is eternal. The attendant points to a section of a wall like all the others. Thyme runs toward it, Jay and Honor right behind her.

QT steps out of the deep, like a mermaid emerging from the surf. The leagues of seawater ought to have crushed him like a tin can in the ocean depths, but he's unscathed. He presents as little older than the three tween fobs, but what he does not appear is wet. QT is completely dry. Impossible.

"It's a hologram," QT says. "The secret passage back to the Nexus is this way. Hurry!"

And like runners racing when the starting gun goes off, all three fobs sprint through the hidden doorway that mimics the sea.

CHAPTER FIFTEEN
1:15
10.11.1980 AD
Quad-City, Delaware

Thyme exits the compression chamber on the other side of 3214 approximately the same age as the day she lost her mother. She feels like she's back to where she started, all those miles and still sixteen, still a new orphan, still grieving for the loss of the one person who meant everything to her.

QT points down a corridor with doors all marked with 1980 on one row and numbers starting at 101 below and ascending into the distance. "I saw them when I came over from 1841. When they entered the compression chamber, one of them was incredibly old. He was carrying a baby in one arm and a case in the other. They both turned into men in their thirties here in Brat Town. They ran that way."

"And you didn't try to stop them?" Thyme asks, exasperated.

QT came over pretty old himself and twitchy as a nervous

cat. No one is going to mistake him for a hero. He seems like he's ready to run or cry or both. Maybe amnesia would be a blessing, for he could forget his betrayal of his duties and misremember the last e-hour of events along with the rest of his life.

Thyme doesn't pause to wait for QT's answer. She runs to the end of the hallway in the secret center part of the Nexus Hotel, pushing open a door that leads into the main run of hotel rooms in 1980. The backside of the hidden passageway is concealed by a cardboard cutout of Jaclyn Smith, Cheryl Ladd, and Kate Jackson posed as Charlie's Angels. The fobs race along the hallway to the lobby and pour out into a main atrium that is kitschy and cool.

The Nexus Hotel was built after the Freeze, so the eighties theme is less authentic and more iconic. Madonna plays over the intercom, "Material Girl" the soundtrack to the decade. A tourist who resembles the androgynous natives from 3627 plays Pac-man in a corner arcade. Two Neanderthals are parked in front of a square television box showing Punky Brewster. A teenager in a miniskirt and blue mascara is probably a senior citizen from 2057 reliving her glory days.

Madonna switches to Cyndi Lauper. "If you're lost you can look and you will find me. Time after time."

"Sylvia Plath?" Honor asks, listening to the lyrics.

"No," Thyme says. "Just, no."

Thyme doesn't recognize most of the artifacts decorating the lobby and entertaining the guests, but there are some familiar items. Care Bears. Star Wars. McDonald's. Coca Cola. A mother sits with her daughter on a long sofa in the lobby, the one that appears younger reading Shakespeare and the older one braiding a Barbie's hair.

"Some things never change," Thyme tells. "There are things that are timeless."

Across the vast lobby, the Chronfederate terrorists emerge from behind a car called the General Lee, advertised on the placard as a full-sized replica from The Dukes of Hazard. It's orange and gaudy and perfectly representative of Brat Town. The Grays both came over into 1980 young and fit. Thyme is sixteen, Honor in her thirties, and Jay maybe forty. QT is elderly. Still, it's two against four.

Then fobs start pouring into the lobby from a half dozen different entryways. Each squad appears as if it originated in a different zone, Chronfederate sympathizers from 215,138 BC, 2057, 1841, 3627, 1929, and right here in 1980. Like gangs, they group with their chronological counterparts in six sets of three or four members each. As if on cue, Jay from 1960 says, "There's gonna be a rumble."

"The feds will be here any moment," QT warns. "You all better skedaddle."

No one skedaddles. Honor, ever logical, turns to Thyme as Thyme realizes what this confrontation means. These Chronfederates allies are meant as a distraction. The fobs have been under the assumption that the fugue-bomb needed a power source and auxiliary equipment, but if they're willing to publicly expose themselves like this when the feds will arrive any moment....

"They have not been running away," Honor realizes. "They have been circling back. The bomb is not in the case. It must be already prepared for detonation. We probably interrupted them on their way to activate the f-bomb. They have led us in a loop almost back to when we began."

"What's in the case?" Thyme asks.

"Maybe the detonator?" Honor guesses. "Or the access

codes?"

"They're really gonna do it?" QT whispers.

"Certainly. They're going to blow it up as soon as they get back to 1841," Thyme says.

Between the three fobs trying to stop them and the two terrorists about to change the world, yet again, are gathered about twenty Gray sympathizers ready to stop Thyme and her friends. QT blinks, turns, and dashes back the way he came. It's now three against twenty.

A voice from behind them says, "That guy took the first chance he had to high tail it and ran away."

Thyme turns. It's Efren Cortez, standing near the front desk to the Brat Town section of the Nexus. He's wearing light blue pants and a silky shirt that looks like some futuristic paint monster vomited all down the front. He seems to fit right in between slush puppies and Teddy Ruxpin.

"I thought I told you to go to New York," Thyme snaps.

"I'm not going to be that guy," Efren says, pointing after QT. "Besides, you told me to go to 1980. Well, here I am."

"Since you're here," Jay says, "we can use an extra hand. We need to get the two Grays in the back. That means we have to get through the rest of them."

Thyme evaluates the field of opponents. She's reminded of a Michael Jackson video from this decade where a bunch of monster-zombies dance in unison. The music is right, but the Chronfederate sympathizers have no rhythm. They rush toward the fobs in a chaotic, uncoordinated mass.

"You're going to get yourself killed," Thyme tells Efren as the enemy charges.

"It almost sounds like you care." Efren wears a satisfied little smirk.

"I've always cared," Thyme says. "You just want me to jump right from point A to point Z. I want to explore the rest of the alphabet, Efren Cortez."

The boy from 1960 stands at her right. She peeks at him out of the corner of her eye and Efren notices.

"You're stuck on the letter Jay," Efren says sarcastically.

And then they attack, two groups of Chronfederates that consist of 'morrows and démodés fighting together so they don't have to live together. All of them are trogs who don't want immigrants polluting infinite timelines. They work together so they can stay apart.

Efren gets punched by a scrappy local in a polyester suit and pink tie. Efren hits the ground, unconscious approximately sixty e-seconds after he arrived. A Neanderthal wraps hands as big as a gorilla's around Jay's throat, lifting the full-grown man off his feet. Honor faces four 'morrows from 3627. A gang of gangsters from 1929 approaches Thyme, wearing white suits with black stripes and matching fedoras, with big cigars stuck out of the corners of their mouths.

Thyme pulls her last bouncy out of her pocket. It's the only thing she has left from the other side of this adventure. New clothes. No more wristwatch from her mother. Strangers had become her friends. Just one remaining beyoncé to get her out of a jamb.

Efren is unconscious. Jay has broken the Neanderthal's grip and now scoots around him like Tyson Fury in the ring with Ali. Honor stands among a fallen foursome from the future, the quartet defeated by the super-scary 'morrow. She stares down a group from 1841 as they advance next. Thyme retreats a few steps as the gang from 1929 gets close.

"They still have bowling in 2803?" Thyme asks Honor as they stand back-to-back.

"We do not engage in pointless activities like 'pastimes,' but I am familiar with the concept."

"Then use that genetically enhanced superbod and point me thataway," Thyme says, indicating the direction where the pair of Grays exited the 1980 lobby.

Thyme activates the beyoncé around her and Honor, ever the intellectual, proves herself equally adept at sports. Honor sprints backward toward a wall with a vintage Jaws poster on it, runs up the shark, and pushes off the surface into the beyoncé, punching the big balloon and launching Thyme across the room. Thyme has to sprint like a hamster in one of those plastic balls, dashing along inside the sphere so that she doesn't fall down and flip with the revolutions of the bouncy. The gang of gangsters gets bowled over like pins. A group of surprised 2057ers scatters before Thyme picks them up as a spare. A Neanderthal tries to grab the bouncy but the slick sphere slips away, momentum and the motion of Thyme's legs taking her the rest of the way across the room.

She deflates the beyoncé and steps out of the inflatable. Thyme steals one glance back and Honor and Jay are outnumbered against the Chronfederate sympathizers. She must do this alone. Thyme races outside. Beyond the front entrance is the border to the next zone. The terrorists have already fled back into 1841. The border patrol agents that monitor emigration across state lines have gone inside the Brat Town lobby to see what all the commotion is about. Thyme can simply step across.

She pauses, recalling the rule of three. It's dangerous to cross the border by herself. Maybe there are wild wolves in 1841 patrolling the border in case of abandoned infants trying to cross timelines alone. Perhaps one of the Grays stayed behind to see if Thyme crosses over old and infirm, waiting to attack. It doesn't matter. She must take the chance. Thyme has to go alone.

If the fates decide to make her a baby as she goes across and she flip-flops helplessly on the edge of 1841, then two large cities will suffer mass amnesia. This young, chronological nation will plunge into another Civil War. It's a good thing Thyme doesn't believe in fate.

She crosses into 1841.

CHAPTER SIXTEEN
16:52
3.29.1841 AD
Quad-City, Delaware

It's different this Thyme.

She stands inside 1841. Her clothes fit a little tighter than all the time zones before. She feels different—something changed from all the ages she has experienced over the course of the journey across America or the sixteen years of her life before the Freeze. She steps forward toward the nearest retail booth, selling vintage 2057 artifacts like a mahogany mirror imported from tomorrow. Thyme studies her reflection, a young woman in her twenties who looks all adult.

Finally.

Countless time zones as a teen and a tween, a toddler or an infant, every age from newborn to sixteen, but never, ever older. Until now. She has finally grown up. Thyme peers back through the scarlet shimmer that separates different eras and sees the reflections of all that has been—her years back in Hollywood, the infinite minute she grieved for her mother after the Freeze, all the endless eras from one coast to the other. Histories and destinies and maybes and could-bes.

Thyme is finally beyond all those moments.

She never wants to forget this. The feeling of things being behind her, instead of stuck in amber all around her.

The marketplace sprawls all the way along the front of the Nexus Hotel, vendors and customers lining the roads through old Wilmington. Pushing through the crowd in the distance along this route is the pair of terrorists, one at the edge of elderly and the other less than ten. In her twenties and fit as a fiddle, Thyme finally has the advantage. She takes off after the Grays.

A large mob in front of a booth selling Beanie Babies slows the escaping terrorists enough so Thyme cuts the gap in half. Instead of through, the Grays go around. Thyme sneaks past a break in the crowd in front of two booths with no customers, competing vendors across from each other hawking scrunchies versus fanny packs. Thyme hears "half price" from her left side and "two-fer-one" on her right as she runs by. The Grays are only twenty yards in front of her, and Thyme is gaining fast.

"Hey, you need a license for that," shouts a 'morrow vendor.

"Weapon," screeches a démodé customer, dropping to the gravelly ground.

Stampede. Like blearing cattle startled and panicking. A wave of tourists rushes toward Thyme, citizens of every era across America and even from over the oceans, a cacophony of centuries flowing in her face. 503 AD. 2311 BC. 1911 AD. 1615 AD. 2775 AD. 215,138 BC. 1942 AD. She loses sight of the Grays in the flow of foreigners. When the panicking patrons finally finish flowing past her, the terrorists are the only two left along this stretch of the marketplace. Like an Old West outlaw challenging the sheriff on the streets of a one-horse town in 1911 Texas, the older of the two Grays faces Thyme with a weapon in his right hand.

The weapon is something from the future, one of the epochs when pacifism is apparently passé. It reminds Thyme of the Magic 8 Ball she passed on a table with other items for sale like Erector sets and Radical Robots. The orb in the graying Gray's hand sparks like a vintage 1930s Van de Graaff generator and sizzles like bacon on a first-edition George Forman Grill from 1994. Electricity leaps out from the ball, and everything stops.

Thyme's entire body seizes up, rigid as the surfboard signed by Duke Kahanamoku inches from where Thyme is stuck in synaptic paralysis. Electricity runs through her, tip to toes. Her brain cannot register impulses, stuck in a loop of memory, an infinite minute that turns 'round and 'round on the same thought — she's all grown up. She isn't sixteen and mourning her mother. She isn't thirteen and crushing on Jay Stone. Thyme is older than ten, where she needs someone taller like Efren to reach things off the top shelf. No more a toddler that needs to run three steps for everyone's one to keep pace with the older fobs. Being a baby is behind her, carried and coddled no more. She's no longer the sad, solitary girl from 19:30 on July the Sixteenth in 2023 who didn't have anyone to talk to — now she has Jay and Honor and Efren and Candy. Thyme is a woman, stuck in an infinite minute where the past is just past and the future can be anything and the present isn't so lonely anymore.

Thyme moves forward.

The Magic 8 Ball's effect is over.

The older Gray holds the line while the younger escapes. Throwing aside the drained electrical orb, he picks up something a little more comfortable to a Chronfederate from 1869. The graying Gray wields the sixteen-shooter Henry rifle like this isn't his first time shooting at someone. Thyme supposes he's a Civil War veteran, bullets striking close enough to ping in the dirt of the road at her feet. At the age of sixty, without glasses, Thyme is surely merely a blur in the distance, and the fact that he still aimed so close is a testament to his skill. If he had come over younger, Thyme would already be shot.

Thyme dives behind a table full of artifacts from the future, prices floating above each item as holographic numbers. Her hands still shake in the aftereffects of the Magic 8 Ball's zap. Perspiration covers her face in a sickly sheen. She pats down hair sticking in every direction. She must look like the Bride of Frankenstein, brought to life with a bolt of lightning.

The Gray takes another shot, a bullet ricocheting off the table leg six inches from Thyme's kneecap. All it will take is a little luck combined with his skills to perforate her new, adult body. She hasn't even had time to enjoy being beyond the turmoil of her teenage years before someone's trying to put holes in it.

The vendor for this booth had run off with the rest of the tourists and locals as soon as the Gray grabbed his first weapon. Thyme's skin still hums from the Magic 8 Ball attack. She flexes her fingers, almost expecting them to leak electricity. Thyme peeks over the top edge of the table, scanning the selection of wares arranged on its surface, each labeled with a virtual description below the price tag. There's something from the future that she has heard of before—a HaLiCon. They're the holographic robots that saved the fobs back in 1929. The control device is the size of a credit card and just as flat. She picks it up, and it activates at her touch. A single red laser beam points from the edge of the device and draws an outline on the gravel road. The neon light becomes three-dimensional. A full-sized Hard Light Construct manifests before her, eight feet tall and looking like a Transformer.

Thyme stands up behind the HaLiCon. At the other end of the fairway of dealers dealing historical wares, the Gray exchanges the nineteenth-century pistol for a modern military submachine gun. He aims and fires. Bullets ricochet off the construct's Hard Light hide. The machine made of solid light moves forward, and the Gray keeps firing, relentlessly, pointlessly. His purpose is to stop Thyme, or at least delay her as long as possible. The HaLiCon acts as an impenetrable shield.

The HaLiCon reaches the Gray and grabs him by the wrists, squeezing hard enough so that he drops his weapon. The machine made of solid light lifts the Chronfederate off the ground. Thyme runs by the Gray, leaving him suspended in the air by the Hard Light Construct. She sprints back into the Nexus Hotel and scans the lobby for the second Gray.

QT has doubled back and stands behind the front desk. He points to the mechanical room next to the bellhop's office. "He's in there."

"You came back," she says with a smile as she moves toward the mechanical room.

"Today is my day," QT replies. He might be from Jay's 1960, but he has made 1841 his home. He's ready to defend his adopted zone.

Thyme nods her thanks. She walks over and opens the door.

The Gray is inside. He's only a kid, no older than ten and ready to forget everything. How old was he in 1869? Had he witnessed such things that made him crave amnesia? What horrors were worth forgetting everything? For a while, Thyme wondered if erasing all her grief was worth making all the other stuff go away, too. But there's good with the bad with the blah. It's all mixed together and muddled. Like the past is the present is the future, all swirled and inseparable.

The Gray boy stands over a device that would fit right in to one of those futuristic movies that Jiji would watch on Saturday nights, like HAL 9000 in 2001: A Space Odyssey. The case is open and he has already connected the last component to the banks and clusters of blinking lights. The case contains the detonator, just as Honor had guessed. His finger hovers over a button, ready to push.

"Before you do it, tell me your name," Thyme pleads, holding her hands out, palms forward.

"What does it matter?" the Gray kid asks. He sounds nervous and scared. "You're going to forget in the next moment anyway."

"Have you ever heard of the infinite minute?" Thyme asks.

The Gray stares, but his finger stays off the button. He's shaking. Curiosity exists from the origins of man to the end of times. Nothing ever really changes. The kid wants to know. Or he wants a reason to wait.

Thyme continues. "It's the moment of the end. When something ceases to exist. They say it lasts forever, a second that stretches into eternity. You know, that bomb will make an infinite minute for you. For me. Wiping our memories is the end of everything we are. Erased. It will be the death of Thyme Mugen. I won't be me anymore. Or ever again. Everything I ever did or knew or felt will be gone. This next moment will be our infinite minute. Our forever. Our last breath. Since we're here between knowing and nothing, you and me, together, maybe I ought to know your name."

"It's Jeb Wheeler."

"Nice to meet you, Jeb," Thyme says. "Too bad we don't have a chance to get to know one another before we only know nothing."

Jeb still hasn't pushed the button. His eyes tell a different story than his face, full of youth and inexperience. There's something familiar in his gaze.

"The infinite minute," Jeb repeats. "What do you know about it?"

"When the clocks stopped, I lost my mother," Thyme tells. "She died. And I was stuck in that moment for a very long while."

Jeb still stays still. Stares at Thyme.

"I look like I'm ten," he finally says. Pauses. "But I'm seventeen years old in 1869. When the Freeze happened. My brother fought in the war. He's the other one you were chasing. His name is John. He's been taking care of me since I was a kid. You see, the last time I looked like this, I lost my folks. A fire. I was ten when they died. And even though time went on, seven more years until the clocks stopped, my heart stayed in that moment. In that infinite minute."

"Maybe we're not so different, Jeb," Thyme suggests, taking a step forward. "Maybe nothing ever really changes. But I wonder if that isn't so bad."

"I just want to forget," Jeb says.

"So did I," Thyme confesses. "But there are other ways. Because there will always be infinite minutes, Jeb. You erase the last one and there's going to be another, eventually. We suffered yesterday and we will suffer again someday. We can't forget every time something bad happens. We need to move on and get to tomorrow."

"How?" Jeb asks, tears blooming and tracing down his youthful cheeks.

"We'll learn how," Thyme tells. "There's a school in 1980. Come with me. We can learn together."

Thyme extends her arm, like a big sister asking her little brother to hold hands and cross a busy road. Jeb stares at the fugue-bomb, ready to detonate. He looks back at Thyme. Jeb can choose the future, or he can choose nothing at all.

The boy reaches out and takes Thyme's hand.

CHAPTER SEVENTEEN
1:15
10.11.1980 AD
New York City, New York

It is Thyme's birthday.

In measured moments, she's more seventeen than sixteen, but the clocks are still stopped and calendars make as much sense as the futuristic language Honor curses in when she gets angry, so Thyme picks a random occurrence to celebrate a new age. Her first day at the Minute seems as appropriate as any to start a new chapter in her life. She's had enough of being stuck at sixteen.

Thyme Mugen even looks a little older. When the fobs crossed over from 1841 to 1980, the border patrol had them go back and forth over the state line, changing age with every pass. It only took Thyme two attempts before she was about seventeen in New York and stayed that way. It took Honor twenty tries. Efren went back and forth for the equivalent of half a day before he finally came across into 1980 appearing about eighteen.

Candy Kane waits outside the classroom, leaning against the wall with her schoolbooks over her chest. There are eight boys

around her, all in love with the pretty blonde from 1948. Among
the ogling teens is Jeb Wheeler, former Gray and almost-terrorist,
back to being about seventeen and learning to live outside the
endless moment of loss. The smile that lights up his face in the
presence of Candy's beauty suggests he's figuring it out, little by
little.

"All right, boys, I think you all better get to class," Candy
says, and they scatter reluctantly but obediently. A pretty girl
and teenage boys. The future is the past is the present. Nothing
ever really changes.

"Our first class at the Minute," Thyme says, addressing
the momentous occasion.

"And it's your birthday!" Candy is wearing a dazzling
grin that leaves no secret why all the boys line up for a look.

"It was time I grew up a little," Thyme tells.

"I think we all grew up a little on that adventure," Candy
says, pushing open the door and walking in.

The first class of the first semester of the inaugural term at
the Mallory Norman Institute of Time is in the subject matter of
history. Of course it is.

Honor Fitzgerald and Efren Cortez sit at the front of
the class, heads together, whispering something that might be
secrets or may be comparing scholarly notes on the nature of
undiscovered centuries. Thyme waits for a pang of jealousy at
seeing the two so close, but there's nothing. Efren stops mid-
sentence as soon as he sees Thyme. There's something there in
his eyes. He still lives in their tomorrow, but Thyme must live for
today.

Honor is expressionless, still serious even after the
adventure is ended. Does she ever relax? She always appears to

be solving a trigonometry problem and composing a symphony at the same time. Honor isn't an easy person to have as a friend. But she's worth it.

"Happy birthday, old gal," Honor says. "You know, back home in 2803, you would be eight-hundred-and-two years old. Seventeen, in comparison, is refreshing."

"Thanks, Honor," Thyme replies. "I'll remember that next time I picture you when I first met you and you were like ninety years old."

Honor frowns, suddenly surly and appearing a lot older than her eighteen years. She will make one fantastic cantankerous old biddy when it's her time.

Thyme has never been a front-row kind of girl. She takes a desk in the back row and Candy sits across from her. Two boys immediately change seats so that one is in front of Candy and the other on her opposite side from Thyme. Like the sun, she will always have planets to orbit her.

Thyme stares at the door. Waiting. Even in a world without seconds, there's still a way to be late.

Ms. Norman arrives as the bell rings. She's about thirty years old in 1980 and lovely in an unconventional way, a mixture of different ethnicities, not unlike Honor. Momentarily escaped and soon recaptured by the Chronfederates in 1960 Las Vegas — able to commission Shepherd the traveler to find her missing students during her brief brush with freedom — Ms. Norman was held against her will all these last e-weeks, until finally liberated by a military strike force from 1841 at the same time Thyme was saving the day from the Grays. The founder of the Minute met her students at the White House where Thyme, Jay, Honor, and Efren were all pardoned by the president for any illegal immigration across state lines.

At the same time Ms. Norman arrived in 1841, Shepherd emigrated with Candy and the girl from 1960 rejoined her friends. The traveler kept to the shadows. Ms. Norman later told Thyme she thanked Shepherd privately, then he promptly disappeared. In a grand ceremony on the National Mall, the fobs were presented with the Presidential Timeless Medal, issued for the preservation of peace between eras. Citizens from 1841 and tourists from every zone made up a crowd of thousands, and Thyme was sure she saw her mother standing somewhere in the sea of people. For a moment, she thought maybe. Then for an infinite minute, she realized it couldn't be. Her heart twisted into a knot, again and again and again.

It never gets easier.

Thyme stares at the door to the classroom as Ms. Norman introduces herself to the class. Efren and Honor listen intently. Candy ignores the boys more interested in their classmate than the class itself, and she nods politely as Ms. Norman speaks. Thyme mastered long ago the art of looking like she's listening while concentrating on something else.

Before they left 1841, President Harrison had met with Thyme Mugen and Mallory Norman personally. "I understand you're the one who convinced the Wheeler boy not to set off the fugue-bomb? Made a connection with the lad? I wanted to thank you for saving my memories. My wife...." The president paused. "Well, the Freeze gave us a little extra time together. I was supposed to be dead already. This is my second chance. I appreciate not losing all recollection of it."

The president is blessed by the Freeze with extra time, and Thyme's mother was cursed with a premature ending. Some gain and others lose.

"The Grays?" Thyme asked the president. "Are you going to retaliate against Jefferson Davis?"

"His bold action might have ultimately failed, but he proved to his allies that he has the means and the will to strike at the Union. It may be impossible to avoid a War Between the States."

"Again," Ms. Norman added.

"For some of us, it will be the first time," President Harrison said.

For some, it will be the first time, Thyme thinks now. Efren wants her to feel a certain way and be a certain person, but the Thyme he marries is not this Thyme. This is all new. All different. This is the first time, not the replay. Her future isn't set. Her tomorrow is not the record filed away in some future. It's whatever she makes it. This is the first time Thyme has ever been seventeen.

The past is the present is the future. They say nothing ever really changes.

"We'll see," Thyme whispers as the classroom door opens.

"You're late, Mr. Stone," Ms. Norman sniffs.

"Sorry," Jay apologizes, smooth and slick.

He's late, but he's here. He slides into a seat in the back of the room beside Thyme. Efren glares from the front row until Honor gives him an elbow, and he pays attention again to what Ms. Norman is saying.

Jay looks at Thyme. Thyme looks at Jay. Ms. Norman seems to pause mid-sentence. Candy blows a bubble with pink gum and it suspends, still, neither growing nor popping. Honor's face sets into an expression that might've been a transition from frown to smirk but looks for all purposes on pause like a smile. Efren stares at the clock on the wall that hasn't moved in an e-year, as if expecting tomorrow any moment now.

The moment goes on and on. Thyme is stuck in an infinite minute. She never thought a never-ending instant could be born of both tragedy and joy. She smiles and Jay smiles back. The whole world stuck in amber around them, they're the only two hearts beating in all the timeless world.

Alone, an infinite minute seems forever.

Together with Jay, Thyme never wants this infinite minute to end.

EPILOGUE
1:15
10.11.1980 AD
New York City, New York

The headmistress and namesake of the Mallory Norman Institute of Time walks through the timeless halls of the school. It's after school hours and the students are all in the dormitory wings of the Minute. The structure was built after the Freeze and borrows from no specific epoch of architecture. It's meant to be welcoming to learners from every era.

The Minute is a round building with the classrooms at the very center. There are twelve sections, eight of which house students based on a very strict algorithm designed to promote as much interaction as possible between citizens from different time zones. Mallory Norman intends to enrich the lives of these young people and set an example exemplifying the idea that citizens from even opposite ends of history can find something in common. As her mother often says, the past is the present is the future.

From a bird's eye view, the Institute mimics the shape of

a clock. The twelve compartments are divided equally, partitions rising to section off each wedge-shaped area like a pie cut into a dozen equal portions. The entrance encompasses two sections, one a greeting room for visitors and dignitaries designed to highlight the accomplishments of the school, and the other a communal gathering area for students to meet and mix. The two sections that make up the anterior of the Minute have walls protruding from the perimeter, so from the sky it seems like the hands of a clock set at eleven and one.

The communal area is always bustling with activity and features a commissary, games both old and futuristic, and artifacts that can make anyone from any zone feel at home. Ms. Norman wants the communal room to be inviting and foster friendships with students across all time zones.

Everyone except Thyme Mugen.

There are certain students that need to be off-limits to Thyme.

So far, the school is a success. Today was opening day. All enrolled attendees arrived safely and classes began without incident. After the dangerous journey of Thyme and her companions, it's something of a miracle that the Chronfederates didn't achieve their agenda in making a violent example of Mallory Norman's students and therefore disrupting her dream of anachronistic peace. But Jefferson Davis was unsuccessful in his attempt to hold her captive indefinitely, and he failed to do harm to any of her students. There might be a war on the horizon, but Ms. Norman and her allies have won the first battle.

It was a narrow victory. In 1841, Thyme refused to come across the border into 1980 unless Mallory Norman agreed to her demands. Ms. Norman had to get Thyme Mugen safely to the

Institute. She's not just any student. Thyme is the most important student at the Minute. Ms. Norman can protect the girl if she's in 1980 and close. Thyme made demands that Ms. Norman had to agree to. There's no price too high to ensure Thyme's attendance at the Minute, but it's the highest price Ms. Norman could imagine.

The chancellor of the school wasn't happy with Ms. Norman's bargain with the stubborn Thyme Mugen.

Ms. Norman passes the science wing. Professor Franklin is writing formulas on the blackboard. Ms. Norman has assembled a peerless group of instructors plucked from across history. Benjamin Franklin heads the science department. Coach Jim Thorpe teaches P.E. Professor Euclid works in the mathematics department. Christopher Marlowe handles drama. Professor Twain has agreed to commute from Washington, DC, to 1980 for occasional writing seminars. This Institute is the paragon of post-Freeze America.

Anyone should feel honored to be invited to the school.

Thyme told Ms. Norman in 1841 that she was ready to go back to 2023 unless the headmistress complied with her requirement. The chancellor would've been upset with either alternative. Ms. Norman couldn't let Thyme go back to her home zone. That was an unacceptable outcome. So Mallory Norman made the only decision she could.

"Either Jay Stone is allowed to enroll at the Institute, or I refuse attendance," Thyme stated in no uncertain terms. "I'll go back to live with Jiji."

Ms. Norman stared at the young woman, and Thyme remained defiant.

Mallory Norman had no choice.

Ms. Norman stands in front of an unmarked door at the

very center of the clock-shaped Institute. The chancellor expects a report. Ms. Norman doesn't really want to confront the actual architect of the Institute. It wasn't a pleasant conversation when Mallory revealed she had to allow Jay Stone enrollment at the Minute in order to get Thyme here.

Surely, there will be more complaining about that situation.

Things won't get better with time.

Mallory Norman touches a panel next to the door that reads her biometric aura and the door opens. It's 1980 outside the walls of the school. The rest of the Institute is timeless, conforming to no one era. But the chancellor's office is decorated with amenities original to her home zone of 2057.

The chancellor sits behind a desk as big as half of Ms. Norman's history classroom. She wears a permanent scowl, as if it was etched into her face long before the clocks ever stopped. Never a happy woman, there's been no occasion for a smile in all the infinite minutes since the Freeze. Mallory's news from her last visit did nothing to lift the chancellor's mood.

"The situation?" the chancellor demands.

"The same."

"Unacceptable," the chancellor says. "Jay Stone cannot be allowed to interfere."

"Would you like to talk to her yourself?"

"Of course not."

"Well, you ought to know as well as anyone that Thyme Mugen is a headstrong and independent young person," Mallory Norman says.

The chancellor glowers. The choices are limited. They can't expel Jay without Thyme going with him. And without Thyme nearby, they can't steer the direction of her future.

"This is all wrong," the chancellor tells.

"Nothing has been right in a long time," Mallory says.

"We barely saved her from bad choices in that terrifying trek across time zones. We managed to call on the USS Hammerhead just in time to save her in 68,437,912 BC, and we called in the HaLiCons at the last moment in 1929. Yet she still careens headlong in the wrong direction."

"She's as stubborn as ever," Mallory Norman acknowledges, staring directly at the chancellor as if the words mean more than they seem.

"We can't let her run from our tomorrow. She can't be allowed to fall for a boy from 1960. This is about our family, Lori. She's supposed to fall in love with Efren Cortez. That girl is supposed to get married and have children."

"I know how it's supposed to be, Mother," Mallory snaps.

"Then make it right." The chancellor stands up and leans forward. The Thyme Cortez from 2057 appears haggard and weary, slivers of silver streaked through her black hair, not at all like the lively girl who made demands of Ms. Norman in 1841. "Take care of the future. By any means necessary."

Mallory nods. Any means necessary. She takes a long look at her mother, so bitter and cold. The teenage Thyme is so unlike what she will be, the girl from 2023 still young and vibrant. And falling in love. What a difference a little time makes.

The End
Is the Middle
Is the Beginning

Edward Newton lives in Florida and enjoys few things more than the beach. An accomplished author, he received the Robert L. Fish Memorial Award from the Mystery Writers of America for the Best First Short Story. His previous works include *Horrorfrost* and the fantasy novel *Truth to Light*, as well as several published short stories. Edward spent a year traveling the continental United States and found something intriguing everywhere he went—this country is an amazing and fascinating place. His heart is his family, and he couldn't do any of this without his wife Treina and his amazing kids Kobe, Gage, Oliver, and Bennett.